Bark of the Tree

A Lazy Dog Mystery

By

MIKE SILVESTRI

BURD STREET PRESS
SHIPPENSBURG, PENNSYLVANIA

This Burd Street Press publication
was printed by
Beidel Printing House, Inc.
63 West Burd Street
Shippensburg, PA 17257-0708 USA

The acid-free paper used in this book meets the guidelines for permanence and durability of the Committee on Production Guidelines for Book Longevity of the Council on Library Resources.

For a complete list of available publications
please write
Burd Street Press
Division of White Mane Publishing Company, Inc.
P.O. Box 708
Shippensburg, PA 17257-0708 USA

Library of Congress Cataloging-in-Publication Data

Silvestri, Mike, 1957-
    Bark of the tree : a lazy dog mystery / by Mike Silvestri.
        p. cm.
    ISBN 1-57249-367-4 (alk. paper)
    1. Drifters--Crimes against--Fiction. 2. Computer programmers--Fiction. 3.
Hit-an-run-drivers--Fiction. 4. Pennsylvania--Fiction. 5. Legislators--Fiction. 6. Dog
owners--Fiction. 7. Dogs--Fiction. I. Title.

PS3619.I553B37 2004
813'.6--dc22

2004057510

For Carol...

The biggest mystery is why
you've put up with me for
more than twenty-five years...

Preface

To be certain, *Bark of the Tree* is a work of fiction and the disclaimer really does apply.

Residents of the greater Harrisburg area will note that the community names listed in this work don't exist. I have taken the liberty to define neighborhoods and suburbs to suit the lives of the characters within my book. The same goes for various state agencies and companies. Fiction writers get to have all the fun, don't they? Of course, Harrisburg remains Harrisburg. Even an author can't get away with naming a state capital something it isn't.

Happily, Abby and Roxanne do exist. Abby is a lazy Shetland sheepdog, though not as lazy as the Abby in this book. Roxanne is a hyperactive golden retriever. Both dogs have agreed to allow their names and likenesses to be used in the book. It's amazing what a box of doggie treats will buy.

Acknowledgments

My gratitude goes out to Tessa Silvestri for her patient editing, to Kate Silvestri for her patient listening, to Harold Collier for publishing this novel, to Jack Kurtz, Park Ranger Extraordinaire, to Dave Bayne, and to the Pennwriters Area 5 gang.

Credit for the excellent cover art goes to Gretchen Giordano. Gretchen's body of work ranges from highly detailed miniature paintings all the way up to interior design. Her "Capitol Tile Cow" graced the Pennsylvania Capitol Rotunda during the 2004 Harrisburg Cow Parade.

Credit for the very cool Lazy Dog logo goes to Matt Sullivan. Matt is a highly talented graphic novel artist.

Chapter 1

A single eye floated on the lens of the riflescope. Following back along the scope's smooth black surface sat the projection's source, clad in tree bark camouflage and barely visible in the straw-hued dawn of an autumn forest.

The snap of a distant branch alarmed him and his masked head swiveled to track the sound. Sweeping eyes surveyed the dense brush that bordered the dirt trail. His hands embraced the weapon's contours. Another branch cracked in the early morning chill, this time closer, louder, and imminently nearing. The rhythmic footfalls of his approaching prey made his heart beat faster. He curled a single gloved finger on top of the gun's safety and clicked it off. With that sound, the rifle grew leaden as if deadliness gave it more weight. His eye returned to its projected perch within the scope as he drew in a breath.

A loud snort and the crunch of new fallen leaves announced the arrival of the target. He caught sight of it behind a tangle of vines and brush. A single nervous breath rose upward in a cool fog. He unsheathed a single pale finger from his glove and wrapped it around the trigger until he felt the cold metal push into his warm skin.

There. There it was. He responded almost without thought. The lone eye in the riflescope blinked. He jerked the trigger. The bullet launched toward the certain death of his unsuspecting prey.

An unsuspecting Mike Daniels rounded the bend of the trail in time to see the flash. A hornet's sound half-buzzed and half-whistled past his right ear. A sapling exploded behind him with an impact so

1

great that it severed the young tree. Mike froze. The realization of what just happened sunk in about the moment the shockwave from the gunshot rippled through him. White-eyed, Mike yelled, "Holy crap." He looked at the tree that had detonated behind him and decided to repeat himself even louder. "Holy crap." Mike turned to confront his attacker, and watched as a camouflaged shape materialized from behind a tree only ten yards from where he stood. The shape shed his mask, revealing a half-boy, half-man. The half-boy was in tears.

"Ohmigod Mister...Ohmigod...Are you okay?" warbled the hysterical teen.

"You could have killed me," screamed Mike as he noted a third figure joining the two's company at the edge of the thicket. From the similarities in both faces, he guessed it was the boy's father.

"What the heck were you doing?" bellowed the blaze-orange and camouflaged parent.

The boy stammered and mumbled.

Mike stood by, relishing the coming parental tirade. An awkward silence hung in the air until he realized that the question was directed solely at him. "What was I doing? I'm out here for a morning run..."

"...In the middle of deer season, you idiot," completed the father.

Mike countered. "I have the right to be out here the same as any..."

"...And get shot," ended the parent.

Mike stood dumbfounded that anyone who came so close to death should be treated so rudely. The man turned his back to Mike in order to comfort his shaking son. They gathered the boy's gear and set off in search of another place to hunt. As they did, Mike heard the father say, "I saw you flinch when you yanked on the trigger. You gotta squeeze the trigger, boy. No wonder you missed."

Mike turned with arms outstretched and found God ignoring him, too. No lightning fell from the sky to smite the heathen. It never did. He let out a long sigh and tried to calm himself. Trying not to end up stuffed and mounted over the fireplace, he headed the opposite way to finish his morning's run. Mike took two steps and promptly tripped over the shattered sapling.

Chapter 2

Abby listened to Mike's venting for the third time. She rolled her eyes skyward.

"...And then he says, 'No wonder you missed.' What an idiot," yelled Mike over the shower curtain. The steam from the shower seemed to increase with the temperature of his exhortation. "Well, he can deer season this." Mike waved the middle fingers of each hand in the air.

Apathetic to Mike's rants, Abby watched his extended digits perform an obscene shadow play on the translucent curtain. While Mike railed at the injustices of his life, she coped with it, although she didn't quite understand why the shower seemed to be the preferred location for his whining.

The shower curtain slid aside with a sweep of Mike's arm and he dried himself with a nearby towel. Making his way to her, Mike cupped her chin in his hand and asked, "Is there no pity for me on a Monday morning?"

They stood, face-to-face, Abby's brown eyes looking back at his, showing him only the slightest bit of compassion.

"Not even a little bit?"

Abby responded with a long, slow lick of his cheek and returned to rest her head between her paws. Abby, a Shetland sheepdog, constituted all the family that remained in Mike's modest red brick Washington Street house in the ever-so-middle-class environs of Bridgeport.

Abby watched the towel curl around her owner in the strange way that humans dried themselves. In fact, she felt that all humans were odd; particularly this one that had the oddest appendage hanging between his legs. The item jiggled invitingly, but Abby suppressed the urge to bite. Recalling a vague memory of an ugly incident during her puppyhood when that activity brought much pain to her and to her owner, she decided to keep her head between her feet.

Abby sought quieter surroundings in the bedroom. The blissful silence ended when her owner came in and started whistling so badly that she wondered if she didn't prefer his whining. The pain in her ears subsided when Mike began to get dressed.

"What do you think, Ab? The red power tie or the green geometric?"

All Abby wondered was why humans insisted on putting collars on themselves.

"Red, today. It'll go with my navy blue suit." Mike slipped on an undershirt and ran a comb through his hair to straighten things out. His face wrinkled at a gray hair stuck in the comb's teeth. "I just keep getting more and more distinguished. Oh well, at least it's still there."

Abby let out a huff. Having endured enough of her owner's daily routine, she rose from her spot on the carpet and trundled down the stairs. Abby sat down in the kitchen and waited. It didn't take long for her to hear Mike's muffled steps coming down the staircase. She knew what was next.

Mike bounded into the doorway with a thud and yelled, "Boo."

Her only reaction was a few taps of her tail to signify a five for technical merit and a two for artistic presentation.

After grabbing some breakfast, Mike pulled Monday's *Harrisburg Post* from its plastic wrapper. "What do you want to hear about, girl? 'Trash Piles Up?' 'Highway Construction Ties Up Interstate?' Nah, how about 'Fourteen Things to do with Canned Rhubarb?'"

Realizing that none of the choices had to do with food or doggie treats, Abby responded with a yawn.

"Me neither," said Mike, his eyes focusing on another story. "How could I be so stupid?"

Abby's head tilted and a single ear tipped over.

"'Record Deer Season Harvest.' Looks like I'm going to have to run on Sundays, not Saturdays, for the next couple of weeks." Mike glanced down at Abby. "Maybe we'll go for a walk next Saturday."

Slumping to the floor, Abby protested with a groan.

"I didn't think you'd be real interested," said her owner with a shake of his head. He tossed Abby a corn flake. "Time for me to go to work, girl. See you later."

The door closed a few moments later, leaving Abby in the deserted house, slowly wagging her tail. Two flights of stairs later, she basked in a sunbeam on the corner of Mike's bed.

* * *

Having run the rush hour gauntlet, Mike stood at the entrance of his employer, Bleeding Edge Consultants, trying to time his entry to the granite-walled and copper-roofed building when Judy, the company receptionist, was most occupied—occupied on the phone. Mike liked the bubbly personality of the pretty administrative assistant, even if she wore five earrings in each ear, one in her nose and God knows where else. What he dreaded was her penchant for having never ending conversations. Hoping to avoid a marathon discussion of the weekend, Mike listened in vain for a hint of the receptionist's soprano monotone behind Bleeding Edge's carved oak door. Hearing only the traffic on Front Street, he gave up on his eavesdropping and stepped inside.

Judy looks like Cerberus, the three-headed dog guarding the gates of Hades, Mike thought as he surveyed her head, headset, and the disembodied voice of her mother wafting over the scratchy electronic speaker. As he neared her desk, the raven-haired woman's spiky new hairdo came into view. *No, not Cerberus*, Mike mused. *Medusa, although I might be myth-taken.* Picking up the pace, Mike beelined to the sanctuary of his office.

"...No, Mom. He's in a band. Yes, he took lessons. No, we haven't...hold on," said Judy to her mother as her attention shifted to Mike's passing.

Mike heard the conversation cease, a bad sign, and halted his stride, as if being still would avoid detection.

"Mike. Oh Miiiiiiikkkkeee. The boss would like to see you in his office at nine. It's not on your calendar," yelled Judy in a high-pitched tone that could shatter ice.

"About?" asked Mike.

All three of Judy's heads shrugged in unison. She threw up her arms to plead ignorance while resuming her phone conversation. "Guitar, Mom. He plays the guitar. He has such nice hands. No Mom, we haven't..."

Just before 9:00 a.m., Mike headed down to the Monk's Cell. Bleeding Edge's stately architecture and riverfront locale were the legacy of a wealthy steel executive and John Weaverton paid a premium price to get it. For his efforts, John claimed the Monk's Cell, a curved apse that once served as a modest library. Crossing into the boss's inner sanctum, Mike gazed at the tall walnut bookshelves and austere Scandinavian desk framing John in his tailored navy blue suit. It always looked like the setting for an executive portrait, complete with John's imposing height, disarming smile and serious eyes. Wondering what was in store, he waited for John to clue him in.

Rising from his leather chair, John strolled to his coffee pot. "Mikeeee," greeted John. "Coffee?"

"Mikeeee." Not good. He wants me to take a swim in a cesspool, thought Mike.

"Cream and sugar?" asked John.

Naked.

"I have a special opportunity for you to look into right away."

And it's stocked with piranha. "You know, John, a special opportunity is not my way of starting the week. What's wrong?" asked Mike.

"Boorman."

"What did you promise them?"

"The team we sent over there didn't overcome some issues," said John flatly.

"Issues? You know how I hate those little code words. Monica used to say that we had issues. They're having problems, right?"

"Monica had some real issues, Mike."

"Let's not talk about my ex-wife on a Monday. Boorman?"

"Yes. I took one look at Boorman Inc. and figured they were lightweights, so I sent in the second team. Well, the second team is missing something out there that needs to improve Boorman's bottom line.

The deadline is looming and we need to get a grip on their inventory issu...problems."

"So you need me to go in and figure out the whole mess? I'm going to have as much hair as you do before long."

"Yes, and no bald jokes. At least I still have the sides," said John as he passed Mike a cup of coffee.

"When?" asked Mike.

"Next week."

Starving piranhas. "Why me?"

"There's two people that can do it. Me or..."

"Me. Why not you?"

"If I show up, Boorman's management will wonder why. Besides, people love to talk to you, and they always listen to your reports."

"You never listen to my reports," said Mike.

"That's different," said John.

Mike smirked. "If I counted the number of special opportunities you've given me over the last seven years..."

"You'd have a good reason to ask for a raise. Don't. I pay you enough. I'll forward you the team's analysis and the contact people at Boorman," finished John.

"Thanks, boss. I can hardly wait," said Mike as he headed out the door. *Special opportunity my butt*, thought Mike as he headed back down the hallway past Judy.

"Yea, he went shopping with me. Yes—shopping. No, Mom, we haven't..."

Chapter 3

After a week of Boorman issues, Mike was happy to be hitting the trails. His Pontiac swayed in the pre-dawn twilight while dodging the occasional grinning opossum that didn't believe in hibernating from the early December cold. A left, and a right turn later, Mike pulled onto the gravel parking lot on Gilbert Sanford State Park's eastern shore. He paused to watch the mist curl up off the lake. Mike looked at the lake the way art patrons stared at their favorite painter's work. After taking a few seconds to savor the moment, he shut the car off and stepped out into the crisp morning air.

A blue jay landed in a nearby pine and told all of its neighbors that a human being had arrived. Mike listened to its cackling and heard four other birdcalls relaying the alarm. He kept an ear out for the one sound he didn't want to hear—gunshots. None were heard. *Nobody's hunting today*, he reminded himself. *It's Sunday.*

Grabbing his running belt from the car, Mike inventoried his supplies: two bottles of water, an energy bar, and a zip-lock-bag full of toilet paper. Bears weren't the only creatures that did it in the woods, and a simple comfort like toilet paper would more than offset the discomfort of using a poison ivy leaf by mistake. Mike subconsciously scratched at his right buttock where the steroid injection occurred two years ago. He slipped his hands into a pair of thin gloves, thwacked the buckles of his running belt together, and began his run.

Dawn provided just enough light for Mike to navigate the trail. Fall had moved the forest canopy earthward, and the depth of leaves forced a cautious pace over the roots and rocks. On he went over hill and dale to the varying accompaniment of chirping birds, scurrying squirrels and wind-churned leaves with the sun splashing through the trees. A branch snapped behind him, and uneasiness crept into his muscles. His head moved from side to side to pick up the direction of an approaching sound. As the volume increased, so did his searching. The sound was vaguely mechanical but humanly rhythmic. Each step forward closed the distance, yet its emitter remained invisible. When he reached the bottom of the hollow, Mike turned to see his phantom pursuer. None appeared, but the sound grew louder. A rolling hiss accompanied a near-continuous crunch and Mike realized his folly at exactly the moment that the sound was upon him. A mountain biker blew past, yelling, "Good morning," sending Mike scampering off the trail. A second rider passed him with the same amount of manic hurry and added a single "Hi." As his heart rate peaked, Mike let out a frustrated sigh. Mountain bikers on the trail were nothing new. However, mountain bikers on the trail at this hour of a Sunday morning were. He stood for a moment and realized that the sounds they made traveled down the hollow and tricked him into believing that they were coming from behind.

Mike's pulse returned to normal once the riders went on their way. Mother Nature cooperated by delivering a bright orange-yellow sunrise that chased a bit of the chill from the trail. Temperatures rose and Mike shed his gloves to offset the growing warmth. *It feels great to be moving*, he thought, feeling the tension from his unpleasant surprise disappear.

By the time the sun peaked over the trees, Mike passed the southern parking lot and spotted some trucks parked at the water's edge. *Fishermen—they're crazier than I am*, thought Mike.

He soon found himself trudging through the park's swampy nether regions and past the closed-for-the-season campground. Ahead, a guidepost signaled a split in the trail. Mike considered his choices. *Left or right today? Well worn and smooth to the left, or overgrown and neglected to the right? The right looks like the road less traveled.* Caught in a Robert Frost moment, Mike chose the right.

Roads (and trails) less traveled were less traveled for a reason, Mike discovered. Softball-size rocks, concealed beneath the leaves, turned his steady stride into a jerky puppet's dance. "This was smart," he said, casting his eyes upward in disgust. Mike's momentary lapse of concentration was rewarded with a misstep that sent him tumbling between the rocks and the hard places. While the chickadees Mike encountered had mastered flight, Mike had not, and he was soon keenly aware of the gravity of the situation. His body slammed to earth on a soft dirt incline between the large gray limestone boulders that bordered the trail. Shielding their owner from impending doom, both of Mike's eyes closed in mid-flight to deny him the memory of landing. Once he came to rest, his eyes flickered open while his brain did an inventory.

Back—okay. Legs—okay. Arms—okay. Nose—full of dirt. Lying still, he was relieved that nothing was missing or damaged. Considering the terrain all around him, Mike realized that he had managed to land on one of the few spots along this stretch that hadn't demanded blood or bone as toll for his impromptu fall. He rolled over onto a pointed rock that positioned itself as one last insult for his lack of injury. Slowly he sat up and found his clothes as intact as the rest of him. Deciding that this was as good a place as any for a break, he reached for a water bottle and guzzled a third of it. He replaced the bottle back in its snug pocket.

Thunk.

A heavy, hollow sound echoed through the forest at exactly the moment Mike's water bottle hit the bottom of his pack. After pulling the water bottle out, Mike reinserted it with the accompanying plastic-on-nylon shush he expected. He sat in silence, looking at his pack for a few moments. The strange sound repeated.

Thunk.

The sound puzzled him, and his mind lingered on it. He closed his eyes and tried to recall where he had heard that sound before. A memory of camping appeared, and with it, some friends building a campfire ring. *Yes, a fire ring where they laid stone after stone atop one another to keep the embers in. Each time they laid a stone...*

Thunk.

The real sound brought Mike out of his recollection. He rose and looked in the sound's direction but found it obscured by a stand of dark green hemlocks. Curiosity got the better of him, and he bushwhacked farther into the woods, following each thunk to its source.

Arriving at the edge of an old stone wall atop a shallow hill, Mike regarded the scene below him like a birdwatcher surveying a pair of wrens.

She stood in a small clearing ten yards down the wall from where Mike stood, her blonde hair glowing from the backlight of the morning sun while her shoulders drooped from an unseen weight. A wool blazer covered her black, mid-length dress. She bent over, letting her hair cascade forward, and...

Thunk.

A second thunk joined the percussion. An African American man dressed in a single-breasted blue suit and tie kneeled nearby, supplying the accompaniment. His disheveled salt and pepper hair glistened with sweat. The suit was covered in dirt and stained with perspiration. The man stopped his stacking until the woman said something, and he resumed.

Thunk—thunk.

Mike wondered, *What in the world is going on? Well-dressed folks arranging stones on a late fall morning?*

A squirrel darted across the forest floor, scattering foliage along the way. The ruckus made the odd pair twitch like they had gotten an electrical shock and they dropped their stones. Their sudden movement jolted Mike into ducking behind the shallow wall. One of the duo approached, investigating the source of the sound. The person stopped close enough for Mike to hear labored breathing, high pitched and feminine. Fearing that the fog of his own breath would give his location away, Mike cupped his hands, exhaled into the rocks next to him, and tried to calm himself. The footsteps renewed their patrol, coming closer to Mike's hiding spot. The instinct to hide faded in Mike's brain. *This is stupid*, he thought. *There's probably a good explanation for these two people to be out here stacking rocks—in December—in business clothes.* Mike decided to stand up and see what was going on.

The blonde woman stood only a couple of yards away, her back facing him, and blocking Mike's view of her partner. His mouth opened to ask what was going on.

The woman hissed at her partner. "Keep going. He's almost covered."

Mike's stomach knotted and he dropped back to the ground with his mouth still hanging open. His mind repeated, *"He's almost covered,"* over and over. The urge to look fought with the urge to stay hidden behind the wall. The urge to look won the fight and he crawled baby-style to the end of the wall so he could get another look at the pair's labors. Peering from behind the hodge-podge of fallen rocks, Mike watched the man's chest heave and shake. *Did I just hear him sob?*

The woman yelled at the man to hurry up. The man obliged and returned to his stacking.

What is it about these two? Who's almost covered? What's in that pile of rocks? Nothing. It's just a pile of flat and rounded stones borrowed from the fallen walls of these old farmhouses, Mike explained to himself. *No, more like a grave—like the way they buried people in old westerns.* The knot in Mike's gut pulled tighter. His analytical sense prevailed despite the building apprehension and his eyes followed the irregular contours of the couple's mound. His lips mouthed what his eyes saw. "Limestone...limestone...mountain-stone...boot...toes...limestone...Oh my God." Fortunately for Mike, the knot in his gut had worked its way up to his vocal cords and managed to choke off any sound. Slamming himself back against the wall and out of sight, Mike lay, trying to keep his heart from jumping out of his chest.

Thunk—thunk.

The rock-meeting-earth bass note of the last pair of thunks shook him. A side of Mike's brain tried to reassure him that he couldn't have possibly seen a pair of feet sticking out of a stone grave. The other side of his brain worked hard to quiet his thumping heart. Despite the reassurance, a surge of cold fear froze him to the ground. Knowing that there was only one way to find out, Mike took a few deep breaths and forced his head up to the top of the wall. His eyes picked up where the stones left off.

God, those are feet. I can barely see them now. Why is one foot wearing a boot while the other one isn't? His thoughts stopped when the couple interrupted his line of sight.

Thunk. Thunk-thunk. Thunk.

The last four sounds signaled the end of the burial. The man quivered as the final rock covered the remains of the person within. Mike ducked back down when the woman took one last desperate look around.

"That's good enough. Let's go," commanded the woman.

An inner shudder reverberated throughout his body and kept him in place until he felt that the pair was far enough away. Rising onto stiff muscles, Mike neared the pile of rocks with a gathering dread and it amplified his mild shudders into a full rolling tremble. Mike tensed as if this particular Lazarus would rise from the dead. The forest's silence reflected the silence of the grave's occupant. No birds chirped. No wind moved. The stillness in the air around Mike seemed to penetrate his skin and calm his trembling for a moment. Standing quietly, Mike considered a eulogy. A crow broke the silence with a guttural "caw." Mike's feet were already moving by the time his brain issued the command to run.

Chapter 4

"Ohmigod...puff...Ohmigod...puff...Ohmigod," chanted Mike to the cadence of his pounding feet. Those same feet pounded past the left turn that Mike intended to take to a picnic grove. "Ahhhhhhhhhhhhhhh..." Panic overwhelmed his sanity until he ground his running shoes into the trail to halt his sprint. All ten of his fingers cradled his face as he gasped for air. "Think. Settle down and think," he screamed to get a hold of himself. The heaving of his chest told him just how hard he had been running and each breath cleared his mind. "Okay, stupid. Let's find a ranger," he commanded himself as if his voice were another person. Heading back to the cutoff, he began to search for a park ranger. *None— not a dang one anywhere*, Mike thought between breaths. In fact, Mike noticed that there wasn't a car to be seen anywhere in the picnic grove that usually accommodated even a few on a Saturday. "Sunday. It's Sunday," he corrected himself out loud.

Finding no one in the lot, he dashed back to the trail, sending squirrels and chipmunks scampering. The path finally returned him to the parking lot where he started. Mike picked through his fanny pack to find his keys. After thumbing the remote, the car's horn began to blare while the lights flashed off and on. *The car is as freaked as I am*, he figured until he took his finger off the appropriately named Panic button. After hitting the unlock button, Mike hopped into the driver's seat and wiped the gushing sweat from his forehead. A quick shift and a spin of the wheel sent gravel spewing as he nosed the Pontiac onto the road. His erratic driving skills on the narrow service road caught the attention of a pair of men coming down the road in a blue car. Both cars barely avoided each other, although the near miss gave Mike a chance to glance at the letters painted on the side of the blue car—D-C-N-R. Each of the letters registered into his harried brain—*D-C-N-R—Department of Conservation and Natural Resources—Rangers—Crap*. Mike spun the wheel again, sending grass and mud slewing as the big car ran out of small road. Jumping on the gas to catch the other car proved unnecessary as the ranger's patrol car was now headed his way, complete with flashing red lights and two stern-faced rangers gesturing for him to pull over.

The driver was the first to leave the DCNR car and head toward Mike's, though the second ranger wasn't too far behind. Mike flung the car door open, and both rangers' hands instantly flicked off the retaining strap on their holstered pistols at the unexpected movement.

"Sir, step away from the car," commanded the driver.

Mike's first feelings of relief at seeing the rangers now turned to the warm rush of fear. Doing as the ranger commanded, Mike spoke, "Thank God it's you guys. I just saw some people burying a guy back in the woods." Mike almost laughed as he watched the two sets of eyebrows opposite him raise up into identical startled expressions. He had their undivided attention.

"Sir, would you mind repeating yourself?" asked the elder ranger whose voice asked one thing but whose eyes said something else to his junior partner.

Looking over at the elder ranger, Mike spied the engraved plastic nametag that identified its owner as "Savastio, Tony" according to the state's eminently personal style. Savastio, Tony stood almost a half head taller than Mike's six-foot frame. Graying temples showed on the buzz cut both he and the much younger officer sported. Mike guessed that Savastio, Tony was older than he was, maybe Italian, and maybe in his fifties. The opportunity to get a look at the junior ranger's nametag faded when the young man slid behind him. The standing arrangement made Mike feel uneasy. Savastio, Tony's head gave an ever-so-slight nod for his partner to move a tad further into Mike's blind spot. Mike realized that the rangers were as uncomfortable with the situation as he was. *I just about ran them off the road and blurted out that there are bodies buried in the woods. How are they supposed to feel?*

The elder ranger looked Mike up and down and finished by looking him straight in the eye, saying, "Now who's buried in the woods? I mean, you wouldn't be kidding ol' Tony, would you?"

Detecting both the seriousness in Savastio's voice and the fact that the ranger's hand hadn't moved from the grip of his pistol, Mike realized what Tony meant. It seemed to Mike that kidding ol' Tony about strange doings in the park was a quick way to a side of Tony that Mike didn't want to see. What Mike did want to see was the nameless ranger who had taken up residence behind him. A quick glimpse behind proved futile against the sun-borne glare.

Mike turned his attention back to Tony and spoke, trying to contain the frantic undertones in his speech. "No, sir. I...I...I wish I was kidding. I watched two people stacking rocks onto a body. They left and then so did I. I've been looking for you guys ever since."

Ranger Savastio stared at Mike for a moment, then scratched his chin. "Daryl, go get a pad and paper and get the location from, from..."

"...Mike Daniels," Mike volunteered. Tension eased from his spine when he realized that Savastio, Tony took him seriously.

"Okay...Mr. Daniels here. Then see if you can find where the spot is. I'm gonna go call Bud," said Tony. Turning his attention to Mike, Tony explained, "He's our park superintendent. He's not going to be happy to come down here on a Sunday. Mr. Daniels, I sure in the heck hope there's a body where you say it is, or me and Bud are going to be pissed."

The junior ranger made his way to the car's passenger side while Tony went for the radio. Mike began to listen to the static-filled conversation emanating from the car and, at the same time, watched the blond-haired young man fumble for a pen and paper. Noting that nametag styles hadn't changed, Mike read "Musser, Daryl" on the approaching ranger's chest. The other curious thing that he saw was that Musser, Daryl evidently needed his Smokey-the-Bear ranger's hat in order to take down his statement. Mike caught Tony's disgusted eye-roll as the senior ranger took one look at his junior's fastidiousness.

Ranger Musser took down Mike's name, address, and phone number, then asked him, "Can you give us an idea where you saw the body, Mr. Daniels?"

"Over on the southwest side near the long stone wall that borders the trail. Look for the hemlocks and a dip in the hill behind them," said Mike as he watched Daryl try to keep up with every word of his description.

Tony stepped out from behind the steering wheel and said, "Daryl, Bud said that you're to take the car as close as you can to where Mr. Daniels says. Wait for your backup and then go take a look around together. No bushwhacking. Got it?"

"Yea, I got it," Daryl said as he flipped the pad closed and hopped in the idling car.

"And Daryl...," added Tony, "you don't need the hat." Tony stood for a moment watching Daryl leave, then looked at Mike and said, "That rookie better darn well listen to me. I don't want to have to go looking for your body and him at the same time. That boy runs off more than my old beagle. Anyway, Mr. Daniels, my boss Bud is gonna come pick us up and then we're all going to go up to the park office. Why don't you park your car back down in the parking lot, and we'll go have a little talk?"

Even though Tony made it sound like a request, Mike interpreted it as a command. He nodded in the affirmative, and both men got into Mike's car.

"You're sure you saw a body out there, Mr. Daniels?" Tony prodded.

"Yes, unfortunately. One hundred percent sure," answered Mike, now wishing that he had taken the road more traveled.

The cramped old Chrysler's back seat and poor view acted together to give Mike a growing sense of claustrophobia. Fortunately, for Mike's cramping legs, the ride to the park office was short.

The park's ranger station was part ranch house, part log cabin due to somebody's artistic melding of the two styles. While the house was painted the government-issue green, the log cabin was done, appropriately, in logs. Like most state park facilities, the building served as the park's meeting place with the public first, and as a ranger headquarters last.

Bud unlocked the front door of the building and slipped inside to turn off the alarm system and turn on the lights. An awkward silence held between Mike and Tony as they waited. Mike felt Tony looking him over in the way a child felt a parent sizing them up for guilt and punishment. Bud came back into the room and ended the moment. He motioned for Tony and Mike to come on in.

The inside of the ranger headquarters didn't match the hodgepodge of its exterior. The counter was clean and organized. The state-issued metal desks stood in ordered rows holding neat stacks of paper in wire bins. Even the brochure holders on the big map of the park were full.

Mike took this all in until Tony spoke to him and said, "Bud likes things shipshape."

Tony's statement caught Mike off-guard as if Tony were reading his mind. It upped the needle on Mike's discomfort meter.

Crossing the door's threshold, they left the model of modern efficiency and organization behind and entered the old park office. The same institutional green decorating the outside coated the interior walls of the hallway of what was a former home. Each man's footstep thumped on the hollow wooden floor as they turned and walked through a doorway adorned in the same personable manner as the nametags, "Savastio, Tony."

Whatever relief Mike had enjoyed during the ride to the park office evaporated the instant Tony turned on the lights to his office. The flick of the switch seemed to send electricity jolting through Mike's body as he rounded the corner and came face-to-face with the open embrace of a black bear standing in the corner.

Tony let a slight smirk come to his lips when he caught sight of his visitor jumping backward. "Say hi to Stella, Mr. Daniels."

The shock receded throughout Mike's body as he followed the stuffed bear's body all the way to its wooden base. "Hi...er...Stella. Friend of yours, Tony?"

"Yea, strong, silent type. And she don't cause trouble on Sunday mornings."

Mike caught the meaning of Tony's words as he watched the ranger circle his wooden schoolteacher's desk and sit down on a quite-new, high-back office chair.

Flanked by a dusty computer and a clean typewriter, Tony began. "Mr. Daniels, why don't you grab a seat and we can get your statement. Once we have that, we can give Daryl a call and see if we can't give him a hand finding your body."

Mike's discomfort meter ratcheted up another notch with Tony's use of the word "your." *It isn't my body*, he thought. The discomfort was punctuated by the fact that the chair he was invited to sit in happened to be entirely within the circle of Stella's outstretched and very sharp-looking paws.

Bud cut in, offering, "Mr. Daniels, let me take your jacket. It's pretty warm in here."

Mike agreed and peeled off his windbreaker, releasing every pungent molecule of his run into the room. Bud, holding his breath, took the coat down the hall while carrying the toxic waste at arm's length.

Surveying the spare office, Mike read the various official notices and warnings that lined the walls. A single bookcase stood next to a row of large gray filing cabinets opposite the desk, its shelves holding official-looking volumes on everything from A to Z. Tucked on the bottom were a few bird and animal field guides. A dual picture frame stood opposite the typewriter on the far side of the desk. Mike could make out a much younger Tony in tan military camouflage toting a scoped rifle along with another man carrying binoculars. The men stood together in front of a helicopter. *The Gulf*, thought Mike, as his eyes angled over to the other half of the frame and what he guessed was Mrs. Savastio, Tony.

"Name...," Tony barked as he saw his surroundings being scrutinized.

The exchange continued to the irregular staccato of Tony's typewriter, one key at a time, until the front side of the form was filled in. Tony paused, pulled the paper from the typewriter, turned it over, and inserted it once again. He cracked his knuckles. "Alrighty Mr. Daniels, what did you see?"

Mike recounted his story, over and over again, to accommodate Tony's speed and proficiency. *I am in hell*, he thought. *I am being held by a bear and tortured with a typewriter.*

Celebrating the completion of the form, Tony tapped the "Return"' key twice, then reached into the top drawer of his desk, and pulled out a badly copied map of the park. "Okay, Mr. Daniels, draw me a picture. Show me where you spotted these folks," directed Savastio, Tony.

Taking the map and marker, Mike drew lines for his direction all the way to a neat little "X" closest to where he thought the body lay. "'X' evidently does mark the spot, eh?"

Tony grunted at Mike's attempt at humor and perused the map. After looking it over, Tony tossed the paper into a wire bin named "Denise."

Tony stood up to stretch his legs and said, "Well, that should about do it. We'll need to wait a bit to see if Daryl and the local police can find your body. If they can't, you're gonna have to take us there."

"My body? I'll show you where they put it," he replied.

Mike watched Tony's face crinkle into a half-smile as he said, "Sorry, Mr. Daniels, but you'd be surprised how many crank calls and wild goose chases we get sent out on. How 'bout some water?"

"That would be great."

"All right. I'll be right back."

Tony returned in a huff and handed Mike a cup of water. Something in Tony's tight-lipped expression and purposeful stride tipped off Mike that more had gone on than just a simple errand. He watched as Tony yanked out a bunch of forms from the back of a filing cabinet, fed one to his typewriter and started stabbing keys.

Mike looked over his cup. "You found him."

Tony replied, "Yep. Musser radioed it in just a moment ago. That's gonna mean a whole bunch of forms for the State Police. Let's get started."

Mike glanced at his watch and guessed that less than a half-hour had gone by since meeting the rangers by the side of the lake. "That was fast."

Tony stopped typing for a second and scrunched his lips together, mulling Mike's comment. "Yea. I guess it was. Your directions must've been pretty good."

Tony finished the remaining sections and turned his head back to Mike and announced, "We're done."

Mike breathed a sigh of relief and smiled.

Tony continued, "...till the troopers get here."

Rocking his head back, Mike looked upward at Stella's open muzzle and thought—*just kill me now.*

Another half-hour crawled by until the shushing sound of tires on gravel announced the arrival of a Pennsylvania State Police cruiser. Mike heard the opening of doors and the renewal of old ties.

Tony went to the front door and greeted Trooper Alvin Hoover of the State Police with a hearty, "Hi, Al."

Mike could hear the muffled small talk end with Tony saying, "...Yea, he's back in my office. C'mon." Mike knew who "he" was.

"Hi, Stella," the policeman said to the bear holding Mike and then introduced himself as "Trooper Alvin Hoover." Mike guessed that mentioning Alvin and the Chipmunks might give a very bad impression to the tall African American that filled out every inch of his uniform with a solid physique. The trooper took the sheaf of papers that constituted all the recorded facts of the case of the buried man so far. He walked around to Tony's chair, took a seat, and murmured his way, page by page, to the end of the paperwork. Flipping open a small notebook and grabbing his microcassette recorder, Trooper Hoover prepared for the interview. He jotted a few things down and turned his full attention to Mike after flicking on the record button.

"Mr. Daniels, thanks for staying with us here while we sort things out," he began. "Tony's told us how you pinpointed the location and that was a big help. I have to ask you a few more questions and then we can send you on your way. This will be an official statement."

Mike nodded in the affirmative, then spoke out loud with a "Yes," as the trooper pointed toward the recorder.

"Mr. Daniels, can you describe the person buried out there?" said Al.

"Well, no, not really, other than he had two feet."

"He?"

"The feet, well, foot, looked like a man's. The other had a dirty work shoe on it," explained Mike.

"You didn't see anything else of the man that you could identify or describe?" probed Al.

"Other than his feet, nothing really. There wasn't a whole lot of him showing when I got there."

Al switched gears and asked, "Fine, fine, now about the two people you talked about. Can you identify them?"

"Identify, no," said Mike, as he was prone to semantics.

"How about describe?" asked Al, whose clipped voice gave away a mild irritation.

"Sure, I noticed the blonde lady first. She was white, probably a few inches shorter than me. She was wearing one of those modest black cocktail dresses. You know, not too revealing. That and a black blazer," described Mike.

"You were checking her out?" chuckled Tony, who had been standing in the doorway.

Mike turned and said, "It's not very often a nicely dressed woman buries bodies in the woods." Mike paused as he went over the scene in his mind's eye as a few more details percolated up. "Her clothes were pretty dirty. Oh, and she had sensible shoes. Black. They were flats, not heels. She was pretty skinny. I could see it in her legs."

"There you go checking her out again," teased Tony.

"I'm a runner and a guy, Tony. I noticed her legs."

"Anything else? Length of hair? Color of her eyes? What was the shape of her face?" asked the trooper.

"It went down to her shoulders, nothing fancy. I couldn't see her eyes from where I was. Her face was like her legs—thin. I could probably pick her out if I saw her again."

Al sensed that the well was running dry on the blonde, so he turned Mike's attention to the other gravedigger. "How 'bout the man? You said he was African American?"

"Yessir. Shorter than you, maybe about my size. Wore a dark blue single-breasted suit—dirty too. He was sweating to beat the band. Gonna be a heck of a cleaning bill," said Mike.

"Hair? Eyes? Anything?"

"Hair was very short and black mixed with gray. Small curls really—what there was of it. He was bald on top. Stubbly beard and a round face. Kinda heavyset." Mike's mind drifted again to the scene. "Wedding band and a gold wristwatch. White handkerchief. He kept using it to clear his eyes."

"From the dirt?" asked Al.

"Actually, it looked more like he was crying," said Mike.

Al's eyebrows lifted. "Anything else?"

"That's pretty much it, sir," finished Mike—or so he thought.

Al had one more set of questions before he'd let Mike go. "Did you see anything else on the trail when you were out there? Was there anybody else out there?"

"A pair of mountain bikers. White; green jacket and blue jacket. I really didn't get a good look at them. They basically scared the shi...daylights out of me," continued Mike.

The trooper jotted a few words down and asked, "How about cars? Trucks? Did you see any other vehicles out there besides the mountain bikes?"

Mike closed his eyes and remembered back to the parking lot after seeing the burial, then shook his head in the negative. Al tapped the recorder so that Mike would verbally say "No" but found him hesitating.

"I didn't see any vehicles after the incident until meeting up with the rangers. I do remember some trucks parked in the lot the fishermen use. Hmmmm—a Nissan pickup that had a boat trailer attached, an old Ford pickup, and Chevy Blazer. The Nissan was yellow, although it was rusting pretty badly. The Ford was primer gray. The Blazer was pretty new and dark red. Other than my Pontiac, that's all I can remember."

"That's pretty good," said Al. "Are you certain? I mean, you've just been through a lot."

Mike tilted his chin down as if he considered Al's question as an insult. Closing his eyes, he thought back to the parking lot and added to his description like a medium at a séance, "The Blazer was parked on the left—away from the Ford and the Nissan. The trailer behind the Nissan looked like the kind that would pull a johnboat— crazy fishermen. And, other than gray, there was nothing special about the Ford."

"Are you sure?" asked Tony again.

"Yes, Ranger Savastio, I am. It's deer season and I was hoping not to see anything in that parking lot on a Sunday morning."

"Gotcha. Yep, that is pretty good, Mr. Daniels. Now, if you'll pardon me for a sec, I want to touch base with Bud."

Al and Tony left Mike alone for a bit. Mike could hear hushed tones and strained to listen in on why they were excluding him from the conversation. He leaned toward the door to try and pick up a few stray words but to no avail.

Tony and Al returned to the room and stood by Mike.

Al said, "Mr. Daniels, thanks for your cooperation. Someone from the State Police will be contacting you to set up a time for you to work with one of our composite technicians."

Mike gave Al a puzzled look.

"I guess you're not up on the latest. Think of a police sketch artist that uses a computer," explained the trooper.

Mike got it.

"We'll need you to help get that description of yours into a reasonable likeness so we can begin our search."

"So, I can go?" Mike asked.

"So long as I can get in touch with you," replied Al, extending his hand, which Mike shook on his way out the door.

Tony stood in the hall and said, "I'll give you a ride to your car. I need to grab my keys. Meet you at the door."

"See you, Stella," said Mike as he looked at his large furry host and headed toward the door. Before he left, Mike heard more murmuring from the rangers' offices and he sneaked down the hall to get within earshot.

Mike could hear Tony speaking to Trooper Hoover.

"You're right, Tony. He didn't do it."

"I told you, Al, his hands were soft. If he moved a bunch of rocks they'd be all roughed up," said Tony.

"What if he used gloves?"

"He has a pair in his jacket pocket and they are as clean as a whistle. Bud took some swabbings of the dirt on the jacket, but that isn't gonna tell us much more than he was where he said he was."

"True enough, Tony. My, my. What a heck of a way to spend a Sunday," said Al.

Mike shook his head in agreement with Al's sentiment and slipped back to the doorway to await Tony's return.

Tony returned and opened the door for Mike. "C'mon, Mr. Daniels. I'll give you a ride back to your car."

Tony and Mike made the return trip to Mike's Pontiac in the same silence he had arrived in, although Tony's occasional sideward glances kept making Mike feel like he was being observed. Once the creaking Chrysler pulled up to Mike's Pontiac, Mike hopped out and fished for his car key.

"We'll keep in touch. See ya, Mr. Daniels," said Tony.

Maybe it was the way Tony looked at Mike when he said goodbye or maybe it was the way Tony phrased it. Whichever way it was, Mike thought, it wasn't leaving him with any more of a warm fuzzy feeling than Stella had given him.

Chapter 5

Abby could have been the model for a small sketch if the dictionary wished to illustrate the word *indignant*. Sitting in the middle of the kitchen, she waited for the garage door to open. She had already prepared her look and was executing it perfectly. The look consisted of a single raised ear, symbolizing her willingness to hear the explanation as to the discomfort in her bladder and, far more importantly, the delay of her dinner. Tracing down the line from her right ear was a single raised eyebrow to notice her owner's arrival, and, to inflict guilt. The left eyebrow shared none of its right's activity at it was set in quiet indifference of his late showing. Finally, her left ear lowered flat against her head to show that she really didn't care what the explanation was. What she did care about was dinner, pure and simple. The look was calculated to get the fastest response to that most urgent need—food. It was not in Abby's character to do the happy puppy food dance. That would never do. Her look would.

When the door swung open, she cocked her head to emphasize her irritation. Pleased with her performance, she waited to hear the cupboard open and the sweet sound of kibbles hitting the dish. Instead, her owner's running bag hit the table and he strode right on past Abby, look and all. Within a few minutes, Abby heard the shower start.

What a complete and utter loss, she thought. Fighting a strong instinct to go up and chew on Mike's favorite running shoes, Abby reconsidered when she felt that such an act would be beneath her—

not to mention two flights of stairs upwards. With a sigh, she trotted up the stairs and lay at the bathroom door, preparing another look.

All of the energy and thought Abby applied to *indignant* was now channeled into *pity* as she heard the last of the routine sounds originating from the bathroom. Lying prone, Abby placed her muzzle between her paws, and her ears lowered to match. Poignantly portraying woe, Abby cast her eyes downward.

Her owner opened the door and found so sorrowful a scene that he could not help but pet her upon the head and ask her, "Oh, what's wrong, girl? Do you sense what I've been through? You're such a sweetie."

Abby's control faded, and she let a loud sigh escape at her second failure. Instinct flared up, and she fought the strong urge to bite the closest thing to a sheep she could find in the hindquarters. Mike's hindquarters, and the rest of him, climbed the second set of steps to the bedroom. Abby regarded Mike's posterior for a moment and followed him up the staircase. She lay down near the door to make sure that her presence was not overlooked.

Watching her owner pace about the bedroom, gathering clothes and ranting at something new, Abby imagined herself wasting away from starvation. The agony of the storytelling outweighed the gnawing in her stomach, and she left to take up a vigil next to her dish. She waited there, wondering whom Mike was talking to, while he continued his story upstairs. The chatter from the bedroom ended, and her owner came down the steps into the kitchen. Desperate, Abby uttered a single "wuff" to blatantly announce her desire. To her amazement, it worked.

"Oh my God, Abby. I forgot all about your food," Mike said, realizing his mistake.

No kidding, she thought.

The meal came with a price, although Abby tried to pay as little as possible. The price was the resumption of Mike's story, which she tried to ignore. When she was finished, she turned to see his troubled face. Figuring that he was upset over missing her meal, she quietly walked over to his left hand and pushed her nose underneath it. Abby enjoyed Mike's after-dinner attention. After all, it was always easier to forgive this species with a full belly. Soon, both man and dog trundled off to the living room and fell into a pleasant nap.

Waking as the December sun fell to the horizon, Mike pressed the on button of the TV remote to help rouse him.

"Strengthen your quads..." Flick.

"Remove dirt and..." Flick.

"Taste the incredible..." Flick.

"Nobody beats our dea..." Flick.

"A homicide in a State Park ha..." Flick.

"As God is my witness..." Flick.

With clumsy fingers, Mike groped for the other end of the channel key on the remote. He pressed the key twice, so fast that he went right past his intended channel and was greeted by a man in a dog suit selling cars.

"There's no dogs on our lo..." Flick.

"We'll have that story and more in sixty seconds," spoke the talking head on the TV.

Mike scrambled around the entertainment center fumbling for a videotape to record the local channel's take on what happened. Hitting "Eject" on the VCR, he hunted in vain for the tape he had labeled "Blank Tape." His mad search ended when he realized that the tape ejected and the blank tape were one and the same. Once it came to rest, he checked the channel selection and pressed "Record."

The anchorman read the stories for the night with a smile on his face. "Here's the top stories Sunday, December, 1st. A power failure at a local mall leaves hundreds searching in the dark for bargains. Let's go on the scene with WBWY reporter, Ben Kidder..."

Fighting the urge to change channels, Mike tapped the channel changer while Mr. Kidder asked all the obvious questions and got all the obvious answers while rent-a-cops chased shoplifters just out of the range of the cameraman's bright light.

"...for WBWY, this is Ben Kidder," finally signaled the end of what Mike considered just a wee bit less important than a man's life.

The anchorman continued, "Thanks, Ben. Today was the annual Christmas Parade in downtown Harrisburg. Let's talk to Margot Beatty, on the scene..."

Mike wondered if the reporter's name should be "I'll go batty," which was exactly how he felt. The shot depicted the reporter receiving a balloon hat from a pair of clowns, which Mike suspected were the station manager and news producer. Margot gave highlights on the parade held in the state capital to herald the coming of Saint Nick. Mike didn't have any problem with Saint Nick unless he happened to be buried in a certain state park sans one shoe.

"...for WBWY, this is Margot Beatty reporting," concluded the balloon-wearing and clown-flanked reporter. The anchor said thanks to the reporter, though she was no longer on the air and continued, "A mystery is unfolding in a Muir County State Park. Our reporter, Kirk Griffin, is on the scene, Kirk..."

"Thank you, David," began the decidedly typical made-for-TV blond man. "We're standing in Gerald Sanford State Park in northern Muir County waiting for further statements from the State Police regarding the apparent homicide of a white male whose identity is currently unknown. Sources tell WBWY that a passing hiker made the discovery this morning and informed the park authorities."

"Hiker? I'm a trail runner, you idiot." protested Mike. Mike recognized the location as the parking lot near the swampy nether regions of the park. The lot was teeming with news crews, each trying to conceal the fact that the lot was overrun with news crews. The camera jiggled and jostled as each news team jousted for an interesting angle to feed the masses. The image stabilized showing a view of Kirk Griffin's midriff and a bunch of cars. After a second or two, the camera panned up to a perturbed Kirk, who regained his composure and said, "Earlier in the afternoon, Sergeant Alvin Hoover of the State Police made this statement."

Mike recognized Al from earlier in the day though this Al had his game face on, so to speak. "A hiker discovered a man along the

trailside at approximately 9:30 a.m. this morning. He notified the
Park Rangers who arrived at the scene and found a deceased white
male approximately fifty to sixty years old. We are awaiting the findings of the State Police Forensics Unit to determine the cause of death.
No other information will be released at this time," said the stern-
faced Al.

"Trail runner," corrected Mike as if Kirk was waiting for critiques.

The clip of Al Hoover ended with Kirk shuffling from foot to
foot, frowning at the camera. Once the cue was given, his face brightened up like he was modeling aftershave in Malibu. "That was Sergeant Alvin Hoover's statement on the homicide here at Sanford State
Park. No other information has been released so far. WBWY will
have more details for you as they become available. This is Kirk
Griffin reporting. Back to you, David."

David, the anchor, spoke each line scrolling up the teleprompter
and left the crime as buried in the news as the poor man Mike had
discovered. Hitting the Eject button, Mike grabbed the cassette and
stuck it on the shelf with all the other tapes marked "Blank Tape."

Something about the telecast nagged at Mike, but he had no
idea what brought on the feeling of unease. He rewound the tape and
played it a second time. Glossing over the earlier stories, Mike watched
the animated reporter at the parking lot and listened to Trooper
Hoover's deadpan delivery of his report. Nothing seemed irregular,
but the nagging remained. He hit rewind again and listened to Al
once more. *No, that wasn't it,* he thought. Thumbing the remote a
third time, Mike watched the tape play in reverse. *Al didn't look that
much different going backward as he did going forward*, Mike mused.
When the tape spun back past the parking lot scene, the feeling returned, but nothing that Mike noticed seemed to be the cause of the
feeling. *Maybe it was just seeing everything on TV.*

After ejecting the cassette, Mike put it on the shelf with his
other tapes, a bit reluctant to let go. His hand wavered with indeci-
sion as to whether he should let go or take another look.

At that moment, Abby stood and shook off the lingering effects
of her nap. Mimicking his pet, Mike put the cassette down and tried

his best full body shake. It worked, at least for the few seconds it took for him to cross the living room. As he reached the light switch, Mike stared at the videotape for a moment and the nagging feeling returned.

Chapter *6*

Images flashed into Mike's conscious mind of a pair of feet protruding from a stone pile while the voice of Tony Savastio echoed, "We'll keep in touch. See ya, Mr. Daniels...We'll keep in touch. See ya, Mr. Daniels...Mr. Daniels...Mr. Daniels..."

"Mr. Daniels...Mr. Daniels," called another voice.

Female, thought Mike—*insistent*.

"Mr. Daniels?" asked the Boorman Incorporated receptionist.

"Er...Oh, sorry. Yes. Um...Oh, yes. I have a meeting with Paul Denning." Mike showed the receptionist at Boorman Incorporated his gunmetal I.D. badge denoting his employment with Bleeding Edge Consultants.

Shaking off his daydream, Mike focused on the task at hand and dreaded it. Looking forward to his meeting at Boorman as much as a dental patient enjoyed having a root canal performed without Novocain, Mike strolled past the receptionist to a small conference room. The exception was that Mike was the dentist, and Paul Denning was the patient. Mike was convinced that Denning had a fairly large cavity between his ears.

Other than the age of the paint or the furniture, all corporate conference rooms looked alike to Mike. A glance at his watch told him that Denning was not on time, which, according to the second team of Bleeding Edge Consultants, was typical. Denning burst into the room fifteen minutes later—a cup of coffee in one hand and a fistful of excuses in the other. Mike glanced upward at the balding man whose tie canted out forty-five degrees due to the expanse of his stomach-stressed shirt. While Denning whined, Mike extended one finger to silence the bluster, finish his thoughts, and offset the make-believe importance of the man standing in the door. He would have never done this at any of the shops he worked at before and was quite amazed with how much deference he was given when a company's upper management turned Bleeding Edge loose. Mike offered Paul a seat and began his interview.

Weaverton's instincts were proven correct once again as Mike listened to Denning's droning. Mike kept his pen ready for a drop of insight to be filtered through the self-importance and bull. Even if he did miss it, the wireless mike on his digital dictation machine wouldn't. Every now and then, a gem would percolate out and he would jot something on his legal pad. Some thoughts would arrange themselves in his brain and he'd play connect-the-dots with Denning's comments and other activities at the warehouse that Mike had watched last week. Nodding in seeming agreement with Denning, Mike listened to the one-way conversation.

With his concentration ebbing, Mike's mind drifted a bit and he found himself stacking rocks on the obese man's body while he was still talking. Shaking off the nasty daydream, Mike refocused on Denning. Time ran out and Mike thanked the manager, who seemed very happy to have had this "little talk."

Mike was very happy when the "little talk" concluded and was happier still at the amount of information gleaned from so much chatter. It verified what he had seen in the reports in the first place; Denning had been hoarding inventory for one particular order fulfillment manager in what Mike called a "back-scratching" relationship. The order fulfillment manager always had big sales while the rest had nothing but backorders. That translated into bonuses and customer service awards. *Interestingly enough*, Mike thought, *Denning got in on some of the cash too because the order fulfillment manager wrote glowing memos to Denning's boss. Yes*, he thought, *a nice, neat little arrangement. Meanwhile, the rest of the company was losing out on sales*. How the so-called second team missed it was beyond him. Of course, Mike knew he would have to sanitize their oversights before he put down anything on email or paper. He would tailor the whole report in business-speak to "identify efficiency roadblocks and increase productivity." The more of these roadblocks he removed, the more Bleeding Edge would get paid. The more Bleeding Edge got paid, the more he got paid, and that thought made him happy. *John would be the happiest*, he thought. Sending Mike on this special opportunity had paid off.

While he mulled Denning's comments, his cell phone chimed with an incoming page. Mike thumbed the buttons and frowned at the message. Judy had sent him a page, "Phone Police—555-8532." The sickly green backlight on the phone's LCD panel made him feel uneasy as he dialed the number.

"Trooper Hoover speaking," answered Al.

Mike let the words hang in the air a moment and said, "Hi, Sergeant Hoover, this is Mike Daniels."

"Well, that's nice of you to return my call so quickly. Judy tells me you're a very busy man," said Al.

And Judy is a busybody, thought Mike as he imagined her broadcasting Mike's message from the police throughout the entire free world.

"I was wondering when you can stop by State Police Headquarters so that we can go over what you saw and spend some time with our composite artist. Would this afternoon work for you? Judy said that you weren't booked," asked Al.

"She did, did she?" said Mike as he paged through his planner. "How about 3:00 p.m.?"

"3:00 p.m. is fine with me. Do you know where we're located?"

"Up on Elmerton near the Post Office?"

"Exactly, Mr. Daniels. Just come in and speak to the guard at the desk. He'll run you through Security and then let me know when you're ready. Thanks," said Al.

"You're welcome," replied Mike, who was not very thrilled at the prospect of identifying gravediggers. He debated the idea of calling John Weaverton to let him know where he was going, but figured that Judy was way ahead of him. A moment later, the phone chimed again with another page. It was from John. Mike viewed the question, "What's up?" along with John's phone number. Judy had accomplished her mission.

Mike drove back to his office along the congested city streets neatly defined by a traffic light per block. For Mike, it would be better described as a red light per block, which always seemed to be his luck. Eluding the last light, Mike pulled into the parking lot of Bleeding Edge.

Bleeding Edge's location afforded him with some of the nicest areas around to jog in, which was exactly what he had in mind as he rounded the sidewalk to the front door. Mike watched Judy's eyes welcome him with a look that, at first, said "Hi" and was followed by another look that said, "What have you done?" Her voice never wavered on the headset-mounted phone during the less-than-business-related call with her mother. Mike took it as a blessing and made for his office.

After picking up his mail, Mike sped down the hall, up the grand curve of the old oak staircase, and into his small office. He dropped his running gear on the floor and lowered his laptop to the desk. The phone on his desk winked at him with a small Cyclops eye indicating that there were messages waiting. John, and whoever else called, could all wait until his lunchtime run was done.

Mike returned after a few miles of exercise that provided enough stress relief to set the day right. It was nice, he thought, to go the entire five miles without finding any of the regular lunchtime crowd burying each other along the river. After showering, he returned to his desk to eat and answer the infernal phone. Mike navigated the answering system, one message at a time. The last call was from John Weaverton, who had called to ask about the Boorman meeting and to see how things were going, which Mike translated into, "Why did the police call?"

Looking out his office window at the apse, Mike saw that John's office light was off and his chair empty. This provided him with the perfect opportunity to return the call via phone mail and eliminated the need for vague excuses as to why he wouldn't be able to tell John about his little discovery in the woods. *Ah, technology*, he mused.

Toiling away the afternoon, Mike wrote reports that few would read and fewer still would give a flying fig about—until the reader figured out how much money there was to save. *Money always got the upper management's attention*, he thought. As his report was nearing completion, Mike checked his watch and found that it was time to head over to the State Police building for his appointment. Sneaking out past Judy, whose head was still mounted in her headset while she talked to her mom, proved easy, and he was on his way.

* * *

Zipping up his coat against the December air, Mike left his car in a visitor spot on the State Police lot and hustled into the lobby. "I'm here to meet with Sergeant Al Hoover," he said to a young trooper seated behind the information desk.

"Name please?" came the query from the serious looking young trooper.

"Daniels, Mike Daniels."

The trooper tapped a few keys on his computer and his eyes tracked down the list until he found a match. "May I see your driver's license?"

Taken a bit by surprise, Mike fumbled around until he found his license.

The trooper looked at the picture and looked at Mike for a long moment. He handed the ID back and said, "Thank you. Please remove any coins, keys or other metal objects from your pockets, place them in this tray and then walk through the detector."

Mike's unease magnified when the trooper's next movement was to don a pair of latex gloves. The mental image of a recent doctor's visit that involved wearing a hospital gown tied in the back raced through Mike's mind and he unconsciously tightened his buttocks. After he passed through the metal detector, the trooper approached him, gloves and all, and proceeded to fish through the tray of assorted coins and keys. The trooper finished, looked up at the wide-eyed Daniels, and sensed his discomfort.

"Hope that didn't worry you. September 11th. We have to be careful these days."

"Oh, right," Mike agreed, relieved that the gloves were being removed.

"Why don't you have a seat, Mr. Daniels? I'll let Sergeant Hoover know you are here."

Al appeared before Mike's posterior could warm the metal seat. "We're gonna meet with Mrs. Fanelli. She's our resident composite artist," informed Al as he led Mike down the warren of hallways and numbered offices.

Noting the same interior design as the bleak office he had visited earlier, Mike obediently followed Al down the corridor until the pair stopped at a plain wooden door bearing a plastic sign engraved "Fanelli." Al knocked and walked in before being granted permission by the occupant. The light washing out of the room was warm and golden as opposed to the banks of fluorescent green mounted everywhere else in the building. Mike viewed the room with a look just short of amazement, as it was an unlikely place to find in such serious and sterile surroundings. The walls were satin beige as opposed to clinical white or institutional green. An honest-to-God floor lamp glowed against the back wall, and another gooseneck lamp lit an easel holding a large sketchpad.

The sketchpad-obscured Maggie Fanelli acknowledged the interruption with a nasally "Be with you in a second. Grab a seat."

Happy to have a seat in a plush chair, Mike surveyed the caricatures of various policemen mounted in frames on the walls. Healthy plants rose out of handwoven baskets, and the homey smell of cinnamon wafted through the air. It finally sank in to Mike that he was in a version of this person's living room instead of their office. The scratching on the other side of the pad stopped and Mike turned his attention to the woman that appeared from behind the easel.

Expecting to see more of the military formality and professionalism that the State Police displayed, Mike found himself staring at the late fifty-something woman clad in black, over-stressed stretch-pants and turtleneck sweater. Mike wondered just what shade of Clairol her dark red hair was. Dangling from her ears were hoop earrings that Mike guessed were large enough to pass a baseball through. The earrings, he thought, were the perfect complement to the varnished wood block and glitzy glass beads of her necklace sitting atop ample cleavage.

Maggie peered from over top of the ornate scrollwork of her reading glasses, realized that she was being sized up, and said, "So you're the guy that saw some folks burying Woodsy the Owl." Her dark red lipstick settled into a Cheshire smile as they rounded their way past the "O" on their way to "L."

Mike snapped out of his analyst mode, trying to forget the layers of makeup around her eyes, and chuckled at the thought of a pair of costume feet projecting from the stone pile instead of what he did witness. It was a good way to break the ice and ease his tension.

"We're gonna have company while we work on drawing the two people you saw. There's this kid in Information Systems that wants to replace me with a computer and he wants to sit in. That okay with you?"

Mike didn't give it much thought and figured that it would be interesting to see some imaging software, so he shook his head in the affirmative.

Maggie picked up the phone and said, "Quit playing Solitaire and c'mon down here, Junior. We got work to do." She hung up without so much as a "goodbye" and opened a drawer in her wooden schoolteacher's desk. She reached in and pulled out a shoebox full of foil bags, each one containing a different flavor of coffee. "You look like a Vanilla Hazelnut to me. Want a cup?" she asked.

Mike was caught off guard by the generosity but liked the idea of a cup of coffee on a chilly day and said, "That would be great. Thanks."

Maggie scooped the coffee into a small coffee maker and started it up. Soon, Mike's nose inhaled the sweet java mélange perking a drop at a time into a beaker.

A knock at the door announced the arrival of Andy Reardon. Unlike Al, Andy waited at the door for permission to enter, which Maggie was not inclined to give, at least for a few moments. Instead, Maggie leaned back in her chair and winked at Mike, who couldn't begin to guess her motive. She read the puzzlement in his face and said, "We have to break these kids in right, you know." Maggie didn't let the time drag on too long and finally granted permission for Andy to come in.

Andy, or "Junior," as Maggie referred to him, looked like the textbook version of the word "nerd." Mike wondered just how much radiation he received from his monitor and how little he received from the sun. The very young man's hair was at least an honest shade of red, thought Mike.

"Fire that thing up, Junior," commanded Maggie in a somewhat frumpy tone. "Junior thinks that his computer can do a better job than I can," said Maggie to Mike.

"I didn't say that, Maggie, it's just that I think it will...," interrupted Andy.

"You just think that I should be using that instead of my eyes and hands," Maggie countered.

"I just want you to give it a try."

"Try? Every six months you guys upstairs want me to try some kind of computer program that's supposed to do my job, and every six months I send you back up the steps with your tail between your legs."

"Maybe not this time, Maggie," Andy said with the kind of naïve confidence that only fresh-out-of-college kids possessed.

"Ohhhhhhh," said Maggie with an emphasis that said a challenge was on. "Well, Junior, are you willing to put your money where your mouth is?"

Junior's confidence wavered for a moment, but then cockiness rushed in where angels feared to tread. "Yea. Sure. What'll it be?"

Maggie realized that her interviewee was being ignored and included him in the competition. "First off, Mr. Daniels will be our impartial judge, if he doesn't mind."

Mike didn't. He agreed and smiled wryly at the thought.

"Okay, Mr. Daniels picks the winner. If he likes your computer creation then I'll toss my sketchpad in the can and run that stupid computer from now on. If he likes my work better, you get to take me to Stumpy's Bar next Tuesday, your treat, and you come with me to bingo afterward," dared Maggie.

"Ummm." Andy hesitated, blanching at the thought of being Maggie's date. Then there was the thought of being her escort to bingo, which he considered a fate worse than death. He swallowed hard and Maggie picked right up on it.

"No balls, Junior?"

Andy's manhood, what little there was, had been challenged. It had been challenged by a pro and backed into a corner. He could pack up his toys and go home, or show Maggie the wonders of technology once and for all. "You're on."

After shaking hands, the pair retired to neutral corners. Maggie gave Mike his coffee in a honest-to-goodness ceramic mug and had him sit between the warring parties. Sitting down at an unused table opposite Maggie's desk, Andy pulled the dust cover off the huge monitor and punched the on button. Mike watched both competitors limber their fingers. Andy keyed the passwords and mouse-clicked away at the various icons and menus that appeared. Maggie simply leaned a small sketchpad against the easel and sharpened her pencil. Each looked at Mike when the preparations were complete.

"Mr. Daniels, is it okay if I call you Mike?" asked Maggie.

"Sure," Mike replied.

"According to the report, you saw two people, a blonde Caucasian woman and a male African American."

"That's right."

"Who did you see first?"

"The woman. I saw her face a couple of times, but her back was turned toward me most of the time."

"Well, let's stick with her. Close your eyes and think about her for a little bit," said Maggie.

Mike took a drink from the mug and did so. At first, it was hard to see her. As he relaxed a bit, her face focused in his mind. In the meantime, Maggie had pulled some binders from her credenza, and Andy had brought up a series of thumbnail pictures on the monitor.

"Mike, how old was the woman you saw? Twenties? Thirties? Older?" asked Maggie.

"Probably thirtyish," answered Mike.

"Was her face thin, fat, round or oval?"

Mike didn't quite know what shape her face was and Maggie picked up on his confusion.

"Here. Take a look through these pictures and see if any of the faces are similar," requested Maggie.

Mike did so and felt the presence of Andy's eyes peering over his shoulder. Maggie spotted Andy's apparent cheating and allayed

Mike's suspicions, "It's okay, Mike, we both have to start at basically the same point. We have to get a general idea from you of the person's basic appearance. These books give us categories of people to look at. Once you pick out the person in there for me, Andy will do the same on his toy over there."

"Toy?" Andy protested.

Mike returned to the book Maggie picked out for him and sifted the pictures for anyone having a resemblance. After five minutes of scrutinizing, he picked out a couple of faces that he thought best looked like the woman. Maggie tagged the two faces with post-its, wrote something on a form and then showed the pictures to Andy, who feverishly clicked his mouse. Maggie turned her attention to the sketchpad and scribbled away.

Turning her attention back to Mike, she asked, "What was her hair like?"

"Blonde," said Mike.

"Okay, blonde, but how long was it? Could you tell if she was a natural or bottle blonde? Was it curly, straight, permed, or kind of tossed like mine? Did she have it up?"

Mike closed his eyes and thought back to the park again. "Straight. Parted down the center. It curved around the sides of her face."

"That's good, Mr. Daniels," Andy chimed in.

The process went on through all the parts of the face with varying success based on Mike's recollection. Maggie quickly sketched while Andy dragged and dropped. An hour jetted by without anybody noticing, particularly Mike, who was on his second cup of coffee and third piece of chocolate from Maggie's stash. Andy was not offered any.

Both artists asked Mike to look at their respective work from time to time to see what he thought. Mike would think about it and guide their talents to relocate a feature or change it slightly. The woman's face materialized on paper and on the computer monitor before his eyes.

Mike viewed both and shook his head, saying, "Yea, that's pretty much the person I saw."

"That may be so, but which composite do you think looks more like her?" asked Andy.

Mike sensed that the question was a loaded one as he watched the pair exchanging narrow-eyed looks with each other. He also knew that there was little difference between both of the images presented to him. "I'd say that both are pretty much on target," Mike said.

"Yea, yea, yea," replied Maggie, who was not pleased with the politically correct answer. She tore the sheet from its loose binding and set it in a folder on her desk. After jotting some things down, she announced that it was time for a break. Andy showed Mike to the rest room and Maggie ambled down the hall to sneak out the back door and have a cigarette.

The trio returned to Maggie's office, and Mike's nose wrinkled at the smell of tobacco.

Maggie apologized, justifying it by saying, "I'm getting old and there are so few vices I can indulge myself in these days." She followed her excuse with a catty wink to Andy, whose eyes widened with the inferred flirtation.

"Al...l...lright, Mr. Daniels, Mike. What about the gentleman?" said Andy, who was dealing with the very unpleasant thought that Maggie was undressing him with her eyes.

Mike picked up on the method laid down by the first run-through and was delivering better descriptions of the features of the man's round face and sad eyes. Both artists moved at a quicker and more determined pace. After all, a bet was a bet. Mike helped Maggie tweak the last of the features he could recall from the brief encounter. It made him feel uncomfortable to see both faces again. In many respects, he wished that he couldn't remember them at all.

Andy continued to apply filters and shading to his creation, hoping to show Maggie just how well he could do. He proudly finished up and sent his composite to the color printer, then retrieved it for Mike. "What do you think, Mr. Daniels?" asked the confident Junior.

Mike scrutinized the print-out and looked over at Maggie's sketch. Each moment hung in the air in silence. Mike's eyes traversed the color print, then swapped to the pencil sketch. Mike looked again at the print-out and said, "I think Maggie's is more on target."

"What do you mean?" questioned Andy.

"I think yours looks like Shrek," said Mike.

"Shrek?" asked the stricken young man.

"Shrek, the ogre from the movie *Shrek*. You drew Shrek with a tan. What happened? You were pretty close before," said Mike.

A single loud "Ha" emanated from a delighted Maggie.

"Noooooooo" wailed from the devastated Andy as the realization hit home.

Whether Mike meant it or not, the contest had concluded. He looked at Andy and found him somehow paler than before, and Mike wondered how that could be physically possible.

"Good try, Junior. You almost had me worried after the first round," gloated Maggie. She rose and walked over to him, cupping his chin with her hand, saying, "Tuesday at six. I don't wanna miss Happy Hour. I can't wait to show you to the girls. Wear a nice tie, okay?" Maggie lifted the unresponsive Andy up off his seat and ushered him out the door. "See ya Tuesday, Junior," said Maggie as she dismissed him with a pat on the butt. Maggie returned to the still-smiling Mike. "Somebody's gotta tame these young punks."

Mike speculated that Andy was not the first, or last, to be brought low by Maggie.

Two hours had zipped by, thought Mike. Maggie filled out the rest of her paperwork and let Mike know that she would be adding finishing touches to the sketches later on. From there, the State Police would circulate the composites amongst themselves first and onto the area's local law enforcement after that. If no leads developed quickly, the composites would be published in the local newspapers for the good citizens of Pennsylvania to peruse. She picked up the phone and called Al, who had been waiting back in his office, "Oh hiiii, Al. Mr. Daniels and I are all done. Yes, he's fine. You know I'm always gentle with first-timers." A wink was shot at Mike. "Wasn't I, sweetie?"

Mike smirked back at the older woman with the twinkle in her eye.

"Al said he'll be down for you in a minute. Thanks for your help," Maggie finished as she offered her hand to shake.

Mike obliged and said, "You're a piece of work, Maggie."

"A work of art, Mr. Daniels; a work of art," she countered with one hand on her hip and the other on her hair in Mae West style.

Al took Mike back to his cubicle where he took down yet another statement and filled out another set of forms. Al apologized for all the paperwork and explained, in gory detail, why he needed it. Somehow, Mike managed to stay awake as another hour went by while every "'I'" was dotted and "T" crossed.

After thanking Mike for his time, Al took Mike back to the front desk, saying, "Maggie's something else, isn't she? She's been around since the sixties when she walked in off the street carrying a drawing of a guy that held up a market in her old neighborhood in Riverdale. It was a bang-on likeness, and the word was that they nabbed him the same day. She's been our composite artist ever since. You wouldn't believe how many bad guys ended up in jail 'cause of her stuff. She organized all of the mug shot books, too, so we could narrow them down by sex, race, age, and facial structure. Not too many like her left. I think that Andy probably hopes that's true."

"It was pretty amazing. We just sat down and talked. Before I knew it, the faces in my mind appeared on paper," said Mike.

"That's her real magic. She gets you to relax and live the moment. Did she offer you coffee or chocolate?"

"Both."

"Both? Both eh? Hehehehe. You'd better watch it, next thing you know, she's gonna ask you to bingo," joked Al.

"Too late for that. Andy's her man."

"Oh man, poor Junior bet her again, didn't he?" laughed Al.

Mike nodded.

"Those bingo ladies are gonna have their way with him yet."

Chapter 7

Mike called Abby in just in time for the pair of them to watch the local dinnertime news. Watching in vain for more news on his incident, Mike found that the event had dropped off the local news' radar. By Wednesday, he had quit trying. Since Sunday, there had been no word on the burial, as Mike liked to think of it. To him, *burial* was a much more gentle word than murder. Regardless of which word he used, Mike still dwelt on the events of Sunday. He tried to counter his recollections by pouring himself into his home routines, which included paying a lot more attention to Abby.

While the television news fell silent within a day of the burial, the newspaper did not. That was due to the paper's middle-of-the-night publishing time. This put the paper at the distinct disadvantage of being almost a day behind any broadcast media. What the paper lacked in timing, however, it generally made up in content. The snippet-ridden TV news never seemed to have the time to give the full story to its attention-span-challenged viewers. Of course, the *Harrisburg Post* happened to have no more content save the interesting line, "The cause of death was listed as 'unknown' pending the State Police Coroner's findings."

Like his channel surfing, Mike scanned the paper's local section for the answers to his questions. *Who, and what, killed the man beneath the stones? Was the man still alive when they buried him? Was it a drug deal gone sour? How about an unlucky husband?*

Leafing through the national news, Mike passed over the wire stories and the mindful and mindless letters to the editor. Bomb scares

in a local high school got relegated to page six while holiday shopping expectations got much bigger headlines on page three. Paging
into the local section, he passed over obituaries and business news
until he almost made it to the sports page. There, tucked into the
nether reaches of the back page, were three muddy sketches and a
short column that read:

SUSPECTS WANTED FOR QUESTIONING IN
STATE PARK BODY DISCOVERY
Body Found in Shallow Grave Still Goes Unidentified
By Bill Renard for the *Harrisburg Post*

The body of a white male about fifty years old discovered in Sanford State Park goes unidentified after the
coroner's investigation. The cause of death has been listed
as suspicious.

The State Police have released sketches of two people:
an African American male approximately fifty years of age,
brown hair and brown eyes, and a Caucasian female, approximately thirty years of age with blonde hair. Both are
wanted in connection with the investigation.

The State Police have also released a composite drawing of the victim. Persons having information regarding
this case should phone the State Police at 717-555-1213.

Tucked next to the article were three sketches. Seeing the inky
display in the newspaper gave the composites a different and dis-
jointed view. Two of the pictures didn't look like Mike's sketches at
all. They looked like every other criminal sketch that he routinely
ignored in the newspaper except for the fact that he had a hand in
their creation. The people depicted looked even more foreign and
strange to him. He had seen them alive, stacking stones just five days
ago and now they were on their way to a Post Office wall. The third
sketch drew his attention away from the others. The lifelessness in
the sketch echoed the character of the person portrayed. Mike knew
he was looking at the victim.

The article told Mike precious little about the crime. In the same
token, his analyst sense kicked on telling him what wasn't documented

said more than was apparent to the casual reader. He remembered back to each step Al told him would occur when they dispensed the drawings. Both the State and local police had their turn at identifying the pair and, having turned up no easy leads, released them to the public. Mike wondered if it would help or hinder their chances. The comment about the cause of death also drew Mike's attention. *That's a laugh*, he thought. *After all, why would burying a human being under a pile of rocks be considered suspicious?*

Having folded the paper, Mike tucked it away under the end table and spent the remainder of the night channel surfing until his eyes got heavy. Rising sluggishly from the couch, he spied the newspaper lying there folded backward with the three faces watching him. "Sorry, " he said to the still nameless victim, "if those two have any sense, they'll be long gone." Mike turned out the light and went upstairs to turn down the sheets. Abby was already in the bedroom, fast asleep.

Mike's eyes opened once he felt the weight on his chest. He moved his arms to push the weight off but found them unresponsive, pinned under the same load. The weight was shortening his breath and he fought his chin down enough to see what had trapped him. His eyes opened farther in the horror of seeing not one single weight upon him, but dozens of gray rocks stacked all around his body. More stones were being stacked around his head and limited his view. Each one made that infernal thunk sound. He tried in vain to lift his head, but the pile had shifted down upon him once more. With his lungs withering against the weight, she finally came into view. She stood there, glowering over him in black stretch pants and turtleneck, with her belly and chest jutting out. Mike could see all the way up her nose from his angle. Tilting her head, she positioned her stone—and thunk. Summoning up what strength remained, Mike asked, "What are you doing?"

"I need you to hold still for your sketch, sweetie," replied Maggie Fanelli.

With consciousness fading, Mike could see Maggie sketching manically. She stopped and turned the pad toward Mike. There, on the paper was the face Mike had seen earlier of the poor man buried in the rocks. Feeling the cold rush of desperation sweep through him, Mike flailed, his limbs uselessly in their rocky prisons. More footsteps approached. He could make out all of the bingo ladies laughing in unison, baying out a high-pitched monotone, "He He He He..."

The edges of his sight grew dark as his view slipped further away. Looking up, he could see Maggie bent over; lips parted and tongue sticking out for a French kiss. While the edges of his vision vignetted in blackness, Maggie's face grew close and her tongue kissed his trapped face, all to the accompaniment of the "He He He He He..."

Mike's eyes flew open, and he found himself wrapped in a cold, damp shroud of his own perspiration-soaked sheets. Glancing at his chest, he saw Abby lying atop him, earnestly licking him awake since the alarm clock's beckon had failed to rouse him. It still warbled out its electronic annoyance to wake the dead from their slumber. Turning in the sweaty covers, Mike gave the alarm a hard whack. He looked into Abby's eyes and said, "Oh, thank God it's you."

* * *

Mike immersed himself in his work to fend off the constant seep of memories from the burial. When lunchtime rolled around, he changed into his running clothes and jetted out the door without disturbing Judy's perpetual conversation.

"Saxophone, Mom. You know; it looks like a "J." No, that's a trombone, Mom. Yes, he does have nice lips. No Mom, we haven't..."

Another cold December day greeted him as he left Bleeding Edge. Azure blue skies reflected off the river's depths. A few hearty runners and walkers dotted the walkway as they always did, all of them taking advantage of the chance to get some exercise. Mike slipped into a runner's trance and his tensions abated with every step. While running was an abhorrent form of exercise to most, Mike generally enjoyed his time on foot. If nothing else, it gave him a change of view from his corner office and a breath of fresh air.

Mike didn't see the man perched on a mountain bike some fifty yards behind him. He mirrored Mike's movements as he turned across an iron bridge that led to City Island where the ballpark and other amusements resided. Stopping at the entrance, the cyclist leaned his bike against a nearby picnic table and sat on the table top, waiting for Mike's return. The island offered a single road around its periphery and only two exits, both of which were plainly visible to the cyclist. During his wait, the cyclist's cell phone chirped to life and he peeled his helmet and hat to be able to listen. He hit the Call button and spoke. "Yes, I'm out here now...I caught up to him once he left work...No, not yet. I'll do it before he gets back to his office. I know, before anybody else gets to him. It won't be a problem. Nobody's out here anyway." The cyclist pressed the End button on his cell phone and returned it to his winter coat's pocket. A cold metal weight rested in the bottom of his pocket, and he moved the cell phone out of its way. Bundling back up, the cyclist resumed his watch for Mike's return.

Ten minutes ticked away with no sign of Daniels. The growing cold and lengthening time concerned the cyclist. The cyclist paused and looked around at the walkers and other joggers he had seen earlier along with Mike on the island to no avail. Widening his search, he glanced frantically past shuttered food stands and an empty football field. Raising his eyes over the rooftops of the food stands, he saw a runner on the bridge wearing the same clothes that he had seen earlier in his surveillance. "Dang it," he muttered as he spun his bike around and gritted his teeth in pursuit of the distant jogger.

Oblivious to the goings on around him, Mike continued his almost routine run. Rather than three laps of the island, he had decided to allow himself in a change of his usual route to amble off the road and through the woods to prove to himself that there weren't bodies being buried all over Pennsylvania. City Island offered a short trail that curled and rolled along the river and led up to an area behind a horse stable. Happy with his choice, Mike turned and ran back across the bridge on his return trip. Passing behind a cyclist, he wondered, *God, how cold must it be before people put their bikes away?*

The cyclist found himself gaining fast though Mike couldn't see him. The burst of speed generated so much body heat that beads of sweat rolled down out of his watch cap. He unzipped a pocket so that its contents would be ready for use as soon as he cut off his prey.

As he neared the office, Mike slowed to a walk to finish out the last fifty yards before he stretched and went back inside. His run had relieved him of the stresses of the morning and he even allowed himself a brief laugh at the awful dream with Maggie Fanelli. Hearing the tick-tick-tick of an approaching bicycle broke Mike's momentary laugh. He moved to give the rider room to pass on the narrow walkway and the bike blew past uncomfortably close. Wheels skidded against the cold pavement as the rider clenched the brake handles and slid his bike across the path, blocking Mike's way. Mike froze as the cyclist reached into his pocket and pulled out a dark gray metal object.

Pointing a micro cassette recorder at Mike's face, the cyclist puffed, "Bill Renard of the *Harrisburg Post*—Would you like to tell our readers about the murder of Bennie Carlson? How do you feel about Clayton Edwards and why do you think he would do such a thing?"

Startled, Mike's whole body shuddered as the metal object came into view. His best response was a wide-eyed expression and a jaw popped open in mid gasp. As his mind caught up with the man's words, a more normal expression returned. Having no concept of whoever Bennie Carlson or Clayton Edwards were, Mike replied, "What?"

Bill Renard repeated his spiel into the recorder and returned it to the six-inch distance from Mike's still agape mouth.

This time it all sank in, and Mike's flustered fog lifted. He realized that the sketches all had names now though they didn't mean a blessed thing to him. Remaining quiet, Mike mulled over how he should respond. Almost immediately, he remembered Al's request not to discuss the case with anyone and considered that the best course of action.

"No comment," Mike replied as he tried to make his way round the bike and rider.

Bill stepped in front again and said, "Mr. Daniels, the public has a right to know what happened on the morning of the ninth."

"That's true. I'm sure the police will share that with the deserving public," retorted Mike.

Bill realized that his confrontation tactic was creating exactly the wrong kind of rapport that a reporter needed to get a story. Rather than make things better, he made them worse. His finger keyed the recorder off and he lowered his arm to his side, saying, "Mr. Daniels, we'll pay you for your story."

So much for it being a public service, Mike thought. "How much?" he asked.

"How does a hundred dollars sound? Maybe more if my editor likes what I write."

"A hundred dollars. Wow, that's pretty good. All right," said Mike.

Renard quickly thumbed the record button and brought the gadget to readiness.

"I was born at Harrisburg Hospital, the youngest of two children to a blue collar family in Bridgeport, Pennsylvania. My mother, Bernadette, worked for the fede..."

"What does this have to do with the murder of Bennie Carlson?" interrupted the reporter whose white eyebrows were raised in a quizzical look.

"You said you'd pay for my story."

"This isn't the *Biography Channel,* Mr. Daniels. I'd like to get your story on what happened at Sanford Park last week."

"Ohhhhh," replied Mike with a tone of mocking understanding. "You have to realize, Mr. Renner, when you ask an Information Systems person a direct question, you have to expect a direct answer. I'll tell you what, ask your specific question again and I will answer it directly."

"It's Renard. R-e-n-a-r-d. Ren-ard. All right, Mr. Daniels. You are listed as a witness in the discovery of the body of Bennie Carlson at Sanford State Park. Would you tell our readers what you saw?" asked Bill.

"N-o c-o-m-m-e-n-t," spelled Mike, skirting around Renard and crossing the street to Bleeding Edge.

Renard's shoulders slumped. "Nice to meet you, too."

* * *

Watching the pantomime going on outside his office window, John Weaverton observed the change in Mike's body language and knew that something was wrong. He picked up the phone, to have Judy tell Mike that he wanted to see him after lunch. Rather than speaking to her in person, he got Judy's phone mail. After hanging up, he walked up to the entrance.

"...yes, Mom. President Clinton played the sax and so does Kenny G. Yes, Kenny G. No, his he's not as cute as Kenny...," said Judy until John came into view.

"Tell Mike I want to see him as soon as he gets cleaned up," ordered John.

"Ulp," gargled Judy as she fumbled for a pen and paper.

"And tell your mom I said hi," said John with a boss's half-sneer and half-smile.

* * *

Knowing it was a big deal for Judy to stop any phone conversation, let alone one that probably involved her mother, Mike figured that things were getting out of hand. A personal delivery of John's message meant that a personal reply was necessary.

"What's his calendar for this afternoon?" asked Mike.

Judy said, "All clear."

"Great," said Mike. "The day just keeps getting better. First I get gang-raped by a mob of bingo ladies, and then the press shows up and accosts me. Now, the boss wants me for a face-to-face."

Judy wasn't sure what she just heard, but decided to tell her mom anyway.

* * *

After his shower and hurried lunch, Mike walked down the steps to John's office.

Knocking hard, he stood before the thick entrance door until John answered with a muffled "Come on in, Mike."

John, sporting his country club golf shirt and tailored slacks, sat at a small conference table surrounded by curved chestnut shelving and cut glass windows, pouring Scotch into two tumblers. John offered a Scotch to Mike and said, "Let's talk."

And talk the pair did. Mike told the whole story even though he felt like he shouldn't. He needed to vent the whole episode from finding the body in the park all the way up to the confrontation with the reporter, although he omitted the gory details of his dream with Maggie. Al Hoover's request was ignored. *It's John I'm telling. Not the press*, he thought.

"So, you've never heard of Bennie, Bennie...What was the last name again?" asked John.

"'Carlson' was what the reporter said, and no, never heard of him. I hadn't seen his face until those sketches made it into the papers," said Mike.

"And the other man, Clayton?"

"Edwards. Nope, don't know him either."

"Funny, it sounds familiar to me. Can't quite place it but it will come to me," said John with eyes squinting in recollection.

Mike knew that John had a knack for names and waited for his boss to come up with how he knew it.

"Hmmm, no. It's there, but I just can't get it. Oh well, I'm sure we'll both hear more about it now that the press is sniffing around," John continued.

"Probably. I'll be watching the news tonight to see what's up, if anything," said Mike.

The conversation digressed from the depths of crime to the depths of business and then onto the lighter side of personal issues touching on Mike's mostly solitary life. The first Scotch eased the words out of Mike, who was shy and private when it came to talking about himself in the post-Monica mode. A second Scotch was offered but Mike refused, figuring that he'd be asleep in his office chair in fifteen minutes if he accepted. Their talk would have gone on for the rest of the afternoon, but business interrupted once more, as it always did. This time, it was the form of Judy, paging John on the intercom to take an important call that couldn't wait. John pursed his lips and shook his head in a kind of dismissal. Mike took the cue and went back to his desk to try and finish his report while maintaining consciousness against an empty-stomach Scotch.

The afternoon crawled by, and Mike was happy when his workday ended. He bumper-to-bumpered his way home to Abby, whose priorities were bathroom, food, and attention, which Mike took care of right away. After her needs were sated, he cooked up a microwave meal and set up a snack tray in the living room to begin his patrol of the six o'clock news. Mike guessed that he still had about five minutes until they began, so he rose up to retrieve an iced tea from the fridge. WBWY won the remote lottery after he punched one of the local channels at random and sat down. The news teasers began with a bright graphic sliding across the screen and a voice that sounded like it was announcing a come-on from a used cars salesman.

"Tonight on WBWY's Y-Witness News, a local politician turns himself in for the hit-and-run death of a Harrisburg man..."

Mike spewed his tea across the room when he saw one of his sketches come to life on the TV.

Chapter 8

Bright green numbers glowed in the upper corner of Mike's TV as images flickered from channel to channel. The remote beckoned for the next talking head to appear as soon as the still photo of Clayton Edwards departed. Caring less about the commentary, Mike focused on the sad eyes and drawn face of the elder black man briefly floodlit by klieg lights on the way to being booked. Most channels cobbled together stock footage of the man who appeared to Mike as being a politician of some kind. He settled on WBWY as the least objectionable of the superficial newscasts. A blond Ken-Doll clad in a stylish wool winter coat occupied the foreground of the police station façade, and Mike caught up with his broadcast in mid-sentence.

"...after a gathering of newly elected and re-elected representatives from Muir County. Mr. Edwards struck and killed Bennie Carlson of the Harrisburg area."

The blond Ken Doll's face was replaced with the sketch of Bennie Carlson. A second still image appeared on screen of a man in a dirty flannel shirt brandishing a bottle of glass cleaner and a towel at a nondescript intersection. "Bennie Carlson had no permanent address and was widely known in the local homeless community. This photograph from the *Harrisburg Post*, taken last year as a part of their feature on the homeless in the capital area, shows Mr. Carlson and the life he led," said the reporter.

The broadcast went on to interview an area resident who remembered how Bennie used to beg for change at the end of the State Street Bridge near the capitol complex. The remainder of the newscast returned to the exact same video clip of Edwards making its fourth appearance as the reporter narrated, "It's a sad tragedy that brought State Representative Clayton Edwards and Bennie Carlson together on that fateful Sunday morning. Now, one man is dead and another may end up doing prison time. This is Kirk Griffin reporting. Now back to you Dave..."

Mike surfed away from the all-too-pretty male reporter and on to the other local channels to see what more he could learn. By the time the channel changed, the only thing Mike could learn was a schedule of holiday events and how to get Christmas shopping done before the 24th. Mike thought back to the first broadcast that announced the discovery of the burial and thought how much he preferred being connected to a news story that was buried in its own way, safely tucked in anonymity in the back pages where no one cared. People were going to care now, and his accidental witness to that horrible event would not leave him, or his life, in the back pages. He reached down to instinctively pet Abby who had moved into position to be petted.

The TV remained on though Mike and Abby really didn't notice the best car-leasing rates available or how to get their credit repaired. Whether or not they saw the weather was also in question. Sports flickered by with no cheers or sneers toward local teams preparing for the Friday night game. It was all trite. A man was dead and another man would be paying the price for the accident that killed him. Still, things tugged at Mike's brain. *There was no mention of the blonde woman. Why did this man turn himself in to the Capitol police?* Mike remembered the line the reporter spoke that talked about some kind of "gathering." Was "gathering" a code word for "party"? *Was the guy drunk? If he wasn't, what did happen?* Mike thought about it again and again. His analytical sense kicked in, and he reasoned that the news folks didn't have that much information to go on. They padded the report by showing the same scene four times along with some second-hand accounts of Bennie Carlson's life. It was just enough to fit into the lead slot, and what a perfect lead slot it was—nothing like a political scandal to stir up the media.

"I hope they leave us out of it," he said to Abby, who had no concerns about the media so long as her head was being gently caressed. The phone rang and Mike pulled his hand off Abby on his way to the kitchen to answer. In doing so, he knocked the tray that held his empty dishes to the floor. After a few seconds of cursing and picking up his dirty dishes, he sprinted to the phone where the answering machine was already acting as spokesman for the Daniels household. "You've reached the Daniels. We can't come to the phone right now. Please leave a message at the beep," followed by a dog's bark.

The tinny speaker on the answering machine said, "Hi, Mr. Daniels. This is Ken Griffin of WBWY news. We'd like to come by your house and talk to you about the Edwards case. Please give me a call at 555-1214 and we'll set up a time that works for you."

Mike expected the message to end with "...and now back to you Dave..." but it didn't. What was unsettling was the fact that a second newsperson had his name, which meant that the report he made had been given, leaked, fed, or distributed to the press. *First it was kids with guns taking shots at me, now the press gets to line up and take their shots at me, too.*

The phone rang again and the machine spoke its part. The message that followed proved to be a cookie cutter of the first but with a different channel's call sign. In the hour that followed, no less than eight messages from the media had landed on his phone. After the fourth call, he had walked back into the living room to try to read a computer journal in an effort to pretend that the calls weren't coming in. A ninth call sparked the machine to life and Mike tuned it out until the name on the line made him pull away from his reading.

"Hi, Mr. Daniels. Al Hoover here. Sorry to call you, but I saw the news tonight and I thought I'd request again that you don't talk to the media. You're a material witness to a felony and anything you say might influence the outcome of Mr. Edwards' case. If you have any questions, gimme a call at 555-1213. Thanks and have a good evening, sir."

"Thanks and have a good evening, sir," Mike mimicked. "I'm a divorced guy alone on a Friday night who witnessed a murder. I'm sure I'll have a great evening, Al. Won't we, Abby?"

Abby looked up at Mike once the petting stopped and realized that Mike was going to roll in self-pity the same way she might be tempted to roll in something in the backyard. Her nose dipped and she raised one ear and eye at him to get an understanding as to why he was headed that way. Seeing his empty look, she decided that more aggressive measures were in order. Arising from her warm spot, she paused for a moment to think what could cheer him up and restore her owner's faith that the universe was in order. The answer came to her, and she finished her walk with a flopping landing against the video cabinet. She pushed against it just hard enough to make one of the magnetic latches click loudly and break Mike's moody spell. *The things I do for my owner*, she thought.

Drifting toward an inconsolable funk, Mike watched Abby withdraw. Rather than leaving the living room, she plopped next to the video cabinet hard enough to make the door pop open a bit. He stood up to close it lest the offending door hang open and annoy him. As his hand reached to push the door closed, he changed his mind and looked inside. Searching past all the action flicks, romances, and dramas, he hunted for the one movie that would restore his faith in mankind. All of the good and bad guys were plainly marked and morality was clearly defined. Add to that enough hardware and explosions to satisfy any male viewer and the perfect movie was within his grasp. He pulled the movie from its case, loaded it into the DVD player, and cranked the sound up high enough to offend Abby, who was already on her way up the steps and into the bedroom. The title crawl marched up the screen accompanied by the swell of John Williams' heroic score. *Star Wars IV—A New Hope* had begun. Mike settled back onto the couch to empty his mind of Clayton Edwards and fill it with fantasy.

* * *

The phone rang sporadically for the rest of the weekend. Mike had disconnected the answering machine and turned the ringers off to ensure that no intrusions would occur. He made it a point to avoid the TV and the newspaper. Switching locations of his trail run, Mike headed north to avoid Sanford's memories. Sunday slipped by with the routine of church and chores spent in preparation for the coming workweek.

Monday arrived as unceremoniously as Mondays always did, although Mike was a good deal happier than most any other employees doing the zombie stroll from their car to their desk. Having neither close friends nor family to occupy his weekend like his coworkers, his job offered him as much social contact as he wanted. While work seemed like that last place to find comfort, Mike thought it would be safe hiding behind the granite walls of Bleeding Edge. He fired up the coffee pot, laid out his work for the day, and turned his attention to the solitary red light winking incessantly on his phone.

Any fantasy about hiding behind his work immediately evaporated with Phoebe's emotionless voice. Phoebe was what the staff called the automated voice of their phone mail system. The bland soprano monotoned every word unless it was coupled with the voiceover of an employee adding their name to the recording, making the personal greeting that much more artificial. Phoebe announced to Mike that his phone mailbox was full. He tap-danced through the list of calls, hitting delete for each one that began with a name and a TV channel. He held the zero key down to speed the removal of the vocal equivalent of junk mail, and Phoebe responded with the silicon ecstasy. "Oh, oh, oh, oh, oh, oh, oh, oh, oh, oh. This command is not recognized." Mike blushed at the sound Phoebe was making as if he were listening to some kind of lurid 900 number. *Great, even Phoebe's doing better than me*, he thought.

No sooner had he cleaned out the phone trash, when John Weaverton knocked on the door and stepped past the threshold. He tossed a folded copy of the *Monday Post* onto the desktop and said, "Here ya go. I told you I remembered something about that guy. What did you think of the news coverage?"

"Well, I tried not to think about the news," replied Mike.

"I figured as much. They'll be all over you if you have to testify," warned John.

"They've been calling the house all weekend and are giving Phoebe fits here."

"Hmmm, they're supposed to leave the witness alone, so the case doesn't get screwed up."

"Maybe so, but I think everybody wants to be first in line to have me as fodder for the evening news."

"That'll be fun. Just don't mention the company. That's all we need is to have Bleeding Edge's name associated with a murder," requested John.

"Fun, eh? John, your idea of fun and mine don't always coincide."

"Which reminds me. How 'bout coming down to Hilton Head with Beth and me after Christmas and tearing up some grass?"

Mike sensed that the invite would have strings attached like the last time he headed south and into the lair of Beth's divorced sister. Considering that likelihood a fate worse than, well maybe not worse than, death, Mike declined. "You know how good a golfer I am. If the course doesn't have windmills and gnomes on it, I'm useless."

"Which is why I like to bring you along. You make me feel like Tiger Woods out there."

"Which you aren't. I just make you look good, which is what I should be doing now. We have the Boorman Inc. reports to go over later today," said Mike, turning the conversation back toward business and away from John's matchmaking.

"Yep, a presentation on Wednesday and we'll bill 'em on Thursday. I love this business," said John with a smile on his face.

"Well then, let me keep you in business."

"Which I will do once you agree to come with us in January," said John, steering things back toward his offer.

"Are there any windmills on the course?"

"No."

"Then count me out. I'd just embarrass myself like the time that twelve-year-old beat me."

"All right. Oh, don't forget to take a look at today's paper. It will tell you more than I could remember," said John as he left Mike's office.

Quiet returned to Mike's corner of the business world, but John had planted a seed of curiosity that prevented him from losing himself in his work. Flipping open the paper, Mike found that he didn't have to hunt and peck for news about his burial. In fact, his burial was no longer a burial; it was a hit-and-run and it adorned the front page with an article and a color photo of a downcast man flanked by police. The article read:

EDWARDS ARRESTED FOR HIT-AND-RUN
By Bill Renard for the *Harrisburg Post*

Exeter residents are still reeling after the shocking news that their newly elected State Representative, Clayton Edwards, turned himself in for the alleged hit-and-run death of Bennie Carlson on Walnut Street in Harrisburg, early in the morning on December 9th.

Edwards, and an aide, were returning home from a party held for Muir County representatives and congressmen after a daylong transition conference at the state capitol.

Police are releasing few details regarding the incident. What is apparent is that Edwards and his aide allegedly moved the body of Mr. Carlson from the scene to Sanford State Park in Muir County in an effort to cover up the accident.

Mr. Carlson's body was discovered by a passing hiker who notified authorities. The hiker was reportedly an eyewitness to Mr. Edwards' activities on the morning in question.

Police have impounded Edwards' 1999 Chevy Blazer.

Edwards' aide, Ms. Brenda Stabler, has been brought in for questioning, but police say that no charges have been filed to date.

Clayton Edwards came to the forefront of grassroots support after a series of white supremacist marches renewed old wounds in the city of Exeter. Known as a peacemaker and consensus builder, Edwards forged an alliance of multi-ethnic community leaders to tackle the issues of race and class. Edwards' history with Exeter goes back to the 1968 race riots when he successfully defended more than a dozen black activists arrested during the fighting. He went on to open a storefront law office for low-income families and built it into a successful practice. When incumbent Representative

Ronald Kepner retired last year, Edwards emerged as a highly popular Democratic frontrunner in a decidedly Republican county. He defeated the Republican candidate, Samuel Houser, a former Muir County judge, by a comfortable margin in the November election.

Edwards is being held in the Dauphin County prison and is expected to have a bail hearing at the Dauphin County Courthouse this morning.

Exeter residents expressed surprise and sympathy for Edwards...

"A trailrunner, not a hiker," protested Mike.

The article went on to quote Exeter residents. All seemed genuinely sympathetic and disappointed at the news. Mike felt bad for Edwards even though he didn't know him. He remembered the turmoil in the man's eyes during the repeated showings of his arrest. Refolding the paper, Mike tucked it away in his desk and looked out the window for a short while at the commuters on their way to work. He envied their detached ignorance where the most important thing was to get to work which he figured he should to be doing. Launching his spreadsheets, Mike resumed his work on the Boorman reports.

Work eclipsed the time, and lunchtime soon rolled around. Mike changed and exited Bleeding Edge on his usual run. The skies were now a winter's gray and the cold a touch more biting, though he didn't mind. When he got to the Walnut Street Pedestrian Bridge, an odd feeling overtook him. He recalled that the newspaper said that the accident occurred on Walnut Street. There he stood with a long view of it as it cut west to east through town. Somewhere along the bumpy thoroughfare, Bennie Carlson's life had ended. The paper gave no indication as to how it happened. Having been target practice for the pedestrian-hating drivers in the area, he had no problem pretending how it could have occurred. *There were probably a dozen blind spots that somebody could pop out of*, he thought.

A shiver slipped through his body. It shook him from his morose musing, and he returned to running. As he did so, he saw a knot of people gathered outside the entrance of the Dauphin County

Courthouse along with a number of Harrisburg Police dressed in riot gear. He ran nearer and saw more police gathered on the riverbank opposite the courthouse standing near their patrol cars. A pair of officers were mounted on horseback. When he got to the corner of Market and Front, Mike got a decent view of goings on.

Two distinct and very different groups were crowding around the courthouse steps. One group was clad almost entirely in black. Black boots, pants, and bomber jackets seemed to be the uniform of choice. Some of the cadre wore black watch caps. Those that didn't had their heads shaved. All of them were white and they marched in an irregular oval, chanting, "Victim's rights...victim's rights...victim's rights" while thrusting their right arms into the air to punctuate each syllable.

The other group was decidedly less organized and much less co-ordinated in their dress code. Men, women, and children, mostly African American, gathered in a loose crowd farther down the block. Suits, dresses, jeans, and sneakers reflected the informal group whose faces reflected fear, concern, and, what worried Mike the most, anger.

Between them stood a buffer of police whose sole purpose was to keep both sides from confrontation. Farther down the bank, beyond the police, stood a row of broadcasting trucks with their dish antennae creating an artificial forest among the trees that stood over the river. Most crews were out of their trucks and had their respective newsperson bleaching in the camera's light.

The gray-black oval of protestors circulated near the courthouse entrance like a storm cloud and served as a dramatic background for the reporters. From time to time, the voices in the crowd would taunt each other and both parties would near the police. The officers did their jobs well and raised riot batons in a show of force. Mike could see a single officer gesture to the offending party, who would then back down into their respective crowd. The Harrisburg Police weren't taking any grief from anybody.

Mike's observations would have gone on except for the distinct growling emanating behind him. While the crowd growled at each other, this sound was distinctly animal and distinctly close. He swung his head around and found himself looking into the shoulders of a police officer whose beefy arm held a very serious looking German shepherd on a tight leash. Neither the officer's eyes nor the dog's said that they were in the mood for any nonsense at the present time.

"You might not want to hang around here for too long, sir," said the officer who had seen Mike stop to look around.

One look at Mike's running outfit screamed passer-by, and the officer wanted him and any others like him out of his way and out of danger. The police dog took its cue from its handler and relaxed its threatening posture. It began to sniff the air around Mike.

"What in the heck is going on here?" Mike asked.

"It's the bail hearing for that guy Edwards. The skinheads caught wind of it and decided to stir up trouble. It's not a real good time to be down here, sir."

After getting a good whiff of Mike, the shepherd sat down and relaxed into a pert-eared look worthy of a picture on a can of dog food. Mike reached forward and petted the dog on the head, which was the one thing most sane people would not do to a police dog unless invited by its handler. Not losing any fingers, Mike continued to pet the willing dog. "Good boy," Mike said into the dog's relishing eyes.

The officer watched the scene with more than a little irritation and asked Mike, "Please, sir, move along."

Mike's pace went from shuffle to run as he left the ugly scene. He turned one last time to look at the crowd and saw a familiar face. Standing at the crowd's edge was a man in a green parka and jeans. His style of clothes had changed from the cyclist's gear of a few days ago. The gray hair and weathered face were unmistakable. Mike knew that he was looking at Bill Renard, who was busy shoving that tape recorder of his into another person's face. Renard's eyes tracked the crowd for a possible interview. Both men made eye contact. Bill gestured with his tape recorder. Mike returned the gesture with a negative swing of his head.

The crowd, and its accompanying cacophony, faded in the distance as Mike ran across the bridge's open metal work. The Susquehanna River's cold green mixture of ice and water hissed over the piers. Winter's grip was deepening on the river, and it would soon be choked with ice and covered in snow. Like the sheets of ice passing underneath him, Mike recalled the sheets of newsprint proclaiming Exeter's racial woes. Problems like those were easy to run by when it was distant and seemingly irrelevant. Now, those problems were underfoot and Mike wondered just how deep things were going to get.

Chapter 9

Both man and dog sat on an oasis of carpet in the middle of a black and white desert of newsprint bound only by the beige walls of the Daniels living room. Mike's habit of keeping the daily papers for a couple of weeks served his curiosity as he scanned each day's columns for anything related to Bennie Carlson or Clayton Edwards. To his dismay, the papers gave up few tidbits other than the arrival of a soft-core porn star, and a pretty good sale on notebook computers at the business supply store. Not being in need of a lap dance or laptop, Mike tossed the paper aside. "Jeez," Mike said to himself when he caught sight of the ink residue on his fingers. *Enough of this.* He had made his mind up to let his computer do the searching. "Abby? Abby?" A disgruntled huff emanated from a tent of newsprint and Mike apologized. "Sorry, girl."

A few keystrokes and some double-clicking later, Mike was surfing the web on his computer. Beginning the search with Clayton Edwards' name, Mike turned up no less than 687 hits, most of which had to do with an American-turned-Italian rock star. He clicked on one of the links and pulled up an Italian fan's website. The Clayton Edwards on the screen, complete with myriad tattoos, leather jacket, flaming pink Mohawk, and pale complexion was not the Clayton Edwards that he was seeking. *My Clayton Edwards is a rock star of a different type,* Mike thought.

Hundreds of hits scrolled by until a brief flash of "Clayton Edwards Campaign" materialized on his monitor. Double-clicking on the link, Mike watched as the banners and pictures of the official

Clayton Edwards Campaign scrolled in from all four sides of the screen. The largest of the banners announced Edwards as the "The People's Choice." Links appeared offering Mike a tour of the man's platform and a short biography touting his accomplishments. Ignoring the platform, Mike, instead, clicked on the biography, which obliged him with a series of pictures and text. Glancing over the factoids, Mike read that Edwards had been born in Baltimore and earned distinguished honors at Jefferson High School. He went on to study law on a scholarship to Stewart Law School in Cardale, Pennsylvania. After college, Edwards took up the Civil Rights cause and spent his early law career defending those arrested in the violent confrontations of the day in and around his native Baltimore. He traveled to Exeter to defend African Americans arrested during the riots of the summer of '69. Edwards married Eleanor Watkins of Exeter the following year.

The remainder of the bio lauded Edwards' abilities as a formidable lawyer and businessman that served the community. Taking in all of the made-for-the-masses politically correct information, Mike noted that they left the part out about him burying another human being.

The rest of the site proved to be what Mike had expected for any candidate's web page. He was seeing exactly what the campaign organizers wanted him, or anybody, to see. It wasn't the kind of data an analyst wanted. There were no details to delve into. He needed something more although he didn't know what piqued his curiosity so. He stood, thinking about what to do next. The answer came a second later.

Mike slid his gloves over his fingers, tucked the ends into his parka and wrestled his zipper up to his chin. Looking at the newspapers strewn everywhere, he sighed. *I'll have to clean this up later.* Mike never caught sight of a rhythmic rise and fall of the entertainment section near his feet. Before he could close the front door, Mike heard a peculiar comment.

"So, you're not dead, Mike," said a woman walking her dog.

Caught off guard, Mike stammered." "I... b...b..eg your pardon?"

"What is it about the male animal that prevents him from dialing a phone?" questioned the familiar voice.

Looking at the slender, dark-haired woman, bent into a reverse "C" by the pull of her golden retriever, Mike realized he was looking at Jen Stevens. Mike also realized he was in trouble. "Oh God, I'm so sorry. I turned off the answering machine and the ringers on the phone..."

"...Did I do something wrong?" asked Jen, trying to still her prancing dog.

"No. Not a thing. I was being stupid," fumbled Mike for something to say rather than dumping his recent experiences on her. Their relationship had been going well, at least until Mike met Bennie Carlson, Clayton Edwards, and the blonde woman in the woods. Mike understood the folly of turning off the outside world as soon as he heard the slight tang of worry in her tone. He liked Jen a lot more than he was willing to admit and felt mad at himself for shutting her out. Things had been great between them ever since she showed up at the Bridgeport Theater's screening of *Casablanca* a few months ago when he was freshly divorced. She was the one person he wanted to be around, he just didn't know how to say it. His silence became awkward.

Jen's eyes darted about, trying to make contact with his. "Look, if I'm crowding you or something..."

Jen's question brought Mike back to the moment. "...Oh God, no. That's not it. I'm an idiot. It's...a...Monica," said Mike, trying to shield Jen from his new set of troubles.

"You turned the phone off because of Monica?"

"Yea, I can hardly wait for her to get married. How's Roxanne?" said Mike, hoping to end one subject and move on to a safer topic.

Roxanne, Jen's rambunctious golden retriever, strained at her leash to come and visit Mike or anyone with a hand capable of petting. "Roxy's ready to run tonight."

"I think you're going to get whiplash from that dog," said Mike as he stepped down the concrete stairs onto the sidewalk.

"What brings you out on a cold dark night?" asked Jen.

"A trip to the library."

"Whoa, sounds exciting. I'm headed that way. Want some company?"

Mike smiled and said, "Sure," and thought about how pretty Jen looked under the porch light. Then again, she looked good under incandescent, mercury vapor, fluorescent, and especially, candlelight.

Jen's face reflected the smile as the pair shared a warming moment on the frozen sidewalk. The moment lasted exactly one second until Roxanne's leash wrapped around Mike's legs and cinched up tight. When the retriever pulled hard, Mike toppled over onto the pavement. Fortunately, his coat blunted the impact. Roxanne stood over him in a muzzle-to-nose pose, ears drooping onto his face. Mike returned the stare as Jen rushed to untangle the pair. She apologized while Roxanne kept watch over Mike.

"You have bad breath, Roxanne," Mike said as his legs became freed.

Roxanne responded with a wet lick.

"You're lucky I'm not a cat person."

Roxanne responded with an uneven canting of her expressive eyebrows and walked over Mike's chest on her way to her owner's side.

"You know, she never does that to anybody else," said Jen, extending a hand for Mike to pull himself up with.

"It's okay." He took her hand and stood up, all the while looking into her eyes.

Jen returned the look. Roxanne bounded up to her. "I think that Roxanne wants to make up with you."

Roxanne sidled up to Mike and settled just long enough to be petted.

Over Mike's shoulder, a lone canine face appeared in the window of the Daniels residence. Pert ears and watchful eyes took in the scene of him petting another dog. The window fogged up with the heat of jealous breath.

"So you're headed to the library, eh?" asked Jen as she wheeled Roxanne around to head toward Bridgeport's library.

"Yea, a little after-dinner research," said Mike without explaining.

Jen resumed the conversation and accelerated into a fast stride. "What are you researching?"

Mike felt that he might be better off running. "Politicians," he replied.

"Now that's exciting. Why? The elections are over."

Mike realized his answer was vague and remembered Jen's aversion to vagueness. Now he had to think fast and said, "Politicians in Exeter."

"Local or state politicians? Maybe I can help."

Mike's fast thinking was not averting the discussion. Jen was the manager of personnel at the Pennsylvania Legislature's Support Center. She knew more than a thing or two about politicians and was wired into the best gossip under the capitol dome. He debated telling her what happened like he did with his boss. Then again, she didn't see him get waylaid by Bill Renard. *That's all she needed—a manager in a state agency caught in the middle of a political scandal*, thought Mike. *No*, he reasoned, *I don't want to screw things up for her.* Mike rethought his approach and said, "Local. Bleeding Edge has some prospects going on down Exeter way and we're trying to see who the players are. You know how city and county govern..."

"...Roxanne, put that down," interrupted Jen, who was a little horrified to see a road kill squirrel clenched in Roxy's mouth.

Mike was thankful for the interruption. "So, how're things going?" he asked, hoping to shift the subject away from him.

"Fine," she replied in a tone that meant anything but.

"Now that sounds like an open-ended statement."

"I know we said, 'No exes,' but my ex is getting serious with her."

Acid dripped from Jen's last word and onto Mike's ears. "You told me Jim and his new girlfriend deserved each other. Has something changed?"

"Not really. I guess the reality of something like this had to occur. It's just weird," said Jen.

"I know what you mean. Monica's wedding is only a couple of months away."

"Wow. It's that soon?"

"Yea, the sooner the better. Besides—they deserve each other."

Jen picked up on the earlier reference and let out a snicker as Roxanne slew back and forth on the leash. The humor broke Jen's brooding.

Jen said, "So, what time are you going to pick me up?"

Mike, caught off guard again, mumbled, "Time? I...er..."

"Hmmm, you forgot about Saturday, haven't you?"

Thinking for a moment, Mike knew that the answer was yes although he answered, "No."

Jen, not fooled by his answer, reminded him, "Saturday is my department Christmas Party. You promised to be my escort."

"Yea, that's it, Christmas Party. Goodness knows how much I'm looking forward to that," said Mike.

"You like office parties?"

"No, I like running an escort service. How much does it pay?"

It paid a punch in the arm, which was what Jen gave Mike for his forgetfulness.

"Ouch. Okay, I'm sorry I forgot. How about I pick you up at 8:00 p.m. and we can arrive fashionably late," apologized Mike.

"That will be fine—don't forget," threatened Jen, her fist still clenched.

Jen and Mike reached the library and neither of them was ready to part. Roxanne, on the other hand, wanted to know what the hold-up was.

"Are you going to be in there a while?" asked Jen.

"Probably an hour or two," said Mike.

"Oh, well look, turn up your ringers and turn on your answering machine. Better yet, call or stop by, okay?"

"All right, I will," said Mike as he turned to go into the library.

Both hugged and turned to go their own way. Mike paused for a second to watch her recede down the sidewalk, paying particular attention to the way she walked. A silly grin hung on his face as he turned and entered the McPherson Library.

* * *

The library turned out to be a treasure trove of all things Edwards. Newspaper archives touted the man as a clean campaigner that was well liked by the middle and lower classes of the largely Democratic constituency. The Republicans, on the other hand, seemed to have shot themselves in the foot with negative advertising, and their candidate, Sam Houser, a lawyer from someone, someone and someone, had no real tie to the everyman of Exeter.

Mike guessed that Edwards had an easy ride during the election. Hate groups had paved the way for a backlash of blue-collar whites that had enough of the racist rhetoric and the community trauma it inflicted. White supremacist marches and neo-Nazi groups protested on the streets while diversity rallies filled churches and halls downtown. The diversity rallies put all the races together and a sense of purpose was born. Borne on that purpose was one Clayton Edwards, storefront defender of the people turned businessman and community leader. Exeter's dual newspapers reflected its dual personality. One paper pooh-poohed him as a neophyte while the other touted him as a "breath of clean air." Each paper's coverage of Edwards faded after the electoral victory. Of course, that was until last Thursday when Maggie's sketches appeared. By Saturday, the same papers' coverage resumed with either disappointment or condescension depending on which side of the conservative/liberal fence their reporter stood on. Both featured a handcuffed Edwards being booked by police. *Politicians weren't even making it to office today before their incarceration*, Mike thought.

"The blonde..." Mike remembered out loud, "...what happened to the blonde?" Closing his eyes, Mike let the pictures from the Exeter papers flicker through his mind. No recollection of the woman came to mind. Nothing in any of the papers indicated her presence, and that set the wheels to turning in Mike's brain. The analyst in him didn't like the absence of data. The lack of data indicated something elusive, something unsaid. *Scandal*, he concluded. *A young woman— a newly elected representative—both out together for a nice round of bury the bum after a quickie. My, my. I guess people don't smoke after sex anymore.*

Going fiche-ing, as Mike called sifting microfiche, was his least favorite way to search for information. It became even more so when he found that the *Harrisburg Post* held no trove of goodies like the Exeter papers had. His eyes tired from squinting at the newspapers flickering past.

Closing time drew near. As he returned the fiche he caught sight of the stacks of newspapers kept by the library until they became fiche or electronically stored. Finding the pile that held the *Post*, Mike took out a week at a time and looked for more information. The earliest paper contained a short column on the Edwards victory. It read like an actor's Academy Awards speech with thanks and kudos going out to so-and-so for such-and-such. While the content was not especially newsworthy, the byline was—Bill Renard. A reporter's name was not something that Mike paid particular attention to. That was until Mike had been accosted by one of their kind. Something else stuck with Mike about the reporter's name, and he returned to the microfiche machine after grabbing the films back from a riled librarian.

Once he loaded the film, he brought up some of the *Post*'s articles about Edwards and Exeter. Each time, the name "Renard" appeared as the byline. Mike considered that fact for a few moments until one of the librarians reminded him that closing time approached. Pulling the fiche from the reader again, Mike dropped it in the return box and headed for the door. The rows of lights turned off, one by one, just ahead of Mike as he left. The librarian was having her revenge, he thought.

The automatic doors let Mike out and the cold air in. The last patrons of the library left within seconds of Mike and all mimicked his quick shuffle to their respective cars. Doors opened and closed. Ignitions started. While most cars were taking people in, one car left a person out. Not that Mike noticed the tall, slender man in a black leather coat stepping out onto the sidewalk from a low-slung old Dodge. Nor did Mike see the same man motion to the driver who drove up the street past him.

Mike had tucked his hands into the pockets of his coat. His mood shifted from the concentrated inquisitiveness of his ferreting to a much lighter tone. After all, it was just a few hours ago that Jen reminded him of their date. Happily humming to himself, he sped up to get away from under Old Man Winter's grip. His ears barely noticed the passing car and his eyes never really saw it except for a taillight. The car turned up his street and disappeared from sight.

Mike's happy mood was the polar opposite of the man following him. Had Mike bothered to slow down, he would have heard curses being silently heaved at Mike's speed and at the cold wind slicing through the man's thin leather jacket.

Mike rounded the corner and saw the lights of home glowing like a Currier and Ives painting. Lingering for a moment under the sparkling stars and moonlit sky, he stood still to appreciate the moment. The quiet appreciation lasted only an instant when the sound of approaching footsteps made him take a look around. The footsteps halted, then resumed. Feeling uneasy, Mike hustled to the house without looking back. He jumped up the concrete steps to his house two at a time, and opened the front door. Warmth, and a miniature collie standing in a desert of newsprint greeted him. For a brief moment, Mike worried about the fate he had tempted by leaving a dog in a room full of newspaper. The thought passed and he jumped up the short landing to get to the bedroom window that faced the street. Peeking out through the venetian blinds, he could see a man clad in a shiny dark coat walk by. Watching the man walk out of sight, Mike noted that the man didn't pause or do anything suspicious. Still, the stranger looked out of place and he certainly didn't resemble anybody Mike had seen walking past the house before. At the edge of the window frame, Mike could make out the red glow of taillights playing off a plume of exhaust. A car door went cha-chunk and the windowpane rattled from the throaty engine of the unseen vehicle. The taillights disappeared into the night. Mike let the slats fall back into place. Something about the scene raised the hair on the back of his neck.

Abby pulled up next to him and sniffed his pants leg. Mike reached down to pet her about the time she locked onto a particular scent and let out a disapproving snort. "Jealous of a golden retriever, eh?" Mike teased. "You might want to get used to it. I have a date this weekend."

Abby's eyes rolled upward, her brown eyes ringed in white, and she sighed.

Chapter *10*

The faces at the table resembled the look prisoners had in solitary confinement, thought Mike. He wondered if his face looked the same to the not-so-revelers sequestered in their folding chairs, abandoned by date, or spouse, to forage for conversation on their own. It looked to him that most would starve by the end of the Pennsylvania Legislature's Support Center Christmas party.

Thinking briefly of Abby, Mike remembered that her face presented a very similar countenance when she realized the short walk she had been taken on resulted in her confinement at Jen's house with the ever-playful Roxanne. Both Jen and Mike thought that it might be a good idea for the "girls" to get acquainted. The burning look of Abby's unblinking brown eyes and lowered ears haunted him until his thoughts returned to the moment as Jen approached.

Jen had swapped the tights and fleece of their winter walk for an almost mandatory black cocktail dress. Mike preferred the dress. His preference went beyond the typical male chauvinist assessment of a woman's figure. Jen had a presence, a casual elegance in her movements that drew his eye to her graceful figure. Watching her talk, Mike noted the growing cadre of conversation partners who gravitated to her. She had a way of owning the attention of all as she spoke and a way of making those speaking feel as though she was giving them her undivided attention. The looks in the eyes of those gathered around her portrayed a mixed bag of humor, pleasantry, joking, and some very large doses of cattiness.

Slipping into the same kind of observational detachment as when he was at the lake, Mike detached himself from the nonexistent conversation not occurring at his table. He knew it was rude, but he also knew that he seemed to be the last person to be lobotomized by the lack of social contact. In his detachment, he could observe and analyze without being distracted. It was a trait that his ex-wife despised.

Watching the group gathered around Jen, Mike gauged their ages to be somewhat clustered in their late thirties. They were probably the up-and-coming middle managers and movers-and-shakers that companies, and state bureaucracies, depended on. From the growing crowd around them, Mike guessed that this group was the kind of clique every hanger-on and wannabe wanted to be a part of. Observing a particular pair of twenty-somethings laughing at jokes that they had no chance of hearing, Mike saw the giveaway signs of a pair of wannabes. There was something about the amount of wine they consumed along with the preening and courtship behavior that reminded Mike of a nature show. *Probably a pair of mating wannabes, which was worse yet,* he mused. He wondered if any of the animals on the shows he watched woke up with a hangover the morning after.

There was a subtle but distinct shift in the crowd behavior as though Moses himself was parting the Red Sea. A late-fifty-something man made his way toward the center of Jen's clique. Mike watched the faces of those parting and figured that this man must be high up on the state food chain. Those staffers in the man's way bowed as they shook hands and gave ground very easily. The looks in their eyes reflected a tinge of fear rather than an ounce of respect. Mike, still immersed in his animal show analogies, defined him as the "alpha male." The definition couldn't have been more appropriate as he watched wannabes and hangers-on depart to find another undisturbed group to attempt to bond with.

The music pulsing in the background quieted for a bit as the man made his way to the core of the unaware clique where Jen stood nestled in the cocoon of office friends. Faces changed from holiday cheer to forced smiles as the man finally made his way to Jen. Mike watched the conversation change to a polite, though strained, exchange. *The older man was used to having the stage,* Mike thought, and *he came to challenge those who would take it from him*. His tone demanded that he become the center of the little universe that Jen and her friends had just occupied. Despite the underlying intent of his actions, the man heaped praise on Jen and her small team of employees for such-and-such and for this-or-that. The crowd politely applauded in response to his comments, then froze when he embraced Jen. Women in the crowd stiffened and a look of subtle desperation emitted from Jen's eyes. That look shook Mike from his observational funk and his mind fumbled for a solution.

Mike looked at the table full of people, most of whom were far more detached mentally to the proceedings than Mike had been. One chatted to another while a third twirled her fork into her leftover salad. A fourth was drinking his fifth glass of wine. Looking at the table in front of him, Mike spotted the wineglasses they had used over dinner. His glass stood half-empty while Jen's stood half-full. Grabbing both glasses, he charged headlong into the crowd.

"There you are. I should have known you'd want to be the center of attention. I've been carrying this glass of wine around for five minutes," he said wondering just how far in over his head he was going.

"Er...I...I thought we were going to meet over here, honey," Jen ad-libbed.

"I leave you alone for five minutes and you have the boss eating out of your hand."

"Yea, that's me all right."

"Well, enough of office schmoozing, girl. You promised me some dance time," insisted Mike.

The band played an Easy Listening rendition of an Aerosmith tune that few found the energy or desire to gyrate to. Jen pushed away from the older man and took Mike by the hand. "I'm sorry, Mr. Lowell. Let's go, Mikey."

Mike and Jen had gone a short but safe distance from the leering Mr. Lowell when Mike stopped Jen and asked, "Mikey? My mother, bless her soul, never ever called me Mikey. If you're going to call me that then I'm taking you back to..."

"...Mr. Lowell and no you're not. How about 'Sir Mikey'? You were my white knight back there," said a relieved Jen.

"Something tells me you could have handled yourself back there."

"Kneeing my outgoing boss in the crotch is not good for promotions."

"Outgoing boss?"

"Yes, 'outgoing boss.' Every time the regime changes, all of the political appointees get cleaned out," explained Jen.

"Hmmm, it looked like that one should have been cleaned out a while ago," said Mike.

"He's been trouble since day one. Most of them are all right."

"...but not all."

"No, and I really don't want to talk about him anymore. You asked me to dance. I didn't know you danced."

"I can't," said a slightly embarrassed Mike.

"Well then, it's time you learned." Taking Mike by the hand, Jen led him out to the dance floor.

Something about her touch and the smile in her eyes made him disregard the awkwardness he felt.

After the third rock tune, the band settled into an old Chicago tune of *Color My World* to slow the evening down. Mike headed toward the tables to allow the married and serious couples their privacy. A tapping on his shoulder didn't let him get very far.

Jen had followed close behind him. "Hey Mikey, you're not going to abandon a damsel in distress again, are you?"

Mike ignored the "Mikey" reference and bowed down in his best imitation of a gallant knight. "May I have the pleasure of this dance, milady?"

"Why, yes, Sir Mikey," taunted Jen.

"One problem, Lady Jen."

"What's that?"

"I can't slow dance either."

"My, what a sheltered life you've led."

Jen wrapped her arms around him, which was a fine start as far as he was concerned. In doing so, she guided him from step to step. The jerkiness of his resistance to her movements faded away as he let her move him to the music. Jen stopped her gentle guidance a few measures in, and the two were moving as one. Mike never noticed how easily they moved together. He was too content discovering just how much he liked dancing and just how much he liked Jen. The music slowed down to its finish and Jen's head rose from where it rested against his shoulder. Mike watched her head rise and her long dark hair cascading back as their eyes met. This time there was much more to see in her sparkling blue eyes. The usual guarding of his inner self slipped away under her gaze. Tipping his head toward hers, he let his eyes go closed and parted his lips. Mike saw hers go closed as she moved toward him.

"You son of a bitch," shouted a pretty young thing the elder boss had decided to favor with an unfavorable touch. The curse was punctuated with the crack of a slap hitting home.

Jen's eyes snapped open and she spun her head toward the shouts. "Oh no, he's at it again," said Jen as she broke the embrace and rushed to the aid of one of her office staff. Mike was left alone again with a pair of still-pursed lips.

All attention shifted to the part of the room where Mr. Lowell stood red-faced as two aides did their best to hustle him out of the room. Mike could see Jen hugging the young woman whose face strained to hold back tears. She broke away from Jen and headed out of the room. Jen and some of the women Mike had seen gathered around her before followed.

"Ah, the fun stuff I can never seem to get permission to write," said a voice behind Mike.

Mike turned to find the person who had directed the statement at him.

"My, Mr. Daniels, you sure do get around," said the white-haired man clad in a well-tailored suit.

Mike recognized the voice, although the last time he heard it, the man was wearing jeans and a winter coat. "And so do you, Mr. Renard." His tone turned icy and his body headed in the opposite direction.

"You even got my name right this time. Seems like you're running again, Mr. Daniels."

Mike stopped, rolled his eyes skyward and said, "Mr. Renard: first off, the police don't want me talking about the case until it's all said and done. Secondly, I don't want to talk about the case. The less I'm involved, the better off I'll be. And thirdly, what in the heck are you doing here—stalking me or what?"

Renard answered each point in turn. "The police don't want you screwing up their airtight case by mouthing off to the press and giving the defense a technicality to get their client off. As far as being involved goes, that went right out the window as soon as you told the park rangers what you had seen. That'll teach you to be a good little citizen. And thirdly, no, I'm definitely not stalking you. I'm here with Patti Preston."

The name had no effect on Mike. His face wrinkled into a question. "Patti Preston?"

"Patti Preston is Governor Cowling's press secretary," explained Bill.

"Oh. Does that give you carte blanche to stalk us?"

"Hardly. Ms. Preston and I have been living together for two years now. There's been times when she stalked me, but that's another story," Bill said with a wry look at the sixty-year-old woman performing damage control with some subordinates.

Mike got the gist of Bill's double entendre and wasn't sure he liked the image he was imagining. Bill caught the smile in Mike's eyes even if it never made it to his lips.

"Norm's always been a fool and he's worse when he gets drunk."

"Norm?" asked Mike.

"Norm Lowell. He's your girlfriend's boss. That was a nice save, by the way," congratulated Bill.

Mike glanced at Bill and wondered if he had been watching him all night long.

"He's got a reputation for chasing the ladies, which is the polite way of saying that most of the staffers think he's a pig. You snuck your lady right out from him."

Mike wanted to correct him on the "your lady" account but liked the sound of it.

"Yea, ol' Norm thinks with the wrong head at times but he's a heck of a fund raiser. The governor gave him the Support Center after the '98 election and has been keeping him from screwing it one way or another ever since," said Bill.

"God, I love politics," Mike said in a condescending tone.

"And well you should, my boy. Nothing gets done without it."

Mike laughed at the term "my boy" and said, "Well, you have it made. A reporter on the inside and all that."

"Inside? Just what are you inferring there, Mr. Daniels?" questioned Bill with another double entendre.

"Not that kind of inside, Mr. Renard. I mean being around all of this," defended Mike.

"This is a kind of a reporter's purgatory. Look at it, a smorgasbord of conversations, comments and chaos. All I have to do is listen and I can fill up a few columns every day, right? Nope. One inappropriate leak of any of this and I get cut off in more ways than one. Not to mention what would happen to Patti."

Mike watched Bill's expression change to genuine concern as he ended his sentence and asked, "And what would happen to Patti?"

"The governor would ask for her resignation and then she'd never get another press relations job in the fifty United States. That's politics, my boy."

"So your hands are tied?"

"Just by the governor, never by Patti. Okay, there was this one time that..."

The third sexual reference was enough to make Mike consider dating retirees as Bill was obviously having a better sex life than he probably had in his two years of wedded bliss. He chased the thought from his mind and decided to get Bill talking about other things. "So you like crime reporting?"

"What makes you say that?"

"You were chasing me around after a crime was committed."

"I used to do a fair amount of political reporting for the *Post* till I met Patti. You're right though, I'm the *Post*'s lone crime reporter."

"Lone?"

"Lone. Lone as in alone, sole, and single. I can tell you weren't an English major, were you?"

"Why 'lone'? Did you scare the rest away?" teased Mike.

"Funny. What the grim reaper didn't take, the bean counters did. Harrisburg isn't the most criminal city around, although you might not agree."

"Do you do the Crime Watchers column?"

"Oh God, no. That gets assigned to one of those pimply interns that they keep below the poverty level. I get to do the real honest-to-God reporting. I go in and get my hands dirty," said Bill as he took the last drink from his Pilsner glass.

"Oh, you set type and ink the presses, eh?"

"You are a funny boy, aren't you?"

"I'm sorry. It's just that you looked liked you'd seen it all," said Mike.

"I have, my boy. I have. Refill this glass for me, and I'll tell you my life's story. I'd rather you keep the beer and tell me all about Clayton Edwards and Brenda Stabler burying that poor old bum out in the park."

"Brenda Stabler?" asked Mike who now knew the blonde woman's identity. Mike also realized that his overt curiosity dashed any hopes of avoiding the one thing he wanted to avoid.

"I'd...a...much rather buy the beer," stammered Mike as he tried to cover up his previous two words.

"Too late, my boy. I'd much rather hear your story."

"There isn't much of a story. That's the funny part."

"That's what you think, my boy," remarked Bill. "You really don't know what you walked into out there, did you?"

"Well, you got a hold of my name and know the particulars of the case. You probably got a copy of the ranger's report. You know more than me. What else could you want?" asked Mike.

"I want the eyewitness account for my column. It's as simple as that."

"No comment," Mike stated as he turned to leave again.

"Maybe I do know more than you. Are you interested in finding out more?"

Mike's departure stopped at the bait Renard had put out.

"You put him at the scene."

"Of course I..." Mike stopped midsentence and found himself hooked. Bill seemed to have access to the knowledge Mike wanted to have to understand what happened that morning.

"I know, you can't comment. Don't. Heck, even if we talk off the record, my editor will be up my butt to write something about an unnamed source. It wouldn't take a whole lot of friggen imagination to guess who that might be. You are the lone eyewitness. Lone as in alone, sole and single. Think about that before you talk to anybody but the police."

"I appreciate your understanding, Mr. Renard."

"Call me Bill. Just do me a favor and come see me when this is all over so we can get it down for the record."

"I don't understand what all the fuss is about though. It's a hit-and-run that got found out. What's the big deal?" said Mike.

"You really don't know what you stepped in, do you?"

"I have whatever you wrote about the Exeter elections and the media reports on him turning himself in."

"Then you don't have squat. Your sketch put him on the scene. Heck, they towed his red Blazer into impound and found hair and fiber inside," said Bill.

"But why were they out in the boonies of Sanford Park? Your column said that they hit that guy in the city after some kind of party."

"The boonies was where they ended up. That's not where they started."

"Where did they start out?"

"They started in ballroom B, right next door," said Bill.

Mike missed the connection.

"Edwards and his assistant, Brenda Stabler, were invited to a pre-inauguration party for all of the Muir County winners at the ballot box. Both sides used it as a way to size each other up for the next few years. Over the course of the evening Edwards got falling down drunk. Stabler ushered him out of there before he made a scene. The word was that they got themselves a room. After a while, they snuck out of the hotel. Edwards decided that he was okay to drive. Bennie Carlson did his usual window-washing routine at the light on Walnut and boom. Bennie's dead on the ground and Edwards scrambled to hide the body. Stabler panicked and agreed to help. I guess Sanford State Park was on the way home to Exeter. You found 'em on their little field trip."

"Poor guy. He probably never knew what hit him," said Mike.

"Got that right, ol' Bennie was pretty well tanked himself. He probably didn't feel a thing."

Mike set his wine glass down. He didn't feel like finishing it and driving Jen home.

Bill continued, "It's a dirty shame too. Edwards had the whole city behind him. I haven't seen anything like it for years. He was a real man of the people. Dang."

"Sounds like you knew him."

"Knew of him. He cut his teeth doing storefront law during the riots."

"I read about that," said Mike.

"He'd fight like heck for the innocent ones and tell the guilty ones to turn themselves in. He did a ton of pro bono stuff too. He became a genuine hero in the black community down there. Word spread and the Hispanics started coming to him too. After that, blue collar whites. Had to expand his practice six times. His reputation with the judges was solid 'cause he didn't waste their time on technical crap."

"A real man of the people, eh?"

"You got that right. Just one person too many," said Bill with a touch of sorrow.

"You mean Bennie?"

"Yea, I mean Bennie. Nobody knew where he came from. Bennie was one of those homeless folks that was harmless enough. He staked out Commonwealth and Walnut as his corner. He'd do car windows with an old sprayer bottle and a dirty towel. He'd get meals from the church folk and drink his cash."

"Not much of a life."

"No, not much but it was the only one he had. To Bennie," toasted Bill with the last remnants of his beer.

"To Bennie." Mike picked up his wine glass and toasted Bennie with a clink of Bill's glass.

"Geez, who invited him?"

"Bennie?"

"No. Sam Houser. Edwards hasn't even been through the courts yet," sneered Bill.

Mike watched the acrimony of the words hardening Bill's face. "Friend of yours?"

"Not in the least. Dang. Talk about bad form. Houser, over there, was—is—the Republican candidate from Exeter. Look at him working the department heads. He was a shoo-in until Edwards showed up. Nasty bugger, too—ran a ton of mudslinging ads during the election. All it did was help Edwards. Now look at him, stroking the crowd like he's already in the door."

"You make it sound like those folks can just appoint him."

"No, nothing like that. There's going to have to be a special election to fill Edwards' seat. Houser's just touching base—consolidating his supporters. Democrats won't stand a chance with the whole Edwards thing going on. It certainly is a bad turn of events."

Mike caught the mix of regret and sadness in Bill's narrowing eyes. There was something personal in Bill's observations. "So, Houser gets a second chance?"

"Second chance? Maybe I can have one," said Jen as she returned. "I'm so sorry. It took a while for me to calm Terry down."

"There's no need to apologize, Jen. Is she okay?" asked a genuinely concerned Mike.

"She'll be fine as soon as Lowell gets put out to pasture."

Bill Renard's back had been turned to Jen during the exchange with Mike. As soon he turned, Jen recognized who Mike was speaking with and wanted to eat her words. Bill picked up on Jen's instant discomfort and soothed her, saying, "Don't worry Miss..."

"Stevens."

"Patti thinks he's a fool, too. I'll have to tell you about the time she kicked him in the balls, but the hour is late and Patti is beckoning. I hope we get to talk again, my boy." Bill exited and left the two of them alone in a room full of people.

Jen repeated her earlier apology, "I'm so sorry, Mike."

"Don't worry about it. Really," replied Mike, who was happy to have her back.

"It didn't take you long to find a friend."

"You mean Bill? He's really not a friend."

"Bill? You call him 'Bill'? Everybody calls him 'Mr. Renard.'"

"We had a drink and he insisted that I call him 'Bill.'"

"All of us in the office have to watch what we say around him. It'll get into the papers or back to Patti."

"Well, he did most of the talking, so I think I'm okay."

Jen tried to size up Mike and his newfound non-friend.

Mike interrupted her assessment with an invitation, "How about we do some more dancing?"

Jen looked at the dwindling numbers of dancers and the growing numbers of empty tables that bordered the dance floor. "I think I'll pass. I've had enough for one Christmas party."

Mike sensed her will to go, but felt a tiny pinprick of disappointment in her reply. He wanted to go back on the floor and find that moment they had shared out there.

"Maybe we can go dancing another time," was his hopeful reply.

"I'd like that, Mikey," Jen said with a tease.

Mike took the barb as intended; especially with the way Jen's eyes lit up with childish mischief, and teased back, "I'd like that, too, Jeneeee."

The drive home was uneventful and quiet as both of them reflected on aspects of their evening that they'd prefer to forget or try to remember. Mike pulled Jen's Volkswagen Beetle up into the driveway and the couple made their way to the door. Grasping for her keys in the dark, Jen led the way in the winter air. Mike was two steps behind and less concerned with the cold. After all, he wasn't wearing a black cocktail dress. The keys were being uncooperative by hiding in the deep recesses of Jen's tiny handbag. She turned around to allow the porch lamp to better light her search. In doing so, she almost stepped right into Mike, who had come to a halt behind her. At first, their faces reflected the awkwardness of the near collision, but it passed into a welcome closeness. Their eyes closed as their lips met softly.

Abby noted the approach of someone near the door by the sound of footsteps vibrating up the walkway. A pair of silhouettes merged on the sheer curtains hung over the entrance's small windows. Realizing what that meant, Abby sprang into action, barking madly, and running about the kitchen. Her frenzy rousted Roxanne into a spasm of flopping ears, and thrashing legs. Roxanne's bass barks bellowed in between Abby's soprano in a canine opera. Now that Roxanne was fully involved, Abby surveyed the kitchen for just the right thing. *Yes*, she thought, *that would do nicely*.

Their lips parted at the eruption of loud barking attempting to warn intruders away. Mike heard Abby start and listened to Roxanne's chiming in. It was loud enough to get the neighbors upset and Jen scrambled to find her keys. Jen pushed the door open to quiet the barking dogs. Abby's barking abated the moment Mike came into the room. Roxanne's had already stopped.

Jen found Roxanne nosing her way through the contents of her toppled trash can that were strewn about the floor. "Roxanne." The dog slinked away to her favorite rug.

Mike watched Abby prance over to him and sit down the way an obedience school trained dog would sit. "Let me help get this cleaned up," said Mike as he attempted to shed his coat.

"No, I'll get it. You'll get your suit dirty and then I'd feel worse than I do for inviting you to my stupid Christmas party."

"It's not a problem."

"Yea, yea it is. You've been wonderful."

Mike caught the inference of her desire for him to leave and asked one more time, "Are you sure?"

"Yes. If I don't clean this up right away, Roxanne will get into it even more. Then she'll be hurling all night long, which will be a lot worse than it is right now."

"All right, then," answered Mike, who felt a twinge of dejection creeping in as he fastened Abby's leash.

Jen walked Mike back to the door and opened it for him. He turned to be a gentleman and say goodnight, but Jen surprised him with another kiss.

Their lips parted again and Jen quietly said, "Call me."

Mike's eyebrows raised and a smile broadened on his face. "I will."

"Like last time?"

"No. I'll call," pledged Mike.

The last thing Mike heard as the door closed was the agitated voice of an owner chiding their pet.

On the way home, Mike never noticed the happy little twitch that Abby's tail made.

Chapter *11*

Christmas fell on a Tuesday. Mike's hopes had fallen long before that.

As promised, Mike called Jen, who answered in the hurried, hollow tones of a person doing the remote phone two-step.

"Did Roxanne get sick?" asked Mike.

"No, thank God." Puff—puff. "Every time she turned over I was awake." Step—step. "Stupid dog." Clunk. "I don't know what possessed her to get into the trash can. She hardly ever does that." Step—step—rustle.

"Who knows what dogs think?" said Mike as he looked at Abby's expressionless muzzle.

Mike picked up on the rushed tone of Jen's voice and the sound of continuous motion through the earpiece. Coming to the point, he asked, "What are you doing for Christmas?"

Step—step—halt. "I'm...headed to my mom's."

"Home for the holidays, eh? Sounds like fun." Mike's chipper tone tried to mask his disappointment.

"Well, I don't know how much fun it will be. She invited my brother's family, too—three screaming toddler boys and his screaming wife. I'll be deaf by the time I get back. But hey, she invited me down there, so what am I gonna do?"

"Down there?"

"Yea, she lives outside Alexandria, Virginia."

89

"Well, there's nothing like going home for the holidays."

"Mom insisted. Besides, with my divorce this year and all that..."

"I can't say I blame you one bit," was Mike's diplomatic reply. Silence hung in the air for a full second and Mike realized that there was nothing more to say. It's not that he didn't want to say more but he felt that suffering any more rejection at Christmastime was more than he wanted to deal with.

"Well, I have to finish packing and get on the road. I'll be back on Wednesday. Maybe we can take the dogs for a walk," said Jen.

"That would be nice, Jen," replied Mike.

"Alrighty, I'll see you then. Merry Christmas, Mike."

"Merry Christmas, Jen."

Mike frowned, hung up the phone and chided himself. "Idiot."

After a long self-pitying sigh, he decided to head over to the video store to rent some distractions for Christmas. Before heading out, Mike sat down for a moment in his living room to look at his Christmas tree—the first one he had been in a mood to buy in two years. A whiff of fresh fir transported him back to his childhood and his mother's playful warning to stay away from the presents. The bittersweet moment lingered for a bit as he smiled at the lights on the tree, knowing that he would be the only one seeing it. Mike's focus shifted to the framed family portrait of the three Daniels hung on the wall near the Christmas tree. Fortunately, Abby had positioned herself near him in case he needed a dog to pet, and it was a good thing because he did.

* * *

Christmas morning for Mike was not the childlike expected glee of opening presents. It was just another Tuesday in another week of another year, or so he wanted it to be. There was something about the emptiness in his house that amplified his loneliness.

He had allowed himself the luxury of sleeping in as a kind of gift to himself but that was interrupted by the bubbling and hissing of the coffee machine. During breakfast, Mike read the morning paper and found that the world was still and happy, or at least the *Post* said it was. That was good enough for him—especially since it contained no references to anyone named Edwards or Carlson. The paper's articles and puzzles allowed him just enough diversion to keep his mind off Jen.

Venturing out into the damp air, Mike left the house for a run under lead-colored skies pregnant with snow. *Running in the snow would be a pleasure*, he thought. *The world is always pretty with a fresh coat of winter white.* Flurries announced the start and his posture shifted from a heart heavy-laden to a certain childlike view of things. His mood shifted out of its dark gray cast as the new fallen snow brightened everything around him. He even sang Christmas carols, albeit badly, all the way from the road to the shower. He didn't stop until he could see the ears of a certain Shetland sheepdog twitching in apparent pain during his rendition of Handel's *Hallelujah Chorus.* She left her owner for quieter pastures downstairs. Mike finished his routine and threw on some sweats with the sole purpose in mind of relaxing while he watched his rented flicks. Coming down the steps, his mood shifted when he saw the mistletoe he had discreetly placed on the kitchen threshold as a pleasant trap for Jen. There lay Abby, recovering from severe ear strain. Figuring that it was as good as it was going to get, Mike walked over to Abby, kissed her on the forehead, and got a lick in return.

Mike turned, plopped down on the couch, and fingered the remote to start *Indiana Jones and the Last Crusade*. He asked himself if there was ever a better adventure movie. The DVD languished on the FBI warnings and Mike's mood melted like snow on a warm day. He cranked the sound up and began watching the movie. As he did, he saw Abby go to the front door and stand, as if Mike should be ushering somebody in. Looking at her like she had some kind of a problem, he turned down the volume and asked, "What's the matter, girl?" Abby stood next to the door, ears up and listening to a soft knock.

She looked like a princess in a fairy tale. Her woolen hood covered most of her long brunette hair. The ends hung down the front of her coat, and the snow atop the hood glistened like tiny jewels. Her blue eyes had been cast downward and now looked up at him with widened glee.

"Merry Christmas," said Jen in a soft voice.

Mike stood dumbfounded and joyous all at the same time. The words finally came to him. "Merry Christmas, Jen," he replied with a face that said so much more. He extended his hand to the princess. Roxanne, seeing that there were warmer places to play, rose and followed the couple inside.

Amid the chaos of Roxanne's dancing feet and Abby's struggle to get away from those feet, Mike managed to hang up Jen's coat before joining her on the couch.

"I'm sorry for not calling. I wanted to see you," said Jen.

"You have no idea."

Jen reached into her pocket and pulled out two small gifts wrapped in curly ribbon. "This one is for you."

Mike fumbled and fought with the ribbon until the box was misshapen enough to allow its removal. He opened it and found a glass ornament with the image of a toy collie on the front. He held it up to the light and smiled broadly. "It's great. I don't have an Abby ornament." Mike stood up and walked to the tree to find a place of honor for the new ornament.

Jen followed to watch the hanging ceremony. Her eyes were drawn to the unusual ornaments adorning the tree and she asked, "Is that a spaceship?"

"Yep, X-wing fighter. The *Star Wars* ornaments are on the right and *Star Trek* on the left." Mike watched as Jen's look swung into one of those Mars/Venus kind of expressions.

"Oh," was the best answer she could come up with.

Both dogs had approached at the sound of tearing paper hoping for something far more edible than glass. Abby was not disappointed.

"Here, you can open this for Abby," said Jen.

Mike fared no better the second time. Inside the wrap lay the perfect sheltie Christmas gift—a large piece of beef jerky. Mike figured that Abby's look was the closest thing to canine intoxication that he had ever seen—and that Roxanne's face bore the wrinkled lips of canine envy. "Roxanne," Mike called. Roxanne spun round in a cacophony of clicking toenails and panting breath. Mike offered the present to Jen. "This is for Roxanne."

Jen deftly removed the paper and plain ribbon, exposing a nylon bone to Roxanne's waiting teeth.

Mike fetched a second box and gave it to Jen, "For you. Something to remember the Christmas party with."

Jen looked with skepticism at Mike's description. She unwrapped the narrow box and emptied its contents on the coffee table. The item was one of those small dartboards sold as "Executive Gifts." Glued to the bull's-eye was a particularly bad picture of Norm Lowell cut from the newspaper. "Oh God, it's perfect."

The afternoon spilled into the evening though neither Jen nor Mike seemed to notice, or care. They spent the time finding out all the little things that made a new attraction so wonderful and ended their night watching the rest of *Indiana Jones*. At the end of the movie, Jen announced that it was getting late and it was time to go home. Both Roxanne and Abby had camped out in the threshold of the kitchen door and both refused to budge when called. Jen walked over to grab Roxanne. Mike did the same for Abby. Both sets of human eyes spied the mistletoe and both forgot about the dogs. Their lips met.

"That was better than the porch," whispered Jen.

"I'll say, and I thought the porch was pretty good."

"I wonder if it keeps getting better every time we kiss."

Mike caught the glint in Jen's eyes and realized that he was going to find out.

Abby watched them kiss and wondered what humans saw in such behavior. *After all, bumping muzzles didn't tell you anything about the person*, she thought. *They should be sniffing butts if they really want to know what the other is in to.* There was a hint of something in the air that Abby couldn't quite place—something subtle but altogether visceral—almost like something smoldering. *Oh God*, Abby thought—*hormones.*

Chapter 12

During December, Mike and Jen inaugurated a closer relationship. During January, Pennsylvania inaugurated a new governor. What Mike didn't know was that, by February, the governor would be seeing more of Jen than he would, at least in the professional sense. Jen's hard work had been recognized by the incoming administration, and she took the career risk of a political appointment in return for a large promotion. Jen's job as assistant to the director ate up a great deal of her waking hours, and Mike figured that Roxanne was none too happy with the longer workdays. Fortunately for Roxanne's kidneys, Mike came to the rescue and took the retriever for walks in the evenings. The rescue was mutual as Mike's thoughts focused on a certain pile of rocks in a certain state park. The memories of his discovery had been refreshed by a three-hour deposition at the county courthouse, courtesy of the district attorney earlier in the day. Mike was happy to get out into the cold and clear his mind.

Although she took it in stride, Abby was none too happy to watch Mike head out the door after work, especially since he was walking that—that—r-r-r-r-retriever. Abby somehow managed to be absent when her owner felt compelled to ask her if she was ready to go for a walk. The idea of a walk on a twenty-five degree night coupled with the antics of that social slut Roxanne left Abby with the kind of taste in her mouth usually experienced with stale kibbles. *No*, she thought, *the only walk I'm doing is to the warmest stretch of carpet in the house*.

The romantic novelty of Christmas snow lay under a foot of drifting February powder. Lying on top of the drifts was one inverted golden retriever making dog angels. Just the sight of Roxanne writhing in the snow sent a chill right through Mike's layers of winter insulation. What Mike didn't know was that the three onlooking occupants of a nearby car caught the same chill. The car had been sitting there for about an hour, which was what it did most nights when its passengers were watching the Daniels household.

Mike and Roxanne always turned left and began a circuit that circled Bridgeport. Tonight was different, as Mike was about to find out when Roxanne caught wind of the unmistakable ambrosia of road kill, and she turned right to locate its source. Mike tugged the leash to go left but the willful retriever would have none of it. Mike's arm, which he imagined to be four inches longer since he began walking Roxanne, settled into its position in tow. Experiencing Roxanne's tug firsthand, Mike knew why Jen's body was always bent into a "C."

The change in Mike's dog-induced direction touched off a minor panic in the car. Paying for their complacency, agitated heads bobbed like worried geese in a pond. The most agitated and fed up of the geese kept one hand on the door latch in case man and dog paid too much attention to their presence.

Mike's attention span was precisely measured at ten feet—six for the length of the leash and four for the number of legs pulling him like a water skier. Roxanne's muzzle made it to the front bumper of the occupied Ford Taurus—not that Mike, or Roxanne, had any idea of the amount of alarm growing inside the vehicle. Just as the most agitated of the passengers flexed a muscular hand to open the door, Roxanne cut in front of the car, tugging Mike along. Once man and dog went down the block, one of the passengers got out and began to follow.

Somewhere along the way, Roxanne lost the scent and settled into a more pedestrian pace, which Mike was happy to take. A few hardy souls braved the cold to get in a bit of exercise to keep away the holiday flab or cure cabin fever. Roxanne, being far more social than Mike, yanked on the leash to be sure to greet each one. Each greeting would cause the man following behind Mike to pause and look nonchalant. The change in routine, coupled with the constant threat of exposure, fanned an ember of irritation into the fire of anger for the trailing man.

Mike guided Roxanne down the streets that made up the south side of Bridgeport's suburban maze and into what Mike considered its most dangerous section—the 2800 block of Bucknell Avenue. Roxanne's leash went slack, which told Mike that her nerves were quite the opposite—not that his were any less tense. The pair stood under a streetlight which marked the outer boundary of the lair of Mitsy, Demon Poodle from the Seventh Ring of Hell. Mitsy was generally let loose by its elderly owner for a bathroom break about the time that Mike and Roxanne had passed. On occasion, their timing erred and Mitsy vented the full rage of every fiber of her apricot curls on any canine larger than her. This was nearly every breed save the Chihuahua. Mike had seen Mitsy run off German shepherds, Labradors and a Newfoundland. Its owner would come outside and chide the owner of the retreating pet for disturbing his dog. Mike wondered if the angry owner ever realized that he had to call his dog home from several homes away.

"Remember, Roxanne, go to the light. Go to the light," said Mike. The position of Roxanne's tail between her legs and the way her eyebrows canted told Mike that she didn't appreciate his mock fatalism. Her look made Mike consider taking another route, but Roxanne's mercurial mood swings might take her into the harm's way of traffic. Instead, he steeled himself and gave Roxanne a gentle push on the behind to get her going. They inched forward and increased to a fast walk. Roxanne was not pulling on the leash; rather, she was content to walk beside Mike in classic heeling posture. It was, after all, the furthermost point away from Mitsy in the event of a confrontation.

House number 2809 loomed and passed from view without incident. As each house passed, Roxanne pulled more on the leash showing Mike that her nervousness was going away. His concern faded as well. Their relief had been a mistake. Mike's overconfidence blocked the simple fact that they had reversed their direction.

Under the nearing streetlight came a high-pitched growl. Mike and Roxanne felt their breaths go shallow with a dread as dark as a winter's night. Mitsy stood, oscillating with guttural menace, the raised hair on her back glowing green from the overhead fluorescence. Roxanne began to back away from the confrontation. Mike held firm on the leash. Mitsy bore in at a full gallop, her tiny legs a blur of possessed pursuit. Her ladylike pink ear ribbons streamed in the wind and an unladylike sneer adorned her lips. Roxanne twisted her head round to lose the leash that bound her to certain doom. Tugging hard, Mike found that all he had left was an empty collar and a limp leash. Mitsy, in hot pursuit, yipped at the top of her lungs. Roxanne picked up speed and ran back along the sidewalk in a flurry of chestnut-colored desperation with a blur of apricot-colored demonic possession closing in. "Roxanne. How am I going to explain this to Jen?" panted Mike as he vainly tried to recover the escaping dog.

As Mike ran after Roxanne, he caught sight of the near collision between Roxy and a walker. What happened next made him shake his head. When Mitsy approached the walker, she ground her painted toenails to a halt, dropped her tail and spun around. All of the energy plowed into her assault contributed to her retreat. It really didn't sink into Mike until he neared the approaching man. Mike attempted to maneuver out of his way. Instead of moving to one side, the man countered Mike's maneuver and remained on collision course. Lowering his shoulder, the man lunged forward into Mike's chest. The block lifted him into the air for a second until the momentum ceased. Mike spilled to the ground, helpless and stunned. The frozen sidewalk proved an inhospitable landing spot, and the initial shock now had a distinct amount of pain added to it. Mike's shock distilled into disbelief that the man had intentionally done this to him along with the certain belief that he couldn't breathe. The air had been knocked out of him. As stars flickered amidst random flashers of hypoxia-induced light, Mike looked skyward. A man's face appeared, lit by a shadowy mix of house and street lights. The man's hood had been knocked back, revealing his worn and rugged features. Mike thought he saw something that looked like barbwire around the man's neck. Brushing the thought aside, Mike blinked his eyes to refocus, this time catching the gleam of a gold crucifix dangling between him and his assailant.

The man spoke with a Hispanic accent edged in hissing fury, "It's gonna hurt a whole lot more if you don't leave Mr. Edwards alone. You got me?"

Mike did not get it; not one bit, but figured that he was in no position to ask for a clarification. He shook his head in the affirmative. The man withdrew, leaving Mike gasping for a chest full of air. It seemed to take forever to get air into his lungs. When he caught his breath, he sucked huge gulps of air through his nose and mouth, then coughed it back up again. Lying on the ground, Mike waited for the stranger to leave. Before the stranger disappeared, Mike saw a car pull up to the streetlight where they first spotted Mitsy. Loud voices erupted from the car and Mike struggled to make out what he was hearing. *Angered shouts—what were they saying?* thought Mike. *What? It's not English. It's Spanish*, he figured, somehow equating a year of high school Spanish with what he heard. The car door slammed shut and the tires spun, leaving Mike vertically challenged on the hard concrete.

Closing his eyes, Mike tried to understand what had just happened. *He was just chasing Roxanne and boom. Roxanne. Where was Roxanne?* Mike opened his eyes and saw another face peering at him from above. A long nose and expressive eyelashes inspected him and a long tongue extended to rouse him from his spot on the concrete. "Thanks, Roxanne," Mike said as he stood up, still woozy from the impact. A throbbing in his head and tailbone joined him as soon as he was erect. He put the collar back on Roxanne and headed for home—past 2809 Bucknell Avenue. Mike looked up on the porch where he saw the quivering Mitsy, curled up on the doormat and unwilling to chase anything. Mitsy's quaking sent a shiver down Mike's neck. The chill took Mike back to the night in December when he saw a stranger walking through his neighborhood. *Could that man and the man that decked him be the same?* he wondered. The more he thought about it, the more he didn't like that the answer was "yes."

* * *

"What on earth happened to you?" asked a very concerned Jen when Mike showed up to deliver Roxanne. Jen could see the tight wrinkles under Mike's eyes and his lips drawn straight to offset the unmentioned pain.

"I slipped and fell on the sidewalk," lied Mike, who wanted Jen to have no part of whatever was going on.

"You fell? Are you okay?"

The way she asked him about falling told him that she wasn't buying it, but he kept trying. "I'm a bit banged up but I think I'll recover."

"Do you want anything? Is there something I can do?" she asked.

"No. No. I just need to put some ice on my back. I'll be all right."

"Why don't you stay and let me take care of it?"

Mike considered the offer as exactly the tonic he needed but also worried about the man that had knocked him down. Mike wanted to leave as soon as possible and go lick his wounds. "No, I just really need to throw some ice on it and then get to work on the...er...Miller project. I'll see you tomorrow, okay?"

"Okay," answered Jen. She wasn't buying his excuse. She gave him a quick emotionless kiss to send him on his way.

The door closed behind him and Mike could feel the growing soreness coming from his lower back. That pain seemed minor compared to that kiss, he thought. He wanted to go back and tell her everything that was going on but fought the idea of involving her at the same time. *Besides*, he thought, *she must want some quiet time of her own after a long day*. Heading down the walkway, he stopped shy of the steps leading to the street. *What the heck am I thinking?*

Jen heard a knock at the door and looked out of the peephole. Standing in oval distortion was Mike Daniels. She opened the door and said, "Changed your mind?" Mike looked much like a whipped puppy dog and it tugged at Jen's heartstrings to see so pitiful a creature.

"You know, the thought of a beautiful woman icing my backside sounded pretty good. How could I walk away?"

"Get in here."

Mike lay on his stomach and across Jen's lap as she held a bag of ice on the small of his back. "This has got to be the most non-erotic position a couple can have," he said, feeling a shiver run through his body as he buried his face in a throw pillow.

"I didn't think that you had anything erotic on your mind when you showed up," answered Jen.

"I didn't. I just wanted some ice."

"You are Mr. Excitement, aren't you?"

"Oh yea. My ex-wife once told me that vanilla ice cream is exotic compared to me."

"She did, did she?" Jen said as she lifted his legs off her lap and took the ice bag into the kitchen.

Mike felt the soothing coldness leave and figured he had said the wrong thing by bringing up quotes from Monica. Jen rounded the kitchen doorway and took up her seat under his legs. The cold rush returned an instant later and he was once again soothed. He turned his face from the folds of the pillow and faced out into the room. Dangling in front of him was a long iced tea spoon with a lump of creamy whiteness on it. The spoon moved toward his mouth. "Mmmm Vanilla," said Mike.

"I like vanilla. It's my favorite, especially under tons of hot fudge."

Mike's brow wrinkled into a question. "Are you still using ice?"

"Nope. Gonna have a heck of a story for the girls tomorrow. 'There I was, eating ice cream off a man's butt...'"

Mike buried his head back in the pillow until the cold spoon tapped his cheek.

"I don't think I want to know where this spoon has been."

"I'm the one that should worry about where it's been," replied Jen with a little slap to Mike's posterior. "Speaking about where things have been, where did you fall?"

"Down on Bucknell," replied Mike.

"Mitsy?"

"Yes," said Mike as he hesitated to say anything more.

"So, Mitsy ran you down? You know, Mike, I get the feeling that there's more to this story than your getting ambushed by a toy poodle."

Mike felt the weight of Jen's comment land on him like a ton of bricks. He turned his face back into the pillow and considered whether he should tell her or not. Finally, Mike lifted his head from the pillow with a long sigh and spoke, "It's a long story..."

* * *

"So this guy slams you down? You have to call the cops," said an excited and incredulous Jen.

"No. I'm not going there. If I tell the cops, particularly the State Police, Hoover will want another description. He'll feed me to Maggie and we'll publish another sketch which will tell whoever slammed me down that I told the police all about our little meeting. He'll undoubtedly have another friend who will undoubtedly do worse to me than slamming me to the sidewalk. Then I'll have to do another report and another sketch and meet with another friend of that person until I can't do sketching anymore. Nope."

"So you're going to do nothing."

"No, I intend to have my butt frozen by a beautiful woman. I get my perks where I can."

Jen landed another slap to Mike's butt and said, "You really should call the police."

"And tell them what? That I ran into a guy and fell on the sidewalk? No, the less I know the better."

Jen didn't like the answer but could also tell that Mike had no intention of calling the police.

"And Jen, don't you go calling the cops for me, okay?" said Mike, who picked up on Jen's silence and guessed what she was thinking.

"If you insist."

"Yes, yes, I do insist."

Jen pushed Mike's legs off her lap, and the cold chill of the ice cream left his lower back. Returning a few seconds later, Jen held her hands behind her back in an effort to hide what she had picked up. Sitting on her knees, she looked face-to-face with the reclining man. "You know, your ex-wife was wrong. You make vanilla exciting. I've never dated a murder witness before."

"Vanilla excites you?"

"I told you, it's my favorite, especially with lots of hot fudge."

Jen produced a jar of hot fudge ice cream topping and a demure smile.

Mike's eyebrows raised and a warm rush of blood let him know that his back was not the only part of his body getting stiffer.

* * *

A while later, Mike's bliss parted and his back resumed being the sole stiff part of his body. He mused over the uses of hot fudge as painkiller and aphrodisiac and figured that he couldn't order a sundae ever again without smirking. As the afterglow faded, more unpleasant memories intruded—particularly of getting slammed onto the pavement by person unknown.

They said quiet good-byes between kisses and Mike hobbled toward home pushed by the memories of his encounter and the need to take care of Abby's needs. He knew he had lied to Jen about not wanting to know more. What's more was that he knew he was lying to himself. There was much more going on around him than he thought, and it bothered him a great deal to know that somebody, somewhere meant him bodily harm just for what he witnessed. He knew he couldn't go to the police. That would start exactly the cycle he told Jen about. He had already told Jen a lot more than he wanted to. Still, he wanted to know more. *If I knew more, I'd know what to avoid or, at least, what to watch for. Not knowing was really the problem*, he thought.

Approaching the lights of home, Mike slipped on the pavement. His first thought was that it was a bit of ice. It felt like mud but it wasn't. It was, as Mike so aptly put it, "Crap."

Making a vain attempt at cleaning his shoe off in the snow, Mike chided himself for not watching the walkway. "You really stepped in it this time," he said to himself out loud. In that instant he knew who he could talk to.

Chapter *13*

Gavin's was everything Mike hated about bars. The matte black wall shunned any light save the shaded incandescent lamps dimly glowing with irregular frequency at each table. The requisite red-checked tablecloths shrouded each table and lay under more glass than Lenin. The tablecloths were probably better preserved.

His entrance brought him into the unpleasant aroma of stale beer borne on a hazy cloud of cigarette smoke. Mike stood undecided in the doorway, trying to control his dislikes. *Besides*, he thought, *a cold beer might numb my backache as much as vanilla ice cream— well, not really*.

Gavin's patrons paid Mike little notice. No heads turned to see the newcomer and their hushed tones never hesitated in their voicing. The bartender, like the patrons, paid little attention to Mike as he strolled toward the back of the bar where the stools ran out and the booths began.

Pairs, threesomes, and foursomes occupied the narrow set of booths. Like the stool occupants, they paid no mind to Mike's arrival save a passing glance when he wasn't looking. Mike's single-breasted suit and business tie set him apart from the patrons' flannel shirts and jeans.

Gavin's was everything Bill Renard liked about bars. The matte black walls obscured prying eyes from the outside, even on the brightest of days. The incandescent lamps lit up everybody's face so that he could tell which ones were observing him rather than looking at whomever they arrived with. The tablecloths—well, a neighborhood bar wouldn't be a neighborhood bar without red-checked tablecloths. He stood in the doorway and allowed himself to be surrounded by the first whiff of beer and smoke. Having given up smoking many years ago, he welcomed a chance nicotine encounter, even if it was secondhand.

Bill strode up to the bar where the bartender met him with a generous mug of lager. "Nice suspenders, Ernie. Is your wife still dressing you in the morning?"

"You wish you looked this good, Bill," replied the bartender. "Is he one of yours?"

The tone of Ernie's instant observational assessment let Bill know that the barkeep's inventory of his regulars remained as accurate as ever. "Yea, what do you think?"

"He looks like a light beer type. Maybe a fruity drink with an umbrella," hissed Ernie.

"Nah, let's give him a little credit. Gimme another one of these."

"He'll be gone in two," bet Ernie.

"I say three. Bet you a penny," said Bill as the men shook on the bet.

"Deal."

Bill plopped a twenty down on the counter. Ernie moved it to the cash drawer and handed Bill a receipt for two chicken sandwiches, fries and a couple of Cokes. It was much easier to get that kind of receipt past the bean counters at the *Post*.

"Remember, Ernie, no filling his glass until it's three-quarters empty."

"Yea, Yea," answered Ernie, feeling like a kid being reminded of the rules of a children's game.

Bill took both mugs to the booth Mike had chosen and didn't bother to put them down. He disliked Mike's choice of booths. "I got you one. I hope it'll do. Let's move over here," motioned Bill with a slump of one shoulder in a direction that situated them annoyingly close to the kitchen door. Mike obliged Bill's whim to move and settled into the seat opposite him. Bill liked this particular booth for its location. Since it was closest to the kitchen door, there were no booths behind it or tables next to it for intrusive ears to listen from. If he, or an interviewee, ever had need of a quick and anonymous exit, the kitchen afforded a short trip to an alleyway next to a suburban neighborhood where either could look inconspicuous. The other advantage was that he could see trouble coming all the way to the door, which gave them time to make their exit. Of course, Bill found all of his dime-store detective preparations amusing in the sense that he had never needed to use them. He liked Gavin's for the atmosphere. It always set the mood for whomever he was interviewing. It gave them a sense of confidentiality and seclusion along with a slight danger of collusion. They were a part of the conspiracy, and their information was vital to revealing whatever truth they felt compelled to tell. The fact of the matter was that most interviewees had little to tell and Bill liked a cold beer at cheap prices. Bill wasn't about to tell Mike that, though. "So, you're ready to tell me what happened out at Sanford Park back in December?" asked Bill.

"No. You know I shouldn't say anything," replied Mike, unfazed by Bill's blunt question.

Bill grimaced knowing that the direct approach wasn't going to work. He decided to fall back and try a game of give-and-take. "You gave me a call last night, Mr. Daniels. I was hoping you'd be willing to talk about the Edwards case. Why did you call?"

"Back at Christmas time, you told me that 'I really stepped into it.' What exactly did you mean by that?" asked Mike.

"How much do you read the *Post*?"

"A little. Why?"

"Then you have everything you need in there about Edwards," said Renard as he stood, intending to leave.

"Hold on a second," protested Mike.

"No, Mr. Daniels, you hold on a second. I'm not the county librarian. I'm not your research assistant. I'm an old reporter that has to fill a couple of columns every day until I retire. You can get what you want from the library, or for a buck a pop off the Internet. The address is www-dot-see-you-later-dot-bye."

Mike grabbed Bill's arm to prevent his departure. "Do you want an eyewitness account or not, Mr. Renard?"

Bill looked at Mike, assessing the sincerity in his face. It looked genuine, but there was something more, something in the eye that showed a touch of fear. Renard stopped his exit and returned to his seat. "Something else happened, didn't it, Mr. Daniels?"

"Mike. Call me Mike. I don't want one word about what we talk about to get into the *Post*, not until after he gets sentenced."

"I can't guarantee that. I can from me personally, but my editor is always after me for the next thing. He may put my notes into a column before I'd even see it."

"Then there's no story, Mr. Renard."

Bill realized the seriousness in Mike's face and knew that this was non-negotiable. "All right. No notes. No names. Nothing until the judge smacks the gavel and sentences Edwards. And it's Bill."

"All right Bill, it's a deal," said Mike as both men shook hands.

"So what happened, Mike? You called me," said Bill as he re-stated his question.

"I got knocked on my tush last night by a guy who took exception to my participation in the case. I was walking my girlfriend's dog. The dog got loose and I tore off after it. Next thing I know, this guy gives me a cross-body block and I'm down. He told me that it was going to hurt a lot more if I didn't leave Clayton Edwards alone."

Bill's eyes widened and narrowed as the surprise distilled into contemplation.

"That's not Edwards' style. Kepner or Houser, maybe, but not Edwards. Did he say anything else?" asked Bill.

"What style should I expect? And no, he didn't say anything else."

"Did you call the cops?"

"Heh, no," Mike said with a sarcastic laugh. "The townie cops would file a report and let it sit in the cabinet until Judgment Day. I don't remember much about the guy and I have no idea who picked him up. Besides, you seemed to have no problem getting hold of my involvement in this little episode. Neither did the guy who slammed me. I'm not about to file another report and get slammed down again."

"Been there. It's funny how the perspective of being laid out changes your attitude."

The beer glasses magically refilled via Ernie's deft handling of the pitcher. As he walked away from the table, he flashed a single finger to Bill who simply smirked back at him.

Mike took a swig and said, "You got that right."

"So why are you talking to me? Aren't you afraid I'll get you into more trouble?"

"No. Your name seems to be on most every *Post* report on the Edwards election and a lot of Muir County stuff too. You have to know who the players are. If you do, then you can tell me and I can do my best to stay the heck away from them until this all blows over."

"You should just call the cops," said Bill.

"And what? Wait for them to find me a spot in the witness protection program for a hit-and-run?"

"They'll check on you from time to time."

"Which will undoubtedly piss off whomever came after me. I need information here, Bill. I don't have a clue. One second, I'm running in the woods; the next, I have reporters and thugs showing up. I live a wonderfully boring existence that I'd really like to get back to," said an exasperated Mike.

"I'm sure you would, but I don't know how I can help."

"You can tell me why one of Edwards' little troop would like to pay me a visit."

"That's just it, I can't."

"What do you mean, 'can't' or won't?"

"That's the thing, I can't think of a reason why Edwards would want you threatened. He's a straight shooter. Mr. Clean. No graft, no skeletons, nothing. If he were Catholic, they'd want to canonize him— that's how clean he is. Deacon in the AME church, actually. He'd never order or condone anything like this."

"I didn't say it was him standing on top of me," said Mike.

"Then who was it? What do you remember?"

Mike closed his eyes to remember the incident. When he opened them, his beer glass had refilled itself again. Mike noted the slight change in Bill's attention and caught a glimpse of Bill flashing two fingers at Ernie. "He might have been Hispanic. His words had an inflection that reminded me of high school Spanish. Rugged face— not scarred or anything, just tough looking. Tough looking and pissed off, actually. He had my attention." In his mind's eye, Mike followed the sliver of light on his attacker's face down to the collar of a worn sweatshirt and he focused on the barbwire laced around his neck. "He had a tattoo on his neck. It looked like barbwire. There might have been other tattoos but I really couldn't see too much. It was pretty dark."

"And he warned you off Edwards?"

"Not quite in those words, but I think that the sidewalk pretty much communicated what he wanted to express," said Mike.

"Sounds like Jorge—Jorge Rembez. He's kind of a self-appointed bodyguard of Edwards. Hang on a sec. I'll be right back," said Bill as he rose and scurried out the door.

Mike watched him head out the door and noted the increase in the number of patrons coming in after a hard day's work. Even the booth next to them filled in. Bill returned carrying a worn briefcase bag bristling with papers, folders and cutouts from the *Post*. He shuffled through the debris gathered in the bag for a few moments and then turned his finding over to Mike.

"How about this one?" asked Bill.

Mike looked closely at the newspaper photo noting a much younger Edwards flanked by two African American men as they walked down the street and replied, "No. Nobody in this picture."

Bill pushed a second clipping toward Mike.

Mike perused it and said, "This might be the guy."

Bill handed a third photo to Mike.

"Bingo," Mike said when he saw the face atop a white T-shirt; neck clearly ringed by a barbwire.

"That's not barbwire, Mike. That's thorns. A ring of thorns to commemorate the crown that Christ wore during the crucifixion. Say 'hi' to Jorge Rembez."

"We've already met. So, he works for Edwards?"

"No, not really. Think of him as kind of an Edwards groupie."

"Groupie? Edwards runs a band?" said Mike.

"Hardly, Rembez and others like him are more like followers. It's not like a cult or anything. Rembez and a bunch of other folks from the East Side just feel like they owe Edwards a lot. When things got really ugly during the campaign, these guys formed a kind of bodyguard. All told, there were five or six of these guys willing to take a bullet for Edwards. That's how much they believed in what he stood for."

"For a state representative? I thought there were Secret Service agents who wouldn't take one for Bill Clinton."

"That's 'cause Edwards put himself out for guys like Rembez. Back in the mid-seventies, Rembez got hauled in on conspiracy charges stemming from some drug busts on Hispanic gangs. The police said that the operation was running out of Rembez's tattoo parlor. The cops didn't have much but that didn't matter. Twelve white jurors were selected. Rembez was as good as in the lower bunk in the county lockup. Enter Clayton Edwards. Up till that point, his store-front practice catered to low-to-no-income blacks living on the West Side. He talked to Rembez. Rembez kicked out his public defender and got Edwards to defend him. Edwards did it for free—pro bono. The trial came around and Edwards got Rembez off the hook. It turned out that Rembez wasn't playing ball with the local gang leaders, so they set him up. Rembez was just your basic everyday tattoo artist trying to make a buck. When Harley-Davidson made its comeback, Rembez was right there to cash in. By the time the nineties hit, white girls were getting their behinds tattooed at the best place in town. My—my. How things change," said Bill.

"That's a nice story with a happy ending, but that doesn't ex-plain why this guy would want to tattoo me using a shoulder and some cement."

"No, it doesn't. It sounds like you pissed him off. He's a bit of a hothead if you get in his face."

"But, I've never seen him before in my life," said Mike.

"Hmmm. Have you had any contact with anybody from their camp about any of this?"

Mike tilted his head toward Bill and gave him a look that made Bill realize that it had been a stupid question.

Bill sighed and said, "Then something must have set him off."
Bill sat back against the black wall and stroked his chin in thought.

"You didn't have anything to do with Edwards getting his wrists
slapped for a bail technicality?"

"Yea, that's it. I'm really a closet policeman. Wanna see my
badge?"

"No, some insignificant detail about the bail was brought up by
the DA. I wanted to hear more about it but my editor told me to drop
it 'cause Edwards is old news."

"That's what really amazes me about your business, Bill," said
Mike as he drank his beer.

"Why should it?"

"You guys report on everybody's problems and splash it out all
over the papers. What are you going to say about me when he gets
sentenced?"

"Actually, Mr. Daniels," said Bill with more than a touch of
irritation, "it's idiot readers like you that get what you want in five
hundred words or less. You could give a rat's butt about Edwards, the
folks around him, or the people that voted him into office. All everybody wants to know is how many years he's gonna get for running
over poor Bennie. They want to know how many times he was porking
his assistant and for how long. After that, they don't give a darn what
happens to him, his family, or how screwed up Exeter is gonna be.
Clayton Edwards is just another slimy politician getting what he de-
serves, right?"

Mike didn't answer. Rather, he sat expressionless like a parish-
ioner during a sermon.

"That's the funny part about this. Nobody here in good old Harrisburg cares one ounce about Edwards. He's somebody from somewhere else. You would have gone merrily about your way if he hadn't
been in the accident. Clayton Edwards would have never come here
if it wasn't what the people in that city wanted, and that's really the
saddest part."

"Why is that?" asked Mike.

"'Cause he's a decent guy. Ask Rembez or any of the hundreds
he's defended over the years. That's why him and Brenda burying
that bum hurts so much."

"Sounds like it's personal."

"It is. Exeter used to be a pretty screwed up place to live, that's why I came to the burg. I watched him come to power on the shoulders of ordinary citizens who actually cared. It was civics class in action. The original Democratic candidate ended up spending the early part of the election campaign in jail for bribery and racketeering. The Republican candidate, Sam Houser, thought that he was as good as in. Then somebody in Edwards' church gets the idea of putting him up on the podium. The Republicans started out with the usual stuff about him being a lightweight, which didn't bother a soul. It actually worked for the Edwards' camp by spreading his name around. I bet that pissed off some people...," said Bill.

Mike continued to watch Bill's emphasis and passion. Evidently, he had left Exeter, but Exeter hadn't left him.

"...Anyway, Houser upped the ante and started some mudslinging. They dug up the whole '69 race riot thing and tried to paint Edwards as some kind of communist for defending civil rights cases and doing cases for free. That was the wrong approach. Once the word got out on Edwards' history, more and more folks got behind him. Heck, churches were holding collections for him—white middle class churches—in Exeter. There's still people in the city that fly the Confederate flag just to piss people off..."

"That's unbelievable."

"No it isn't. Probably some of the same folks were the ones phoning in the bomb threats twice a day. That's when Jorge Rembez and his buddies formed their little ensemble. All of the guys involved ran small businesses downtown. They weren't about to be intimidated back to the good old days when they got told to do something or got beat up—or worse. They kept tight security while Edwards' wife, Eleanor, ran everything behind the scenes. Man, was she a political organizer. She was so savvy that it made the Republicans tremble every time they had to square off against them. Every time Clayton would box them in on an issue, you could bet that Ellie had prepared him just right," said Bill.

"I'm surprised they pulled it off."

"You shouldn't be. Heck, the white businesses downtown rely on any customer that walks in the door these days. The only color that matters anymore is green for most of them. Besides, once the white supremacists showed up and supported Houser, the campaign was all Edwards," said Bill.

"White supremacists—like the Klan?"

"The Klan was lightweight compared to who showed up. There was Aryan this and skinhead that. You name it—they were there. Heck, you saw exactly the kind of folks at the courthouse a while back. Once the low and middle-income whites felt a Republican vote supported racism, they voted for Edwards. It really choked the Republican chain."

"I'll bet it did."

"Oh, yeah, once the supremacists showed up, the defections started too," said Bill.

"Defections?" asked Mike.

"Yeah," said Bill between long pulls on his beer. "The most visible was Brenda Stabler. She was an assistant to Houser himself and she jumped ship once the skinheads started screaming rhetoric from the city hall steps. She wasn't your local signature-getter or gopher. She was a Poly/Sci major from Abbotts Ridge University and a good one at that. A real catch for the Edwards camp. Once her and Ellie got to work, they were pretty unstoppable."

"Earlier, you made it sound like she and Edwards were screwing around," said Mike.

"Yea, the two of them were always seen together, especially as the campaign wore on. I guess they decided to celebrate a bit too much by the time you met them."

"I never have met them. Not formally anyway."

"Neither have I, but, as we like to say, 'We have our sources.'"

Ernie showed up with the pitcher a third time. Mike watched the brew fill the mug and announced, "No more after this, Ernie, or I won't be able to find my way home."

Ernie frowned and dug into his pocket for a particular wheat penny and then flipped it to Bill. Bill watched Ernie slink away from the lost bet, brandishing a single middle finger this time.

Mike opted to sip at the third beer as his face grew numb. "So you won, eh?"

"Yea, this time anyway. This penny's made a lot of passes between Ernie and me. You're pretty observant."

"I don't know about that. I just watch people's faces when they talk or when they're listening."

"Sounds like you're a reporter," said Bill with a twinkle in his eye.

"Nope. Wasn't that in your report on me?"

"Just where you worked and where you live. What do you do?"

"I'm a systems analyst," said Mike.

"Geez, you're a geek."

"Hardly, I'm a consultant geek as far as you're concerned."

"Consultant? Heck, you should be buying the beers."

"Like at the inauguration party?"

"All right, now you're buying the beers. You've gotten quite a bit from me and all I have is your promise that maybe you're gonna tell me what you saw back in the woods."

"Okay, fine. I buy the beers. So, tell me about the inauguration..."

"...pre-inauguration," corrected Bill.

"What's the difference?"

"Millions of dollars probably."

"Money," said Mike.

"Very good, my boy. Oodles to be exact. Lobbyists and consultancies pony up the cash to splurge on all of the winners. It's a schmoozefest to see who is on board with what. The horse-trading happens later during the term when one county wants one thing and has to trade favors to another so that they can get things done. That's why Stabler was with Edwards that night. She probably had already charted the waters for him, not that any of that matters anymore."

"True enough."

"Now aren't you going to ask me the bonus question?" baited Bill.

"What's the bonus question?"

"Oh, come on, my boy. Think scandal, intrigue and all that."

"As in Edwards and Stabler?"

"Clever boy," said Renard. "It just so happens that I have a copy of the check-in registration of one Clayton Edwards and a witness that described Stabler to a tee. Edwards was so drunk that he was leaning all over the girl. She didn't mind though. They checked in at 2:30 a.m. and left a little after 6:00 a.m. Then you got to see them in the park, right?"

Mike had been listening closely despite the undercurrent of murmuring going on around him and a beer-induced buzz in his ears. He almost found himself responding in the affirmative to Bill's question, which would undoubtedly put him in tomorrow's paper. "See who? Good try, Bill."

"Well, you know I gotta try."

"Yea. Like I said, after he gets sentenced you can have your way with me."

"By then, nobody will care."

"Then it's up to you to make it interesting enough. You're the writer," challenged Mike.

"Oh, I can make a Greek god out of you but it won't mean anything if the readers won't read it. That's the bad part about my job. When Edwards gets sentenced, it will be the end of the story. Your eyewitness account will be nothing more than a footnote. Nobody will care," explained Bill.

"Pity, Bill? Do you want me to tell you what I saw out of pity?"

"I thought it was worth a try. You can't blame me, really," smiled Bill as his final attempt to get a few words out of his witness fell short.

"I need to keep the Edwards' story perking along until he gets sentenced."

"Then ask the bellhop which porn flicks the happy couple watched during the night."

"That's not a bad idea. Where did they teach you to ask questions by the way—geek school?"

"No, in geek school, they taught us to look at the answer and then figure out the problem."

"Funny, if I wrote that way, I'd get in trouble, but it would make my job a heck of a lot easier," said Bill.

"It's not as easy as you think, which is the heart of it, really."

"What is?" asked Bill.

"Thinking," said Mike.

"Well, at least tell this tired, old, somewhat drunk reporter about geek school."

"You must be the most desperate reporter on earth, Bill," said Mike.

Mike spent another hour going over the droll little details of his life with Bill, who chimed in with anecdotes and jokes about his own life. Dropping his guard from time to time, Mike talked without reservation about politics, business and women. When the subject got to women, Bill, whose hand never stopped a single drop from Ernie's pitcher, rambled on and on. It seemed to Mike that both men had stepped away from the walls they shielded themselves with. Bill was affable and intelligent. He would be witty in one instant and wistful at another. Both shared a way of observing human nature at its best and worst, just in different venues. After hearing some of Bill's stories, Mike found that he preferred the business venue. Mike looked down at his watch. The conversation was winding down and Mike thought it would be a good time to say his good-byes.

Bill beat him to it. "What time is it?"

"Five of 8:00."

"Oh man, I gotta get. I'm calling the numbers at St. Mary Ann's tonight."

Mike saw the panic in Bill's eyes as he gathered his papers haphazardly into his satchel. Spying a gold foil box with a crumpled golden bow, Mike looked closer and thought he saw the word "Godiva" printed on the box before Bill could close the satchel. He thought about it for a few seconds, adding bingo to Godiva, and said, "Tell Maggie I said 'Hi'."

Bill snapped his head around and gave Mike an eyebrows-raised look. Mike knew the comment hit home. Bill smiled and pursed his lips, knowing that Mike was on to him. "My, my. You are a clever boy. I'll tell her. By the way, be careful—she said you had a nice behind."

The beer went sour in Mike's stomach. "Oh, God. Thanks for passing that along."

Bill and Mike rose from their table just as two men rose up behind them, leaving untouched beers on their checkered tablecloth.

All four lined up at the bar to pay their checks. Mike paid the tab and slipped a five-dollar bill into the tip jar, which didn't go unnoticed by Ernie. After saying their goodbyes, Bill went left to bingo and Mike went right home—neither of them realizing that they were being followed.

Mike was met at the door by Abby who was doing the exploding kidney dance in an effort to get let out as soon as possible. Mike watched as her nostrils caught a whiff of his beer-and-tobacco-infested clothes. She sneezed three times and headed to the back door for a much-needed tonic of fresh air.

Mike changed into sweats to relax and catch up on news. Opening the paper, he scanned the headlines for anything connected to Clayton Edwards. He found it. It amounted to a miniscule blurb about Edwards being reprimanded by a judge for not appearing on time for a court-mandated meeting. It was, technically—a violation of his bail qualifications. Mike shook his head as to why that would get him a meeting with the very solid Mr. Rembez. Folding the paper, Mike went to let Abby in from her outdoor activities. He cracked the door an inch and found her pushing her muzzle through to get in as fast as possible. She ran with the nape of her fur up, ears and tail down, all the way up the steps. He called after her from the doorway. His frozen breath hovered in the frigid February night for a moment before it too wanted to be inside and away from the same unpleasant thing that Abby had sensed. As his chilled breath retreated, a shudder rippled through his body. The thwack of the deadbolt did little to fend off the feeling he was having.

After climbing the stairs, he found Abby next to his bed and curled into the tiniest ball of a dog that he had ever seen. He slid into bed, reached over to turn off his lamp and decided to leave it on.

Chapter 14

Watching the winter days pass from his corner office, Mike was anxious to return to the trails now that the snows of February faded into the mud of March. He viewed his return to the woods as a kind of liberation from the confines of his neighborhood and the grip of paranoia he felt since his encounter with the sidewalk. That event worried him every day. It forced him to keep an eye on Abby every time he left her out. Mike spoke with Jen, or stopped by her house daily, to make sure she was all right. Every errand out had him looking in his rearview mirror for vaguely familiar cars with vaguely familiar faces. As his bruises healed, his life slipped back into its wonderfully mundane routine—until today, the day Clayton Edwards would be sentenced.

Mike had long ago decided to show up for Tuesday's hearing. It was his way of finding closure with the case. Other than a deposition given to the DA, Mike had very little to do with the machinations of the judicial system. What little Mike did hear came by way of Bill Renard. Little news occurred other than the not-so-surprising word that Clayton was representing himself and that his plea would remain "Guilty" for the hit-and-run of Bennie Carlson. Bill also told Mike that the courts were downplaying the case to avoid the racial issues stirred up during his arrest. "Edwards pleads guilty and the DA doesn't have to do a whole lot. You probably won't even get to sit in the witness chair, my boy," Mike remembered Bill saying. *All that remained was the sentencing,* thought Mike—*today.*

Mike clipped off the distance to the courthouse in the warming March morning. He felt uncomfortable wearing a suit while walking the pathway he frequented in shorts and sneakers. As he neared the courthouse, he looked for signs of trouble like the day he had run past when the protesters were there. There were none. Bill was right—the Edwards case was now old news.

Looking up at the brass art deco reliefs of various symbols and occupations, Mike entered the tinted doors of the courthouse. The security guards gave him a requisite screening after passing through the metal detector and he was off in search of the courtroom that Edwards would soon be occupying. After several wrong turns, a uniformed security guard led him to his destination.

The coarse marble outside contrasted sharply with the polished light gray marble lining the walls of the hallway. People stood in small groups outside the closed doors of the hearing room, murmuring like distant relatives at a viewing. It had precisely that kind of feel for Mike too—removed, detached. Mike looked at each group and guessed why they were there. The news media were the easiest. They stood in a kind of cluster, all dressed in nice suits clutching pads and pens. They joked occasionally but tended to shift apart after a casual laugh. They all had the same thing in mind—today's story. Socializing would wait till later. The next group was probably members of the Edwards' family and their supporters, or so Mike guessed. The racially mixed group stood stiff and sullen—lips closed tightly and arms crossed in a kind of unspoken barrier to the press. Mike scanned their faces and found no sign of Jorge Rembez, much to his relief. The last group really wasn't a group. It was the leftovers of anyone that hadn't belonged to the first or second parties—among them was Bill Renard. Mike thought it was funny that Bill set himself apart and decided that this was where he fit in until Bill squinted his eyeballs and motioned him off. It took Mike a second to realize that talking or sitting with him might start the other media mavens wondering who he was. Instead, he stood off, alone and waited for the courtroom to open.

The doors opened and all of the groups funneled in. Mike chose to distance himself as best he could. It would be difficult in the small walnut-paneled courtroom. A county seal hung over the officers of the court, who were milling about and making jokes with the court stenographer.

Each group outside the door reassembled themselves inside the confines of the courtroom and sat themselves according to a similar set of rules that were set down for weddings. Mike found his mood drifting toward nervous irreverence. He was expecting one of the bailiffs to usher him to a seat, "Prosecution or Defense?" in much the same way that he might be asked, "Bride or Groom?" His revels stopped when his gaze reached the rounded features of Clayton Edwards set in solemn sadness. All of the relief he expected to feel was replaced with a tight knot in his stomach as he regarded the poignant scene.

Edwards' teary eyes somehow managed the strength to hold back any flow. His wife, Ellie, wept enough for the both of them. Clayton looked at his wife. She must have felt his strength and dignity, and it quieted her. Clayton saw the reflection of that strength in her eyes and it quieted him too. Mike felt as though he was intruding in a very private moment and turned away in time to catch Bill turning away at the same time.

The sentencing began with all the expected pomp and formality and Mike wondered why it was necessary. To him, it was all cut-and-dried. Paying little attention to the courtroom motions, Mike found himself drawn to other faces in the room. He watched Bill's eyes look up and down each time a person spoke while furiously transcribing the proceeding to a steno pad. Few of the press contingent were so diligent. Clayton Edwards' family and supporters alternated between dropped chins and sighs. Ellie Edwards dabbed her eyes from time to time but maintained her air of dignity. Her head rose from watching the events unravel in front of her to take a look around the room. Her head panned until her eyes met Mike's. Watching her eyes narrow in seeming recognition, Mike felt the full weight of her penetrating stare. The last time he saw anger like that was in the eyes of his ex-wife Monica during their last days together.

Ellie's stare broke contact when Clayton was offered the opportunity to address the court. Her face softened back to the realm of sadness as she watched her husband rise and speak.

"Thank you your Honor. It is with the utmost humility and shame that I present myself to the court. I deeply apologize to Mr. Bernard Carlson for my transgression that unfairly took his life. I apologize to my supporters who believed in me as their spokesman for a better Exeter and Muir County. I apologize to my wife for putting her through this living hell. I sincerely regret my actions and await the judgment of the court."

The words, by and of themselves, would never carry the depth and eloquence on paper that Clayton Edwards conveyed in person. Each word, Mike thought, seemed delivered with honesty and genuine emotion. Mike had watched Ellie Edwards shrink lower into her seat with the weight of each syllable spoken by her husband. The only other sound Mike could make out was Bill's scribbling. The rest of the press had frozen in Edwards' address. The courtroom remained hushed for a few seconds until the judge cleared his throat and pronounced a sentence of twenty-three months. Mike watched as the judge's pronouncement overwhelmed Ellie Edwards. She convulsed into open mouthed anguish and tears streamed down her face. The judge allowed Edwards to comfort his wife and then remanded him to the sheriff for processing as a ward of the state corrections system.

Whatever feelings Mike had brought with him to court were left behind when the sentence was handed out. The retribution he wanted—the closure—seemed even more distant. It had been so simple to think of Edwards as some kind of philandering schmuck caught in his own web of deceit. Mike preferred him as a two-dimensional character made out of newspaper and ink—distant and artificial. The problem was that he saw the man's look and knew his regret to be real and heartfelt. Ignoring the scene would have been much easier had he watched a TV broadcast or read one of Renard's columns.

Bill Renard left the courtroom soon after Mike and found him in the hallway.

"When do I get my interview?" Bill asked, half-chuckling.

Mike raised an eyebrow and resigned himself to fulfilling his part of the deal with the devil, saying, "Whenever you're ready. I'd prefer to wait till after work."

"How about tonight?"

"That's pretty quick."

"By Thursday, nobody will care," said Bill in a matter-of-fact tone.

"It's that simple?"

"Oh yea. Edwards admitted his guilt and went to jail—end of story. He didn't wheel out a celebrity defense to strut before the national media. He didn't dodge, weave or otherwise try to kite the system. The public hates an honest man. I'll be lucky to get a paragraph on the front page of the local news. Folks will read that paragraph, say 'what a shame' and never read the rest of it buried between obits and the community calendar."

"So, he goes to jail for a couple of years and that's that."

"You got it. And he's going up for twenty-three months. Not two years."

"Why not two years or even ten? He killed somebody."

"He had an accident so far as the courts are concerned and he was the elected representative of one of the most volatile towns in the state. Both the DA and Edwards want this case kept low key. The deal was that Edwards pleads guilty and gets the minimum sentence. Edwards takes the fall for Stabler, and his family avoids any more scandal. No muss—no fuss. Two years, or more, puts you into the state system and nobody that knows Clayton wants him doing hard time. There's plenty of folks that would go out of their way to hurt him in the state prisons. Heck, a couple of them were sitting in the gallery."

"Who was?" asked Mike.

"You didn't see them? No, you wouldn't have known, would you?"

"You got me there, Bill."

"Sam Houser and his campaign adviser/lawyer/scumbag, Truman Dunn."

"The other candidate? Why would he show up?"

"I'd guess that it's a kind of rude satisfaction. Nothing like seeing your political enemies going up the river for a couple of years."

"And the other guy?"

Bill swallowed as his face pitched down toward the floor and his demeanor changed the instant Mike brought up Houser's lawyer. "Truman Dunn. Think of all the bad lawyer jokes you can and you have Truman Dunn. He's been a fixture down Exeter way for years—been a leading Republican supporter since he was in diapers. Word was that he fronted the Houser campaign with a lot of cash, but it went beyond that. Dunn had quite a winning streak until Clayton Edwards came to town."

"Dueling lawyers?"

"Oh, God yea. Talk about butting heads. Dunn was a good lawyer. Edwards was an excellent one, but that's old news as they say," said Bill who was getting more and more antsy to make his deadline. "The new news is Clayton Edwards' sentencing. How 'bout my interview?

Mike wondered if Bill was avoiding something, but decided to leave it go. His attention shifted to his lengthy agenda for the evening, which consisted of feeding Abby and letting her out, followed by television-induced unconsciousness. Deciding that Bill's offer was better, Mike said, "Gavin's?"

"Gavin's would be fine. Seven o'clock?"

"Sure. You're buying this time," said Mike.

After watching Bill scurry off to do whatever reporters did, Mike turned his attention to the rest of the attendees who were emptying out into the gray hallway. When the procession ended, Mike turned to leave and found his way blocked by an older black woman. Her pursed lips, tipped-up jaw and penetrating stare showed all the body language necessary to predict trouble. Mike braced himself.

Ellie Edwards hissed, "What's the matter—didn't get your money or did you have a change of heart or something?"

For a split second, Mike had no idea she was addressing him.

"I'm talking to you," said the woman.

Mike figured it out by the way she pointed her finger as though she wanted to stab him with it. "I beg your pardon."

Her volume increased. "You can beg all you want. It don't matter. He turned himself in, so just leave us alone now. You got that?"

Mike's attention was fully focused on Ellie's rage but he hadn't a clue what she meant. The way she looked at him in court made him feel like she knew him in some way. He tried to remember if they had, but he was sure he had never met the woman. He focused for a moment and tried to formulate a rebuttal. "Er..." was the only sound that made it out of his lips until three very large African American men stepped between him and Ellie. Mike caught sight of two of the men grabbing Ellie by the elbows and hauling her to the elevator. The third man came and stood between Ellie and Mike. Mike's view was now limited to a well-pressed white button-down shirt and narrow, unadorned tie. The body inside the well-pressed shirt and tie filled out the man's dark blue suit. It reminded Mike of the way football players wore their clothes for sports banquets.

The man spoke four very distinct words, "Maybe you should leave."

Mike heeded the advice. *So much*, he thought, *for getting closure*.

* * *

Pausing for a moment to take another pull of his beer, Mike took a breath, and continued his story to Bill. "...Then the sketches hit the papers and Edwards turned himself in. End of story."

Bill was less than satisfied and said so, "That's it? I've been waiting for three months to tell my readers the same stuff that was in the official police report?"

"Yea, that's it. Heck, you knew more about it than I did. I just happened to trip into it."

"Geez, this isn't gonna sell a dang paper now."

"I tried to tell you a long time back that what happened to me was pretty unexciting."

"Well, it was exciting then, not now. I'm going to call my editor and get things rolling."

Mike watched Bill cell phone his editor and have a snippy exchange. A pair of cheese steak sandwiches arrived and Mike started in on his.

Bill hung up and said, "Dinner's on you tonight. My editor's unhappy enough not to okay my expense report."

"Then that's your last beer and I'm going to get Ernie to wrap up my other cheese steak."

"What?"

"Only kidding," said Mike.

"You'd better be. Besides, we have to hoist a few to the end of this whole mess."

Mike stopped chewing and glanced off to the side for a moment. Bill caught the look.

"What's wrong?"

Mike hesitated, then spoke, "Did you ever talk to Clayton Edwards about this case? Did you ever talk to him about me?"

Bill regarded Mike's serious expression and replied, "No. God's truth. The whole Edwards camp wasn't making statements or handing out interviews. They circled the wagons and fought us Indians off. Why?"

"After you left, Ellie Edwards came up to me and said 'Hi'."

Bill narrowed his left eye at the sarcastic way Mike said "Hi" and said, "Something tells me she said more than 'Hi'."

"You aren't kidding. And Bill, we're strictly off the record and I mean it. Okay?"

Bill reluctantly nodded in the affirmative.

"Ellie came up to me looking like the way a cat eyes up a dog right before all hell breaks loose and told me to leave them alone."

"What's that supposed to mean?"

"You tell me. You're the reporter. I haven't a clue. She said something up front about money and a change in heart, but I don't remember it exactly. She acted like she was gonna rip my head off till some pretty large guys stepped in."

"Large black guys?" asked Bill.

"Yeah. Advised me to leave, which I did."

"Those are more of those bodyguards I told you about. They keep the nasties away from Edwards. They also keep an eye on Ellie. She's got a heck of a temper when she gets going. What'd you do to piss her off?"

"That's just it. I haven't a clue. Other than the pics you showed me, and the newscasts, I've never met her before. She acted like she knew me and wanted a piece of me all at the same time," said Mike.

"That's pretty odd."

"Tell me about it. You know what else is odd? Where has Edwards' little blonde assistant been during this whole thing? I didn't see her at the trial or outside the courtroom. Nowhere."

"Ellie can be pretty confrontational, which is why we haven't seen Brenda Stabler anywhere. The rumor was that she quit and is working for some little public relations firm. Ellie wanted her out— way out. She didn't want her within a mile of Clayton after the accident. My guess was that Edwards cut a deal with the district justice to take the full blame of the hit-and-run in return for leaving her out of it. She should have gotten charged as an accessory, but it didn't happen."

"I can tell you firsthand that Ellie is confrontational. She was right in my face. It was like she knew me and that bothers me a whole lot."

"That's the way this stuff goes, my boy. There's always loose ends and unanswered questions. It may not be that way in the computer business, but it sure is the way things work in mine. You're the witness that put her husband away. Do you think she'd want to be your best friend? Maybe you two can swap email," explained Bill.

"No, but dumping some kind of veiled accusation on me is not what I expected."

"What did you expect? Heck, her life is ruined and she probably needed to take it out on somebody."

"Well, I didn't expect an accusation. I just wish I understood," said Mike.

"Ask her."

"Oh, like, 'Hi, this is the guy that put your husband away. Would you mind telling me what you meant today at the courthouse?'"

"Precisely," said Bill.

"You're out of your mind, Bill. I'd get further selling her aluminum siding or long distance service."

"Look, you're the one who's bugged by all this. I'm telling you what I'd do. Call her. What's the worst thing that could happen— yelling? You already got that."

"Jorge Rembez," said Mike with a touch of fear in his voice.

"You haven't seen him since the night he knocked you down. I told you, it's not Edwards' style. Be honest and straight with her and you'll get an honest, straight answer. That's the Edwards' style," said Bill.

Pondering Bill's suggestion, Mike bit into his cheese steak. The conversation digressed from the events of the day and wandered their way to whatever subject entertained both men. The evening grew late and they headed up to the bar to pay the tab. As promised, Mike picked up the check and left a more than suitable tip. The pair exited Gavin's and said their goodbyes.

"Well, my boy. See you in the funny papers," said Bill as he offered his hand.

Mike shook it and replied, "It's been fun," in a slightly sarcastic tone.

Mike started the Pontiac and drew a deep breath, feeling the first true relief of the day. It was good to have it all behind him. What was also behind him was a man tapping on the steering wheel of his car, waiting for his associate to get out of the bar so they could follow.

* * *

Sitting in the kitchen, waiting for Abby to return from her nightly duty, Mike thought about the abrupt face-to-face with Ellie Edwards at the courthouse. "Just leave us alone now. You got that?"

Mike heard Bill's suggestion in the back of his mind, "Ask her."

Thumbing through the phone book, Mike hunted down the phone number of Ellie Edwards. Whether it was Mike's thirst for knowledge or his beer-reduced inhibitions didn't matter. He paged down the "E" section until he found "Edwards, C attny offc 555-2148—res 555-8830," and dialed the residence number. Not knowing how far he would get if he told her his name outright, Mike decided on a white lie to get his foot in the door like the many salespersons he encountered.

"Hello," answered a woman's voice.

"Is this Ellie Edwards?" asked Mike.

"Yes. And this would be?"

"This is an acquaintance of Clayton's."

"I'm sorry, I don't recognize your voice. Clayton's...not here I'm afraid. And your name is..."

"Mike Daniels," said Mike, remembering Bill's suggestion about honesty. "I wonder if I may talk to you for a few moments."

"Daniels? Daniels. Oh, you awful man. I told you to just leave us alone."

"Don't hang up, please, Mrs. Edwards. You said you didn't recognize my voice."

"No, I didn't."

"Then why did you ask me to leave you and your husband alone at the courthouse today? I witnessed what happened in the park. I had no idea who your husband was."

"Leave me alone or I'll call the police."

"You can do that if you like, Mrs. Edwards. Before you do, let me ask you one question." Silence blared from the receiver and Mike pressed on. "You said you didn't recognize my voice. Do you think that I contacted you about your husband's accident?"

"Yes," replied Ellie.

"I know you have no reason to believe it, but I've never spoken to your husband or called you until tonight."

Mike listened to the phone grow silent again, fearing that Ellie would hang up without him getting the information he needed. "Mrs. Edwards, what was said to you? What was said to your husband? Was it about money?"

"Someone—you—called and told me that you had seen what happened at the park and that Clayton needed to be more careful," said Ellie.

"That's it?"

"No, there was a second call. You said that Clayton needed to play ball or he was going to jail."

"Mrs. Edwards, I want you to know that I never made such a call. I saw what happened at the lake and only talked to the police," said Mike.

"Why should I believe you, Mr. Daniels?" asked Ellie.

"Well, as strange as it sounds, because I'm telling the truth." Mike let the frankness of his words assure Ellie that he was being sincere.

"Then if it wasn't you, who was it?" asked Ellie.

"Someone else who saw the accident or read the report I made," said Mike. "You mentioned money," he continued. "How much did they ask for?"

"They never talked about money. You just told us to play ball."

"Then no other calls?"

"Not a one, thank God."

Mike reassured Ellie of what involvement he had, and ended by saying how sorry he was that her husband had to go to jail. Ellie graciously accepted the sympathy and said her goodbyes.

"You just told...You called...You said....," repeated Ellie's voice in Mike's head as he sat at the table, stroking Abby's head. Something bothered him about Ellie's phrasing—something familiar yet distant. *What was it?* he thought. Then it came to him—*Your body... your burial.* He realized that the closure he expected at the beginning of the day wasn't going to happen.

Chapter *15*

Mike couldn't get over just how much things had changed in four months since he last drove to Sanford State Park. Having chosen the second Saturday of April as his return date, Mike spent his trail-running time in the surrounding mountains for the last month to avoid Sanford's mud and muck. Although he wouldn't admit it to himself, he was also avoiding the memories of the last time he was there. As the attention to the whole Edwards incident quieted, Mike knew that he could return to the lake and face the memories of December.

It was warm for April and Mike didn't mind a bit. The sun peeked above the tree line, sending shafts of golden dawn through the trees. Mike stood outside his car taking in the scent of flowers and watching geese glide on the lake. It was a fine homecoming.

The forest had no memory of his previous foray with the likes of Edwards or Stabler. There was no sign of the park rangers other than the presence of their headquarters high on the opposite shore of the lake. *It was good*, Mike thought, *to lose oneself in the wood.* Gingerly tap-dancing over the exposed rocks and roots, he ran hard. A few sections were still sodden and the cold mud splashed up on his calves. Soon, his shirt sported moist patches where the sweat soaked through. The whole experience let him know that he was, most certainly, alive.

So was the copperhead snake on the path ahead of him. Both man and reptile froze on the trail, each awaiting a move by the other. The snake decided to make discretion the better part of valor and slithered into the woods. Mike wasn't sure if it was mating season or just that it was looking for a warm sunlit rock to work on its tan. Following the creature's undulating track until it disappeared from sight, Mike waited until he had the trail to himself.

The trail meandered on and Mike along with it. He came to the hollow whose rebounding echoes fooled him into being startled when a pair of mountain bikers had passed. They wouldn't fool him again. Mike listened, but no mechanical sounds or rhythmic pumping were to be heard. Instead, he crested the short hill without incident and in total solitude. Some mechanical chatter grew louder as he made his way to the forest's edge where it met with the road. This time there would be no surprise as the first of two mountain bikes sped past. The second hurried on behind the first, yelling, "Hi." The first biker dropped his hand as a sign to stop. He halted the bike and straddled it as Mike came round.

"Welcome back."

"Excuse me?" replied Mike to the stranger.

"I said, 'Welcome back.' Aren't you the guy my wife and I nearly ran down last winter?"

Mike remembered some fleeting glimpses of the bikes and their riders from that fateful day in December and bobbed his head up and down as the recollection took hold.

"Er...um...wait. Back in the hollow. It was you two?"

"Yea. I always wanted to apologize to you. You looked pretty freaked."

"Yea, freaked is a pretty good word for it," Mike said, thinking all the while just how freaked that whole day ended up.

"Well, sorry for scaring you. We didn't see you till we popped around the bend."

"Oh, no harm done. Just a few more gray hairs."

"At least you have yours," said the mountain biker, who snapped his helmet off to reveal a bald head.

"I guess we're each cursed our own way," said Mike.

The conversation ended and Mike set out on the road for a short distance before returning to the wooded path. He turned to watch the couple arrive at their maroon Blazer to begin hoisting their bikes atop the cab and into the bike rack. Mike stopped. His hair stood on end as he looked at the Blazer. He watched the couple finish their post-ride chores.

"It had to be a red Blazer, didn't it?" Mike said to an audience of two chipmunks that were not interested in conversation. The whole time, he had fought wave after wave of remembrances and recollections of his last trek. The chipmunks ran away, and he decided to do the same. Coming to the split in the trail he had faced in December, Mike opted to go left instead of landing smack in the middle of another hit-and-run cover-up. The branch of the trail led him toward the camping areas and back along the lakeside. Leaves along the path had compressed and cushioned the way. Electric green moss bordered the side of the well-worn trail. All around, buds were forming and life was settling into the spring routine. Mike neared the vacant camping areas and remembered the smells of campfires frying up bacon and eggs. Fortunately for the campers, it was too early in the season for the campground to be open or a ravenous trail runner might have raided their camps. The trail swung away and back into the woods past the remains of an old farmhouse that stood watch over the farmlands converted to campground. Mike slipped on a pair of sunglasses to offset the brightening sun.

His course took him through the most traveled portions of Sanford's network of trails. Treading on wood chips and gravel, his feet thanked him for going left. The path wound past the concrete set of dominoes that formed the last vestiges of a former toboggan run. He slowed at the sight and wondered how it would have looked fifty years ago before there was a lake and a state park. Now, the old supports looked like an American Stonehenge awaiting discovery by tomorrow's sensationalists as a sign of extraterrestrial visitation. The thought of that made him chuckle. He considered the comic value of stomping out a kind of crop circle in the reeds nearby until he caught sight of a variety of some copperhead snakes sunning themselves on the boulders surrounding the pillars. This time the man yielded to the reptile.

The groomed path kept its good nature all the way to the park's nature center before it gave way to an open field for picnickers. There were no human occupants at the tables, only an occasional squirrel opening an ancient walnut, or a gaggle of geese picking at the grass.

The lake reflected the blue sky and puffy clouds in postcard fashion. It was truly a fine day to be out in the wilderness. A sense of ease flowed through him and his final few miles were easily covered. He made a side trip to a scenic outlook of the lake and a boating inlet. Mike took in the beauty of the lake for a few more moments, and had a look at where his car was parked. There were many more cars and trucks in the parking area, which was nothing new. What was new was a DCNR patrol car parked next to his. Unease replaced the ease he had been feeling. The memories of December crept back in again.

Shuffling off the last hundred yards, Mike slowed to a walk where the parking lot met the trail. Mike unclipped his water bottle at his car and looked around casually for the driver of the patrol car. There, in the distance, was Ranger Musser, Daryl toting a clipboard and jotting down notes about the dozens of moored boats. Mike decided that his unease was unfounded and went to work stretching his legs after the long run. His thoughts drifted back over the morning's events and how so many of them reminded him of finding Bennie Carlson. The happy feeling of returning to his favorite set of trails was now tainted with those memories, and he wondered if he would ever leave them behind.

Mike finished his stretching, pulled a dry shirt from his bag, and swapped clothes. A voice addressed him as he pulled the clean shirt over his head.

"We were wondering if we'd ever see you again, Mr. Daniels," greeted Daryl.

Mike snapped out of his thoughts and back into the real world, not quite ready to have a conversation.

"Tony said you'd be coming back one of these days," said Daryl, squinting into the sun and donning a pair of sunglasses.

A reflection in the glass caught Mike in the eye. He blinked and held his hand up to block the glare. "I don't think I'd bet against Tony. How are you doing, Ranger Musser?"

"I'd be fine if I wasn't working on a Saturday morning like this."

"I know what you mean. Do all the rookies have to work Saturdays or are you a glutton for punishment?"

"I lost the rookie designation a month after we met, thank God. Nowadays, they turn me out on my own to inventory boats and picnic tables," said Daryl.

"Oh. So, how's things been since...ah..."

"Since you stopped us last year? Quiet. Real quiet. There's not a whole lot going on except for hunters over the winter. How 'bout you?"

"The same really, without the hunters though."

"It's funny. Tony talks about you every once in a while. You should stop by and say hi sometime."

Mike, at first, had no remote desire to visit the park ranger that babysat him while the other rangers scoured the countryside. Still, Tony had been professional and even friendly. "Maybe I'll swing by sometime," said Mike, mainly to appease Daryl's invitation. The glare from Daryl's sunglasses caught Mike again and he pitched his head down to avoid it. Daryl realized the irritation he was causing and stepped a little to the side to give Mike a break. Mike's head lifted and he caught his reflection backlit in the morning sun on Daryl's lenses. The sunglass lenses gave Mike's image a saintly glow and it made Mike laugh a tiny bit. Beyond that, a flutter in his stomach began. What was it about seeing himself in Daryl's sunglasses? He couldn't place it. The silence hung for an uncomfortable moment and Mike realized that he was the cause of the awkward moment. "You said he was up there this morning?"

"Yep. Stop by. Heck, he's pushing paper on a day like today. He'd like the excuse not to use the computer," said Daryl.

"He would, would he? All right, you twisted my arm."

The two men parted as Daryl went back to counting boats or doing whatever he did when he wasn't sent searching for dead bodies found by concerned citizens.

Other than budding trees, little had changed since Mike's last visit to the log-faced park office. His tires rumbled over the gravel parking lot, making the same sound as the elderly Chrysler that had carried him there before—although his car smelled much better. Parking places were at a premium, though, and Mike had a hard time finding a spot. Mike found all of the cars' occupants inside where a disproportionate ratio of visitors to rangers buzzed and chattered. Mike guessed about twenty people filled the foyer, most standing with arms crossed in an impatient indifference. A loud din filled the room with questions, directions, and objections. Mike wondered if Daryl planned his boat inventory just to get out of the office. Mike surveyed the rangers hurrying to attend to everyone as fast as they could. He could see a man giving a terse lecture to a woman ranger about cell phone quality in the park and how better antenna placement would most assuredly help. From the reddened look on the woman's face, Mike figured that she had already assessed the best place for said antenna. Mike could just make out the customer friendly nametag on her chest pocket—Yetter, Denise. Mike's attention shifted to a far different scene occurring at the other end of the counter where an older male ranger was reciting boating regulations to a young couple. The elder ranger seemed to carry an air of authority that dictated a one-sided conversation. The couple meekly nodded their heads. Mike didn't need to read the older ranger's nametag. He already knew the name—Bud Packard. The couple folded their papers, gathered them into an irregular stack, and turned away to allow the next person their time with a ranger. Mike could hear Bud's direct, authoritative tone address the next customer whose ears seemed to fold back against their head due to the park super's presence. Bud's eyes focused hard on the next man in line who stammered out his request. Bud's eyes flickered toward the ceiling in what Mike thought was either exasperation or a prayer for patience. When Bud's eyes leveled, they caught sight of Mike standing at the rear of the throng and narrowed in recognition. While the customer fumbled his paperwork into a semblance of order, Bud shouted out, "We were wondering if you were going to come back sometime."

Mike noted the slight cant to Bud's lip as the closest thing to a smile he had seen from him so far. Bud's recognition brought a smile to Mike's face and he called back over the crowd, "I couldn't resist the urge to turn over some more rocks."

Bud cast a sidelong glance at that remark and said, "Don't go doing that. You gave us enough excitement for the next ten years."

"I promise to stay out of trouble. Hey, is Tony around?"

"No. He went down to town to get lunch for us. Heck, it was quiet until he left, too."

"Too bad. I thought I'd say hi, but I guess that's the way it goes."

"He should be back soon. Just come round the back there and wait in his office. You remember the way?"

"Er, yea. Thanks. You sure it won't be a problem?"

Bud tipped his head down and raised his gray eyebrows in a gesture that said two things: the first was that it wasn't a problem, and the second was that the problem was all around him needing his attention. Mike shook his head and walked past the half door that excluded the offices from the foyer.

Leaving the brightly lit Visitor's Center, Mike walked down the office's dimly lit corridor. Looking up, Mike saw the same bare bulb lighting his way. At first, he didn't remember the way but then journeyed back in his mind's eye to the same setting a few months ago. "Yes, Bud. I do remember the way," he murmured to himself. Tony's office appeared where he remembered it should be and the same jolt that greeted him when he sat in Tony's office hit him again. "Hi, Stella," said Mike after his heart settled down after sighting the stuffed bear. He walked through the open door and sat himself in the same chair he had given his report from. The office looked unchanged except for the pile of folders in the basket marked "Denise." Mike wondered if the "Denise" on the basket meant the "Denise" out front debating cell phone antenna placement. By the shear number of folders in the basket, Mike also wondered if she was going to tell Tony where to put them.

Five minutes of waiting lingered on to ten and then fifteen minutes. Mike's eyes swept the room noting manuals, books, binders and knickknacks—all the accoutrements of any office anywhere. There was nothing else to cast a bored eye upon, so he rose, strolled around Tony's old wooden desk and peered out the window. The bright sun shone in his face and he squinted from the sudden exposure. He looked toward the floor, seeing multicolored spots flicker to life when he closed his eyes. His mind flashed to his bright reflection in Daryl's sunglasses, and the same peculiar twinge tugged at him again. What was it about that moment? The phantom lights in his closed eyes subsided and he turned to leave. Since Tony hadn't arrived yet, Mike decided to depart. As he stood he noticed a small label on the bank of two four-drawer filing cabinets in the back corner of the office. The rearmost middle drawer read "Incident Reports—1992-1993." Mike followed the year's advance up one cabinet and down the next until "Incident Reports—Current" came into view. *Incident*, Mike thought. *I'm an incident.* The thought that his experience had been reduced to mere reporting irritated him. It was a small indignation to apply the term "incident" to the death of one man and the ruin of another. Mike shook his head and headed for home. Before he did, he took another look at the cabinets. Thinking back to his conversation with Ellie Edwards, Mike remembered his comment about the only people knowing what had happened were him or the police. His incident lay in a filing cabinet nearby. *What did they put in it about me?* thought Mike. He hesitated for a moment and considered yielding to a prying whim of nosiness. Having sifted company records before, sometimes with permission, Mike went back and forth about opening in the cabinet. He declined on the whim and worked his way back to the foyer.

The foyer was packed with still more visitors than before. Bud was busy taking care of as many people as he could while Denise was still listening to a technology sermon being delivered by the same man. Evidently, the antenna was not properly installed yet. Mike's way out was blocked, so he turned around and headed back down the hall in search of an alternative exit. He strolled back down the hallway turning his head from side to side looking for a door to the outside. He didn't find one at first although he did find that the part of the building he was in was devoid of people. A hushed little voice started whispering to him in the back of his mind. "Incident Reports—Current." He disregarded it. It spoke again, softly, subtly, like the little voice that spoke to him when there was chocolate or donuts in the break room at work. Standing in the hallway, Mike had a debate of conscience and hated it. Just like chocolate's call to a whetted appetite, the voice wouldn't be satisfied until satiated. He considered the punishment should he get caught. The voice chimed in again and told him, "What are they gonna do—yell at you and kick you out?"

The filing cabinet was neatly arranged like everything else in Tony's office. Folders were arrayed from most recent all the way back to January of 2001. Mike tiptoed back to the doorway and peeked around the corner, his hearth thumping loudly in his chest. Sneaking around was not his forte. He returned to the cabinet full of manila months and let his fingers fold the tabs over until he reached December. With his hand hovering over the folder, a little voice whispered, "go ahead." The folder was as well organized as the file it was a part of, entirely in chronological order. Mike browsed each report.

December 1 08:32:14—Parking violation...—*nope*.

December 1 23:10:45—Public drunkenness—remanded to local auth...—*nope*.

December 2 14:22:33—Indecent Behavior—Warning—couple found in flagrante delicto on campground beach...—god that had to be cold—*nope*.

December 2 15:07:40—Illegal Fishing—Fine...—*nope*.

December 2 16:19:03—Indecent Behavior—Fine—same couple found in flagrante delicto near boat mooring area #3...—*yeesh, what are these people, rabbits? For crying out loud.*

Thumbing through a thinning list of tickets, warnings, and infractions, Mike reached a genuine incident—his incident. He pulled his incident report from its place. A creak in the floorboards made him jump, and he scurried over to the door to make sure that no one was coming. No one was. He returned to the desk to open the report up again and read everything that Tony had taken down.

December 9 10:02:28—Homicide—Body of unidentified Caucasian male, approximately five foot four found approximately seventy-five yards southeast of the Katessen Day Use Area entrance. M. Daniels (eyewitness) who was hiking in the area...located the remains.

"Trail runner," corrected Mike out loud followed by a swift single finger to the lips to quiet his outburst. The report ran on in an odd combination of police terms and ranger official-speak. Mike read the clipped sentences and clinical measurements. After reading the summary, he proceeded to peruse the documents attached to the top sheet. He found a copy of the report that Tony typed while he recounted the episode and found it worded in the same fashion. Mike held the document and thought it was funny that he would be reading the paper distillation of December 9th with all the excitement of an inventory report. It finally sunk into him that this was just another event on another day in another year. Tony's cabinets were full of them. He just happened to be the sole occupant of December 9th.

Stapled behind his eyewitness account was the map where he had pinpointed the location of Bennie Carlson. A singular red "X" marked the spot, right where he told Tony. He flipped over the map and found copies of Ranger Musser's crime scene reports. It took him a few moments to realize that the rangers had to be police while still being guides and watchdogs of the area around the park. Musser's reports consisted of crisp and clear type—the unmistakable hallmark of a laser printer. At least Daryl had no fear of computers. They were a joy to read over Tony's muddied type. The last sheet of paper was a copy of Daryl's handwritten scribbling that Mike remembered dictating to him before the search. Mike had a hard time translating Daryl's chicken scratch into legible characters but reasoned out "...stone wall...hemlocks...SW..." from a group of pen marks vaguely resembling the English alphabet. Staring at the copy, Mike tried to distinguish any other words but came up empty.

The relative quiet of the ranger's office changed with the ruckus of the foyer breaking out of its confinement by the opening of the office door. Mike's head snapped up, startled, and unready for the surprise. He heard the sound of approaching footsteps and froze for a moment. Regaining his composure, he flicked the folder shut. As the footsteps came closer, his head spun wildly, looking for a place to hide the report. Mike knew that he couldn't make it to the filing cabinet, and closing it would tip off whoever was approaching that he had been snooping. The footsteps stopped down the hall. Mike leered out of Tony's office at the approaching figure. He didn't quite know how to act and his face wore the guilty smirk of a child caught in mischief.

Daryl Musser did a double take at Mike's peering from Tony's office. "So you decided to stop by, eh?" asked Daryl as he went over his paperwork from the boating area.

"Er, I stopped but he's out getting food or something. I've been waiting a while and thought you might be him. I guess not, so I'm going to head on out," Mike replied.

"Oh, he just pulled up. Just hang on a few more minutes."

Mike's easy exit had been cut off and he agreed to remain. "Okay."

Daryl went into his office to attend to the chores of his paperwork. Mike heard the door swing open again.

Tony's voice called out, "Holy cow, Daryl. Did you see all the people out there? You'd think we were giving away free cars or something."

"You have a visitor."

"A what?" asked Tony.

"Visitor. Check your office."

Mike did a repeat leer out of Tony's office.

Tony smiled. "I was wondering if you'd be back. We were taking bets."

Mike smiled in return and said, "Who won?"

"I did. Figured you'd be back once the trails dried out. Find any bodies today?"

"God no and thank goodness for that."

"I prefer to hand out tickets for fishing."

Or people humping like bunnies in the freezing cold, thought Mike, fighting the urge to say it out loud.

"I wish that's all you had to do back before Christmas," replied Mike.

"Yea, it was a bad turn of events, but what can you do? At least you saw what was up and reported it. There's a lot of people that would have run away from that situation."

"Maybe I should have been one of them."

"Nah, you strike me as one of those folks that has more guts than you think," said Tony.

"Thanks. I'll take it as a compliment."

Tony rounded his desk and plopped down. He threw a brown paper bag with an oily stain on the outside. Lunch, thought Mike. The smell of oil and onions on a sub full of luncheon meat and lettuce instantly set his taste buds on salivate. Mike watched Tony give his desk a scan as if something was out of place. Mike fought a growing nervousness in the pit of his stomach. Not having enough time to relocate the folder back into the right spot in the cabinet, Mike ditched the folder in the one spot he hoped nobody would notice.

"So how were the trails? It takes us all week to check them out sometimes," said Tony.

"Still muddy in some spots. Fine in others. The rain's let up and there's plenty of runoff still washing over in spots. It makes for some sloppy footing," replied Mike, lifting his right leg to show Tony the splotches of mud adhering to his calf.

"It's beyond me why you runners and them mountain bikers like to play in the mud."

"Because it's more fun than running in traffic, Tony. Better on the legs, too."

"I guess so. Can't stand running myself. Haven't run since the Gulf. Back then, we ran pretty fast when we had to."

Mike used Tony's memory of the Gulf War to deflect attention to something else on the desk and away from the hiding spot he had improvised for the folder.

"Is that where this picture was taken?" Mike watched Tony's eyes make a subtle shift and his face a touch melancholy.

"Yea. Saudi Arabia. That's my buddy and I, before things got ugly."

"Sorry, didn't mean to bring up an unpleasant memory," said Mike.

"Don't worry about it."

The door opened a third time, allowing the din of the crowd to fill the corridors of the offices again. The hollow flooring played out a percussion of hurried footsteps that stopped behind Mike at Tony's door.

"Bud says that you two are to get your asses...," began Yetter, Denise, stopping when she realized that a stranger was in with Tony.

"Bud says that you two are to get out front right away," she said in a more politically correct manner.

"Aw, there goes lunch."

"There's time for that later. Bud said, 'now.'" Denise, having relayed Bud's command, stepped into the room and grabbed the folders out of the wire basket with her name emblazoned on it.

"All right, Denise," complied Tony.

Tony returned his attention to Mike and said, "Looks like we'll have to chew the fat some other time. Don't be a stranger."

Mike read the tone and manner as dismissal and was thankful for it. Daryl hurried toward the foyer and Tony stood to join him. Mike rose, said, "Goodbye, Stella," and walked one step ahead, back into the noisy foyer. Both men said their good-byes and Mike headed toward the door.

The door's hydraulic closer hissed a sigh of relief as the pressure in the cylinder pulled the door shut. Mike breathed in much the same way. His venture into nosiness had gone undetected. He hopped into his car with an air of smugness, feeling like James Bond on a successful mission. Soon, he was on his way home.

* * *

The springtime rush of visitors to their park soon abated and the park office settled back down into its quiet routine. Denise had finished first and went back to her desk to begin shoveling out from the blizzard of paperwork that had accumulated. Bud finished next and did the same. Tony and Daryl doled out information and handled complaints from the last two visitors until both were satisfied and departed.

"Sheesh, that was fun," said Daryl, relieved that the crowd was now at an end.

"It always is at this time of year. Everybody thinks that this is the only day of the week we're open," replied Tony.

"You two finish your lunch then come right back out here so Denise and I can do the same," commanded Bud.

Tony and Daryl headed for the offices and their waiting subs until Denise headed Tony off.

"Oh, hey Tony. What's this doing in here?" Denise held up a folder and forced it into Tony's hands.

Tony had no idea what she was talking about. He took a look at the tab. It read "Incident Reports—Current."

"Daryl, did you pull this folder?" asked Tony on the way back down the hallway with Daryl.

Daryl read the tab, and said, "Nope. Wasn't me."

Tony tossed the folder onto his desk and pulled out his now sodden sub. He unwrapped it and took his first bite, looking intently at the folder and wondering how it had somehow migrated into Denise's In-basket. The thought of how it got in there wasn't agreeing with him anymore than his soggy sub.

Chapter 16

All four of Abby's feet were cemented to the floor, awaiting the signal that she thought would never ever come. Her owner would blink, but always return focus to what looked to her like a beam of sunlight reflecting off the window.

What hung in Abby's mind was far more essential, much more elemental, and definitely more visceral. Of course, Abby would use one syllable instead of many—food. Rather than focusing on some elusive transcendental contemplation on sunbeams, it was simply—food. Abby fought back the urge to tug on Mike's nose to get her message to him. *No,* she thought, *I'd rather not go to the effort. The same result could be accomplished with far less energy.* An opportunity presented itself a few minutes later when a car screeched around the corner near the house. "Woof." Abby barked in measured reaction to the car's annoyance. Her owner, shaken from his trance, blinked away the lingering glare from his eyes and turned to Abby to try and understand what had upset her. Abby, now seeing that she had her owner's undivided attention, sauntered in the direction of her dish. Surely, she thought, this would be a clear indication of her need, even to her particular Homo sapiens. Abby turned when she reached her dish, expecting to find her owner bringing food to her empty and expectant stomach. He was nowhere to be seen. *God, these humans are frustrating,* she thought.

She left her spot at her dish to seek her errant owner and found him sitting on the couch preparing to press the on button of the TV remote. That would never do. If he made it to the History Channel,

dinner might never occur, she fretted. After considering some stri-
dent action, Abby returned to the kitchen and barked again. To her
relief, she heard him rise off the couch before he could turn on the
TV. Abby, hoping that her bark would lead to a bite—of food—stood
near her dish again. She figured, since he had come all this way to
see nothing, that he would see her poor starving self and have pity by
giving her an extra portion. To a certain extent, Abby's ploy worked.
She watched her owner look out the window, and walk past her, stopping at the cabinet that housed her food. Hearing the kibbles rattle
into her dish, her tail went a-wagging. *Food. Oh good, wonderful
food*, she thought.

The celebration stopped short when her ears detected the clicking sound of the front doorknob being turned. She trotted out to the
living room and raised an eyebrow to watch the knob's movement
and to listen for intruders. Both sound and movement issued forth
and Abby called out the alarm in her best Sheltie dialect. After all,
she needed to earn her keep by protecting her owner, and more importantly, her food. The ruckus she raised prompted another stomping walk by her owner, who whipped the curtains aside and jumped
backward from the face pressed against the windowpane.

Abby heard the deformed oval visage say, "Trick or Treat?"

"Jen, you scared the crap out of me. It's April, not October,"
said Mike.

"And it's nice to see you again too. How was your run?"

Before Mike answered, Roxanne nosed her way through the door
and performed a twenty-toenailed welcome dance to greet Mike and
Abby. Abby, who was not amused, shrugged "bitch" in Sheltie and
strolled over to Jen and gave her a good sniffing. While Abby sniffed,
both Jen and her owner spoke.

"The run was good. I liked being back. Heck, it was like old
home week," said Mike.

"I'm glad you went back. I could tell you were missing it."

"Yea, it was nice, but weird in a way too. I stayed away from
where they found Carlson."

"I don't blame you. What was that about old home week?" asked
Jen as both humans and dogs sat down on the couch.

"Yea, got to see both of the rangers that picked me up back then. They were pretty happy to see me, actually."

"That's nice. Were you happy to see them?"

"I guess—in a way. There were pretty busy, though," said Mike.

"Making sure nobody was smuggling squirrels out of the park?"

"No, there were nine million tourists there." Mike paused for a moment, looking pensive.

"What's wrong?" Jen picked up on his thoughtfulness.

"I...er...I...I did a bad thing."

"You were smuggling squirrels out of the park?"

"No. While they were busy, I sneaked a peek at my report."

"Your report? The hit-and-run report?" asked Jen.

"Yea. I don't know, why, really. Stuff is just nagging at me."

"If you need someone to nag you, I can come over more often."

"No, not that kind of nagging. It's just all the stuff that went on. Stuff that went on today."

"Like what?"

"That's just it. I can't say," said Mike.

"Can't or won't? You know, like not wanting to tell me about any of this back when that guy beat you up on Bucknell Avenue?"

"No, that's just it. I can't even figure out what it is that's bothering me. Sorry, it's really dumb."

Abby had positioned herself as the sole pet between Jen and Mike and languished in puppy heaven as both humans stroked her head. *It was so nice of that retriever to leave us alone*, she thought.

"Are you sure that it just wasn't jitters with being back at the park? I mean, you were in your old haunts and you even said you met back with both rangers. It had to bring it back all over again," said Jen as she tried to reassure him.

"It could be. Maybe...I don't know. I just wish I knew more about the whole thing," thought Mike out loud.

"Why would that make a difference? Heck, you didn't even have to go to court."

"That's it, I didn't have to go, but I did show for the sentencing. Ellie's little outburst at the end still kinda hangs with me."

"Sounds like she's just a hothead. Speaking of 'hanging with you,' that's why I'm here. I'm headed to market and wanted some company. You game?"

Mike thought about it and agreed.

"All right, I'll drive. Let me take Roxanne home and we can get going," declared Jen.

Mike grabbed a jacket and headed toward the door right behind Roxanne and Jen. He turned to Abby and said, "Hold down the fort, girl."

Abby was all too happy to do so. She watched the door close and trotted off to her supper dish. The thought of a long nap under the influence of a full belly brought the closest thing to a smile that a dog could portray. She positioned herself over her dish and prepared to take her first bite. It would not happen. Her dish was empty. A loud howl emanated from the Daniels residence. Translated, it was a combination of a lament and a vile curse toward all golden retrievers.

* * *

Once again, Mike stood transfixed, this time running down the items on the shelves of the supermarket aisle—marshmallow, pineapple chunks, maraschino cherries, sprinkles and...

Jen pulled up alongside without a sound. She chided him with mock outrage. "Pervert. I saw you staring at the hot fudge."

"Oh, sorry. I was having a...moment," explained Mike.

"I'll bet you were. Did you want the hot fudge or were you considering another topping?"

Mike's face began to redden.

"You know, you're getting like that guy in *Close Encounters of the Third Kind,*" commented Jen as they walked away from the ice cream toppings and appropriately onward toward nuts.

"What?"

"The guy that sits around all day making Devil's Tower out of mashed potatoes. I'm not going to have a problem with you in the instant mashed potato aisle, am I?"

"Sorry. I keep thinking back to the lake today. I'm being stupid, I guess. Usually, I get this feeling at work and it means that I missed something. You know, like when you're hopping on a plane for your vacation and something sticks in the back of your mind that you forgot something, then you show up at your destination and find out your underwear is still home."

"Can't say I ever left my undies at home, but I know what you mean."

"Well, it's that kind of feeling."

"Are you telling me that you left your undies at home?" asked Jen with a smirk.

"No," denied Mike.

"Too bad."

"Be serious."

"I am."

Mike swallowed hard at Jen's last phrase and debated the merits of returning to the ice cream toppings aisle.

Jen turned the conversation back toward a serious tone by saying, "Maybe you should say something to the rangers."

"Like what? I'm having a funny feeling. Can you help me?"

"No, silly. How about asking to see that report again?"

"Somehow I don't think they'll let me see official ranger business. Besides, that file looked a lot more like Ranger Savastio's personal pile of mementoes," said Mike.

"What makes you say that?"

"Because I doubt that the park office would store all of the official reports in his office."

"So why not ask the ranger for his copy?"

"I don't think that would fly with him somehow. It would be like desk-checking what somebody else did at the office, and they never ever like that. Now, imagine me, someone with absolutely no police experience, asking to look at his file."

"I see what you mean. Maybe you should just let it go. After all, it's old news," said Jen.

"Funny, that's kinda what Bill Renard said the last time I saw him. Then he made me pay the check."

"You're gonna pay the check?"

"Only if I can buy these," said Mike as he brandished a box of instant mashed potatoes.

"No," yelled Jen.

Mike had to admit that it was the best food-shopping trip of his life despite his thoughts about the park. It was even better than the time his mom allowed him to buy some awful sugar-coated cereal just to get the little plastic airplane inside. He helped Jen get her stuff out of the car and flung it to her on command as she stored it in her small kitchen. "How 'bout a movie tonight, Ms. Stevens?" asked Mike.

"That would be fine, Mr. Daniels. Let me get Roxanne her supper and I'll meet you over at the house."

"It's a date."

With Jen's chores completed, Mike headed home with a bag of groceries in each arm. His steps were light and happy like an actor's in a movie musical. Rounding the bend near his house, he walked up the sidewalk in the late afternoon light. Mike saw a denim-jacketed older man wearing a Red Man baseball hat approach and gave him a nod of his head as the two passed. What he didn't see was the second man who had slid in behind him. Feeling his arms get pulled behind him, Mike flung his groceries in a vain effort to get away. He turned his head back toward the first man in time to see the man's fist flying at his stomach. Crumpling to the ground, Mike writhed with his breathless mouth open like a fish out of water. He managed to right himself onto all fours. With his head hung down, he never saw the hard boot that kicked him in the gut, punctuating the vacuum in his lungs with searing pain. Mike's arms gave out and he plunged back down to the sidewalk as another kick caught him in the side. Lights flashed in front of Mike's eyes. One of the men bent down near enough to Mike's ear that he could feel his hot breath.

The man said, "You'd best mind your own business, Mr. Daniels."

Mike's grip on the conscious world began to fade. His mouth opened wide to get any molecule of air while his lungs burned between throbs of pain. Empty gasps bit at the air until his diaphragm decided to breathe again. Taking in huge gulps in wheezing relief, Mike pushed himself up on all fours again until the air resumed. Pushing himself over, he sat down on the sidewalk, looking for his assailants who were long gone. The metallic taste of blood lingered in his mouth from a bit lip. He touched his hand to his chin and found that bleeding too. Gathering his composure and his scattered groceries, Mike staggered into his house.

Mike threw what groceries he had gathered onto the kitchen table and threw himself onto the sink where he heaved in anguish into the drain. Again and again he vomited while wrapping his arms around his torso to lessen the pain. Mike barely heard the knocking at the door over his own bodily noises. Grabbing a towel, he wiped his mouth and went to the door.

"Oh my God. What happened to you? I can't leave you alone for a moment," cried Jen.

Mike offered no explanation at first, just a painful look upward. He then said, "Oh, I just ran into somebody."

Jen helped Mike to the couch and dashed up the steps to the Daniels medicine cabinet for first-aid supplies.

"Ow," yelled Mike as the antiseptic wet his cuts.

"Hold still."

"It's hard to when you're prodding me like that."

"Well, it needs to get cleaned out. Now, are you going to call the cops or do I have to?"

"Neither. Don't you dare call the police or anybody else. The last thing I want is for you to get involved any more. Heck, I didn't even want to tell you about the whole park thing, let alone this," said Mike.

"Well, thank you for being so noble. I don't suppose you have any idea why they paid you another visit?"

"Probably because I was nosy," reasoned Mike.

"They must take their paperwork seriously down at Sanford."

"You aren't kidding. It's funny though."

"How on earth can it be funny?" asked Jen.

"A couple of hours ago, I was perfectly happy to try and put this all behind me."

"And now?"

"Now, I'm pissed off. I'm tired of being a punching bag. I need to know more..."

"...but I thought that the man that kicked you said...," interrupted Jen.

"...to mind my own business. The thing about it is that it is my business. I saw what happened out there and have gotten stomped on twice for it. The way I see it, I'm entitled to know why, if for no better reason than to avoid getting stomped on a third time."

"And how are you going to find out?"

"I have no idea," said Mike.

Chapter *17*

With ibuprofen blunting most of the misery in his body, Mike sat in his den, hypnotized by the screen saver on his computer monitor as it spun and flickered. The motion of an animated drop of color plunging into a larger pool was exactly the kind of mindlessness he preferred at the moment. It beat the heck out of thinking of the beating he had gotten the day before. He thought back to Jen's earlier call. Knowing that all he really wanted was to be left alone, he assured her that he was fine. She had told him that she understood, but Mike knew that she didn't. He couldn't tell her that what he really wanted was a time to hide and lick his wounds. Although he hid from the world, he allowed the television to bring news from any place except his front yard. The anchorman handed off coverage to Rome, then Cuba, and on to Afghanistan. The story on Afghanistan centered on the renewal of minesweeping by the group that the late Princess Diana sponsored. The report showed the bloodied bodies of injured men, women, and, by far the most horrific, children. *At least I have something to be thankful for*, thought Mike as he realized that all of his limbs were intact. He watched the broadcast as the camera pulled back to show a farmer's fields dotted with red pennants—the indication that there were mines present. *That's what I need*, he thought, *some red pennants to tell me where I shouldn't step*. The only red flag he could lay claim to was the report in Savastio's filing cabinet. *Why would Tony Savastio have me beaten up just because I looked at a report?* he wondered.

The problem was the same as the night before—Mike had no idea where to begin. Allowing himself to hide from the things confronting him, Mike elected to not think about the problem at hand. Instead, he sunk into routine and decided to back up his computer files. Mike slipped back into his mindlessness where his only focus was the blue status bar on the monitor. He could see his reflection in the monitor, empty eyes looking nowhere. The image of an Afghani man washed across his thoughts. *If only you had those flags earlier*, Mike thought; *if only you had the knowledge of where they were*. Mike dwelled on the mental comment he made—the knowledge of where they were. *How can I know what to avoid if I avoid this whole mess?* Mike blinked a few times, took a deep breath, and roused himself from his trance. "It's time to plant some red pennants," Mike said to a sleeping Abby.

Once the backup finished, Mike brought up the Internet browser on his computer and entered "Clayton Edwards" into a search engine. The hit count tallied over five thousand. He thought back to when he had originally sought out the Edwards name and found about six hundred. Filtering off all the references to the American-Italian rock star, Mike delved into the myriad news articles that had mushroomed since his last viewing. He read through dozens of cookie cutter reports that looked as though the same person had written them all. There was none of the kind of depth Mike needed. *It's not the joke, it's the delivery*, Mike thought as he changed his approach. Pursuing a different tack, Mike decided to look away from the man, Clayton Edwards, and to look at what he was involved with. Finding the Clayton Edwards for State Representative website still fully intact, Mike delved into each and every link the site had to offer, this time paying attention to the party propaganda and public relations pictures. After reading each article, Mike copied it onto his computer and began to do what he did best—analyze.

Each picture, clip, and article was duly listed in a cross reference of everything Edwards, just as if he were investigating a manufacturing plant or retail operation. He repeated his actions dozens of times, accumulating the raw data for analysis. After Mike scanned the typical "why we are better than them" articles, he realized that he had exhausted what he was going to get out of the site. It had occurred to him that he discounted the us-versus-them information as party propaganda and decided to backtrack. A list ran down the page of reasons why the viewer should vote for Edwards as opposed to Houser, the Republican candidate. Mike realized an error in the way he was looking at things. *A political site for a candidate would obviously portray that particular candidate in a nicer light than a wooden saint in a church,* he thought. *What would the other candidate say?*

Mike copied the list of reasons to vote Edwards, then keyed in a search on Samuel Houser. Houser had been the latest candidate in a series of Republicans that had represented Exeter and Muir County to the Commonwealth of Pennsylvania. Edwards' election had changed that, Mike thought. Houser's site must have been revamped, thought Mike after he clicked on a link the author left to list changes. Mike read the January date and a droll sentence that read, "Alterations and Modifications for Special Election." Surfing back to the homepage, Mike bounced from link to link, copying the dry charts and policy statements. It struck him funny that there were no negative ads or statements to slam his opponents. From what Bill Renard had said, Mike expected to see at least some of it. "Maybe they learned from their mistakes, Abby," said Mike to his slumbering pet. Mike copied the factoids until boredom got the better of him.

Mike resumed his search and pursued some of the other links on Houser, which included the Muir County Courthouse. The page spouted some legalese about an assault charge brought against Houser and the dismissal of the charge. After cutting and filing, Mike plodded through useless link after useless link. Growing tired of irrelevant items, he could at least assure himself that the end was in sight. A few words appeared on the screen and flickered right on past as he scanned his hit list. The words "1998 Annual Muir County Lobbyists Dinner" appeared and took him to a short photo documentary of the group's annual dinner.

Once the pictures came into view, Mike looked past the attempts at witty captions until he got to the last picture. There, standing in the midst of an assortment of male attendees, was a younger Brenda Stabler—standing next to Sam Houser. Both wore the kind of fake smiles given when photographs were posed. Mike saved the picture and added entries in his spreadsheet for both Samuel Houser and a new column named "Brenda Stabler." The hard drive clicked and whirred and Mike pressed on with his search, this time hitting on the lobbyists' menu. The article accompanying the pictures was almost an exact copy of the 1998 version except that some of the names were different. Two pages in, Brenda Stabler appeared with the erstwhile Representative Clayton Edwards amidst another knot of revelers. Both people displayed the same fake smiles in a pale of fake light for the camera. The computer's hard drive whirred to life again, saving the pictures and article that Mike had copied. Mike paged backward through the entire album of pictures he had saved, looking again at the people in the photographs. This time he looked more into the background of the shot. If he found Brenda Stabler in one shot, maybe she might be in others, he thought. As it turned out, his assumption was wrong. She appeared only twice.

While uselessly scanning the remainder of the pictures, Mike came across a mild surprise. In the background stood a somewhat annoyed looking Bill Renard. Mike thought that Bill's face showed a good bit of irritation at a man holding Bill's elbow. The man's back was turned. A few clicks later and the picture had been saved. A column named "Bill Renard" now appeared within the spreadsheet. After reviewing all of the pictures on the lobbyist site, the trail ran cold. There were a few more hits referencing the two men. Few had given him any raw data and fewer still looked promising. "The devil is in the details," Mike said aloud. A groan from the floor told Mike that Abby had enough of his commentary. Seeing Abby stand up and head for the steps, Mike figured it was a good time to finish up his searching at the computer. He threw a CD into his computer's CD burner and backed up all the files.

Attempting to rise from his office chair, Mike found all of his aches painfully present. He took a deep breath and sprung up quickly to avoid a slow torture. It worked until the pain caught up with him again, forcing another exhaled groan that echoed throughout the house like moans in a fifties horror movie. Flipping on the lights, Mike ambled out of the den and into the darkened hallway. He headed into the kitchen where an expectant Abby waited near her dish. The kibbles of her food clattered into the measuring cup and then into her dish as Mike poured.

Mike nosedived onto the couch with as much enthusiasm as Abby had with her food. Distorting his face into a palsied mask, Mike let the cushions cradle his slumping body. Every muscle relaxed into the inviting cushions and he quickly forgot about the aches in his abdomen. Groping for the remote, Mike commanded the TV to spring forth entertainment like a king waving a scepter at the court jester. It was half past eight and the only thing the jester was issuing forth was commercials. Every channel conspired to show only products the public deserved, rather than entertainment of any kind. Abby sauntered out into the living room and took up station near the pillow swallowing Mike's face.

"You're my good dog," said Mike as he petted Abby on the head.

"Urrrrppp," replied Abby in the dog version of gratitude although something was lost in the translation.

Mike's eyes looked upward in mild disgust after Abby's emission when the phone rang.

"How's it going?" was Jen's seemingly innocent question.

Mike knew that she wanted to know much more than how his day was going and replied, "I'm fine, Jen, really."

"Fine? Lemme see. At work, we call that 'fouled up, insecure, neurotic and erratic.' Which one are you?"

"I think I'd use another F word first."

"It actually does start that way but I figured that we were on the phone," said Jen.

"Well thanks for being genteel. I'm f...ouled up and a bit insecure at the moment but have no neuroses and I'm hardly ever erratic," explained Mike.

"That's good to hear. I was worried about you."

"I appreciate that. I'm sorry I didn't invite you over. I just needed some time..."

"...the last guy that told me he needed time was spending it with two other women in two other cities," said Jen with mock injury.

"I just needed some time to hash out recent events."

"So when are you going to go to the police?"

"I'm not. I did some looking around on the web trying to find out enough information to keep me out of harm's way. The best defense is a good offense," said Mike as he pressed the remote.

"The web? You really are a geek, aren't you? I really wish you would tell the cops."

"No way. If Edwards was willing to bury somebody once, I doubt that he would have any restrictions on doing it twice. Besides, everybody seems to have access to this whole affair but me."

"And me, but I prefer to keep it that way. I just care what happens to you," said Jen.

That thought caught Mike off guard and it warmed him from within. He couldn't ever remember Monica saying anything like that.

"I...I appreciate that. Look, I'll be fine. Not F.I.N.E. Just okay. In a couple of days the pain will fade and things will settle down. Okay?"

The conversation ended and Mike hung up, thinking about what Jen said about caring for him. A smile filled his face and the pain was forgotten. What wasn't forgotten was the infernal commercials occupying all one hundred thirty channels of his cable service. He finally stopped on a Chevy truck commercial showing manly men in vigorous pursuits. Mike lectured to Abby, "None of those trucks can go where..." His lecture stopped mid-sentence, not that Abby cared. She clearly didn't, as she lay against the couch, sound asleep. Lifting his open-mouthed, slumping face off the pillow, Mike stared at the commercial. The commercial showed a pair of mountain bikers getting into a red Chevy Blazer. Ignoring the lingering pain from the attack, Mike leapt off the couch and ran over to the entertainment center housing his TV and electronics. He flung open the glass door and started hurling a stack of videocassettes onto the floor until he held a cassette marked "Blank Tape." Feeding the tape into the VCR, Mike punched the play button and stood back in front of the TV. Once the picture appeared, he fast-forwarded the tape to the news broadcast he copied on the day of his grisly discovery. Mike slowed the tape to normal speed and watched the array of talking heads discuss the events at the lake in featureless generalities. The broadcast soon ended and he thumbed the rewind button and watched it a second time. He was looking for something that he knew was on the tape, but the scene remained elusive. He watched a third and fourth time to no avail. The fifth time proved to be the charm. Stabbing the pause button when Kirk Griffin, the WBWY reporter began to speak,

Mike looked hard at the scene. The man stood in the park's boat mooring area parking lot, the lot where he had seen the mountain bikers earlier on Saturday. Mike stabbed the play button again and watched the camera zoom onto Griffin's face. Mike thumbed the rewind button again and then hit pause. He caught the camera in mid-zoom and took a deep breath when he saw what he had been looking for—a red Chevy Blazer. It was the same one he had seen yesterday at the park.

Chapter 18

Gavin's Tavern had a slow Monday night under way. Mike walked in, nodding to Ernie, who was busy arranging glasses behind the bar. He slid onto the aging vinyl seat that protested with all the vigor of a whoopee cushion. Although embarrassed by the noise, Mike could see that nobody cared.

While he waited for Bill Renard to arrive, Mike sipped on a Yuengling lager that had magically appeared from Ernie's deft hands. The brew's cold bite relaxed Mike's anxiety over his discovery on the videotape. His mind drifted back to the jerky image of the reporter and the 4x4 in the background. Mike's recollection ended when Bill Renard finally showed up.

"Black and Tan," ordered Bill, sliding onto the seat without so much as a squeak.

Mike watched the way Bill balanced his weight forward and off the seat until the last moment. Now he knew the trick. "How are you doing, Bill?"

"Are you buying?"

"Sure," agreed Mike.

"Then I'm wonderful."

"Did you order?"

"Yea, Ernie will bring it over when he gets a chance. Too many folks getting off work right now."

"So why did you invite me over?" asked Bill.

"'Cause I have a bunch of questions about the whole Edwards episode."

Two men dressed in workman's dungarees squeaked across the vinyl seats in the booth behind Bill and Mike. Mike smirked at the sound and was happy that he wasn't the only one that made it. Bill didn't quite get the joke. The noise broke the conversation's initial course and both men digressed into small talk until Bill's beer arrived.

"So how's the running going, my boy?" asked Bill.

"Pretty much the same old thing every day. I went to Sanford Park on Saturday."

"Old home week, eh? And how was beautiful downtown Sanford Park?"

"Spring was springing and the chipmunks were running. Same old stuff except for..."

Mike's sentence ended when Ernie showed up toting Bill's beer. Bill thanked Ernie and pointed toward Mike as the recipient of the check. Mike waited politely for Bill to finish his swig before continuing.

Bill's face soured like he had sucked on a lemon as he put his beer down. "That's nasty."

Mike realized that Bill wasn't enjoying his Black and Tan. "Something wrong?"

"Beer's a bit nasty," Bill commented as he doodled on his drink napkin.

"That's what you get for mixing brews."

"A Black and Tan is nectar for the gods, my boy. It would appear that Mr. Gavin neglected to mix the right spirits again."

"What do you mean?"

"This, my boy, is a Half and Half. Half Guinness and half Harp. Can't stand Harp. Too bitter."

"Oh," replied Mike, who was now the wiser in bartending etiquette.

Bill rose from the table without making a sound and took his beer up to the bar. Mike could hear Bill talking to Ernie.

"Ernie, I asked for a Black and Tan. You gave me a Half and Half."

"I gave you a Black and Tan, Bill. Half Guinness and half Harp," stated Ernie.

"No, it's Guinness and Bass."

"Only fake Irish Americans drink it that way. The right way is Harp and Guinness."

Mike looked on as a small difference of opinion was now well on its way to an argument.

"Fake? Are you calling me some kind of fake? Just make it the right way, Ernie," demanded Bill.

All the eyes in the room were on the looming showdown.

"I did make it the right way. If you don't like it, then you can go find a place that does it the wrong way," retorted Ernie in a tone that could frost nearby mugs.

Bill's face reddened and he slammed the beer glass down hard on the bar top, sending its foamy contents all over the counter.

"All right Bill, you don't have to be this way. Out."

"Just pour me a Black and Tan..."

"Out," shouted Ernie with one arm extended to a single finger, pointing out the door.

Mike watched the spectacle end with Bill's stomping departure punctuated with a door slam. *That went well*, he thought and wondered what he was going to do next. He certainly wasn't going to order a Black and Tan. Spinning back to face the nonexistent Bill, Mike grimaced and wondered why such a little thing had boiled over. He reached down to take another swallow when he saw the scribbled word "Mike" scrawled onto the napkin along with an arrow pointing down. Flipping the napkin over, Mike read, "Finish your beer and leave. Wildwood Nature Center 7:00." A warm rush coursed through Mike as his stomach knotted. He had no idea why Bill was playing Cloak and Dagger with him, but it didn't matter. What Mike did know was that he was seeing the equivalent of a red flag.

The beer had somehow lost its taste as he tried to become more wary of his surroundings. He wondered what Bill had seen that made him hightail it out of the bar. Not daring to look around, Mike focused on following Bill's instructions and drank. When he hit the bottom of the mug, he wiped his face with Bill's message and tossed it into the beer glass.

Feeling that his actions were clumsy and unnatural, Mike worried that an early departure might tip off whoever was watching that they had been spotted. He searched for a way to keep his cool amidst his growing panic. Mike walked his beer glass to the bar and looked up at the round schoolhouse hanging over the bar. It was twenty after six. He did a bit of calculating to figure out when he should leave for the nature center. It took a moment or two until he decided what to do next.

"Another Yuengling, Ernie," Mike asked as he handed over the empty mug.

Ernie gave Mike a very short smirk and poured him a beer.

Mike returned to his seat and nursed his drink for another twenty-five minutes, hoping that his lackadaisical pace would tweak his minders. Another casual glimpse at the clock put Mike into the time frame where he'd have to make his exit. The trouble was that he hadn't a clue as to how in the world he was going to pull it off. There were more than twenty patrons in the bar. Which one would he have to avoid in order to meet Bill?

With his heart racing, Mike got up, paid Ernie, and headed for the door. As he did so, he counted five men standing up to pay their tab. *Five*, he thought, *ohmigod, five*. Thinking that his heartbeat was loud enough to be heard in the pub, Mike hovered at the door, undecided as to leave the safety of a public place or to side with the urge to flee. He picked neither; instead he chose to walk out of the bar just like anybody else and head to his car. To his surprise, no one followed. Mike started the car and continued to look around. He let the car drift out on the street, watching for any cars trailing him. There were none, and he took a long, deep breath of relief.

Ernie's eyes looked up enough to see the fleeting taillights of the Daniels car. No one noticed his glance: not the three regular patrons that had somehow grown into complaining whiners questioning each drink on their tab or the two men in dungarees who eagerly wanted to follow Mike Daniels.

* * *

Wildwood Park was an island of green marshlands sandwiched between the bleached concrete of major highways and bleak grays of an industrial park. Mike experienced the incongruity of the park's location when he left his car at the visitors' center and heard the quacking of ducks in one ear along with the roar of trucks in the other.

Painted an institutional off-white, the inside of the park's nature center seemed a bit sterile to Mike as he passed a young clerk at the gift shop counter. The clerk looked longingly at the clock and Mike caught the hint—closing time was near.

Following a set of black bird footprints glued to the floor, Mike began his search for Bill. After three rooms dedicated to the life cycle of the marsh, Bill had remained missing. The trip wasn't a complete loss. Mike learned a great deal about slugs and snails—more, really, than he wanted to know. The three rooms ran in a semicircle that led Mike back to the same ardent young man, diligently preparing to close up shop and head home. Mike spotted a doorway leading to a part of the building he hadn't investigated and figured that it couldn't hurt; at least he hoped it wouldn't. Walking through the doors, Mike was treated to a panoramic view of the marsh through large windows. Seated at the end of a long table was Bill Renard cradling a pair of tethered binoculars in his hands.

"Was that fun or what?" Bill asked as he swung the binoculars at Mike.

"Or what?" replied Mike dryly.

"Where's your sense of adventure, my boy?"

"I get all the adventure I need from *Star Trek* reruns, thanks."

"Oh God, you actually watch that stuff?"

"All the time," said Mike.

"No wonder you're divorced."

"Actually, we met at a Trekkers' convention."

Bill pulled the binoculars away from his face and shook his head half in pity, half in amusement, and said, "So, did you know those guys following you?"

"I didn't even know I was being followed. Is that what the whole beer episode was about?"

"Yea, Ernie and I have a signal worked out. If anything looks or smells wrong, particularly when I'm talking to somebody, Ernie pours me the wrong beer..."

"...and you get into a Harp and Bass argument," concluded Mike.

"Yep. I'm lucky he didn't mix Guinness and Rolling Rock."

"You can tell the difference?"

"Oh, most definitely. You can't?"

"Nope," Mike admitted as though it were a point of shame.

"Then you have much to learn. Anyway, you didn't call on me to discuss the subtleties of various brews. What's up?"

"I got paid another visit," said Mike as his hands slid down to the sore spot on his side.

"By Rembez?"

"I don't know. I barely saw them. They blindsided me on the way home from my girlfriend's. They told me to 'mind my own business,' right before a nice kick in the gut. It didn't sound like Rembez."

"My goodness, you're popular. What I don't get is that the case is over and done with. Why would they pull the intimidation routine on you again?" asked Bill.

"'Cause I wasn't minding my own business."

The last sentence silenced Bill and piqued his curiosity all in the same moment. Bill looked up at the clock, saw that closing time was only five minutes away, and said, "Let's go for a walk, my boy."

The clerk at the gift shop locked the door as soon as Mike and Bill left. They walked down the trail and into the woods as the sun began to fall.

"So, you weren't minding your own business how?" asked a very curious Bill Renard.

"Are we on the record?"

"Here we go again. You know, the last time we talked, you got a whole lot more out of me than I got out of you. That's not how it's supposed to work."

"I know, but I need more information and I don't know where else to turn."

"So you called me. Why?"

Mike reached into the black business satchel slung over his shoulder and pulled out a muddied image printed from his recent collection off the Internet and said, "'Cause you're on the inside. You're in the know. You're wired in."

Bill looked at the black and white picture and smirked, "I've been thrown out of better places."

"Thrown out?" asked Mike.

"Yea, the guy with my elbow was basically a bouncer. I tried to crash the party. I guess I had forgotten my invitation. He didn't want to give me my elbow back either, as I recall."

"So you were there?"

"Enough to see Edwards already putzed and being led around by his girlfriend, shaking whomever's hand she introduced him to. So what does the guest list of a little political soirée have to do with you minding your own business? Seems as though you want to mind my business too," said Bill.

"I came across that shot on a lobbyist's web page during some research."

"Somebody beat you up over a picture of me? I'm flattered, although I do look nice in a suit."

"No, I looked this up after I got beat up," said Mike.

"Maybe you need to tell me a little more detail here."

"As long as it's off the record. I don't need to read about this in tomorrow's paper and have more visitors," demanded Mike.

"I can't say why I'm agreeing to this, but okay. We're not on the record with this."

Mike began, "I was at the Sanford Park on Saturday. I went there to run trails. Ran into one of the rangers who helped find Carlson out there. He invited me up to the station to say hi."

"So?"

"So, I went up and said hi. I got to sit in the other ranger's office a while and I got curious. I read their reports on the incident, but couldn't put the folders back in time."

"Oh. So what does that have to do with you getting beat up?"

"Believe it or not, I usually don't get beat up in my line of work. I took a peek at their paperwork, and, bam, somebody shows up and tells me to mind my own business."

"That is too much of a coincidence," said Bill.

"Tell me about it. The way I see it, I keep stepping on land mines. Instead of trying to ignore all this, I need to do the opposite—I need to find out more. That's why I called you."

"You don't think I'll beat you up?"

"I hope not."

"My editor wanted to beat you up after your story crapped out."

Mike chuckled at Bill's remark. Soon, they had walked the length of the short trail and returned to the parking lot.

"You know, it's the reporter that's supposed to get the story, not give it away. Besides, we've had this conversation back before Christmas," said Bill, musing over the thought that he was the interviewee.

"You mean about the details of this whole thing. Stuff like the red Chevy Blazer?"

"What's that supposed to mean?"

"It's supposed to mean that the red Chevy I saw and the red Chevy the police impounded are two different Chevys."

Mike now had Bill's undivided attention.

"What makes you say that?" asked Bill.

"You said that Edwards' Blazer had evidence on it somewhere. I saw folks getting into the Blazer I saw back then. Their Blazer wasn't Edwards'."

Bill considered Mike's concerns and said, "There's lots of Blazers in the world. Lots of red Blazers. Coincidence."

"That's a heck of a coincidence, don't you think?"

"Before you jump to conclusions and connect Edwards with the JFK assassination too, you might want to try and remember that the police found hair and tissue."

"Inside the truck. What about outside—a fender—underneath?"

"It was him, Mike. He confessed," stated Bill in an effort to allay Mike's suspicions.

Mike paused in his line of thought and allowed the scene with the bike riders to play out in his mind. The more he thought about it, the more he realized that he had totally overreacted to everything. "So the cops and I got lucky?"

"More or less. Was that the reason you wanted to meet me?"

"More or less. You know, Bill, I can accept a coincidence about the Blazers, but what I don't get is why I keep getting slammed and how you keep popping up. Do you get thrown out of that party every year?" asked Mike as he produced another picture of Renard at the previous year's to-do.

Bill looked at the picture with a wary smile. His body language grew stiffer as his eyes traversed from left to right.

"Something wrong with the picture, Bill?" asked Mike when he saw Bill's reaction.

"I guess I should check the web more often. I didn't even know he was there that night."

"Clayton Edwards?" asked Mike.

"No, one of my favorite people, Truman Dunn, " said Bill with a voice that grew distant as he said the name.

"Something tells me that..." Mike paused trying to remember the name.

"Dunn. Truman Dunn, attorney at law," finished Bill.

Mike thought back to the trial when Bill avoided talking about the man. "You mean this Truman Dunn?" said Mike as he fished another printout of his web page findings.

Bill read the list of sponsors of the party and nodded his head as each name went by. The nodding stopped when his eyes landed on "Dunn Associates."

"You found this all on the web?"

"Yea, the lobbyists' group was touting their connections," said Mike.

"Well, good ol' Truman has a lot of those."

"You're on a first name basis?"

"Hardly. Truman and I go way back. It's funny to see these pictures too. Look at this year's pic," said Bill as he tilted the sheet of paper toward Mike.

The sun had all but set though Mike could make out Edwards and his assistant, Brenda Stabler, in the foreground of Bill Renard's forced departure, "So?"

"A year ago, that wouldn't have happened. Brenda Stabler was a dyed-in-the-wool Republican doing gopher jobs and whatever else Sam Houser's gang would throw her way. Old Sam stepped in when

Ronald Kepner got caught with his hand in the cookie jar. Seems as though old Rollie was handing out favors for cash and got burned. Stabler lost the faith and turns up on the Edwards campaign—or so the story went. Rumor was that she gave the Edwards camp the inside skinny on how the Houser folks were going to come at them. In the grand scheme of things, it really didn't matter."

"Backlash?" said Mike.

"Goodness gracious, you are perceptive. Nobody in the city of Exeter felt like voting for the Republican candidate—not that being Republican is any worse than being a Democrat. The whole thing left a bad taste in the voters' mouths. One of Kepner's pet projects deliberately missed getting permits and some planning info to cut construction and demolition costs. A backhoe cut the water main to a third of the city for a week. Boy, were people mad. Imagine ten thousand people who can't flush their toilets."

"I bet they were pissed off."

Bill winced at the comment and went on, "Anyway, Clayton Edwards pops up on the community radar preaching truth, justice, and the American way and rides a big wave of popular support into a seat at the House."

"Hopefully not on a wave of raw sewage."

"Are you done?" asked Bill.

"Sorry. You do know a lot about Exeter politics."

"More than I want to," replied Bill.

"What's that supposed to mean?" inquired Mike.

"It means that Exeter is a little town with a lot of big issues, many of which aren't screwed around with."

"Now that sounds ominous, particularly coming from you."

"You've gotten your nose rubbed into some prying that you've done. How would you like to have a gun barrel in your mouth instead?"

"Not my idea of fun at all."

"It wasn't, especially since it was my first big story after getting out of college. Exeter was on fire at the time. The city hospital looked like a MASH unit and the National Guard patrolled the streets. Whites and blacks were armed to the teeth and ready to fight the Civil War all over again," said Bill.

"I had no idea. When was this?"

"Sixty-nine. I was fresh out of Penn State and stupid enough to think I could change the world."

"And I was in diapers then."

"Quit making me feel old," carped Bill.

"Sorry. You had a gun barrel in your mouth?" asked Mike.

"Yea, and a well maintained one at that. I could taste the gun oil. I got to leave with an unpublished story. Vince Garmon never left."

"Vince Garmon?"

"Vince Garmon is still in Exeter. When I say 'in', I mean in six feet of it. He was going to give me one heck of a story," said Bill with a touch of melancholy.

"I take it that things didn't go quite as you planned."

"Your gift for understatement is much better than your sense of humor. No, things didn't go as I planned. Vince Garmon was a white grocer on the front line of the race riots. He was going to spill the beans on a white supremacist group that he bought protection from. Gangs of them roamed the streets back then. Vince figured it was the safest way to go until those guys started taking potshots at blacks in the neighborhood that had nothing to do with the riots. By then it was too late. I ran into him at a bar and we got to talking about it all. I convinced him to tell the FBI, and me, his tale. A black kid shot him during a holdup the next day. The police caught the kid. By morning, the kid had hung himself. By the next night, Garmon's grocery and the whole block it sat in got torched."

"And somebody didn't want you talking out of turn," said Mike.

"There you go with the understatement again. Yep, I got a visit something like yours except they shoved a gun in my mouth and pulled the trigger. I could feel the hammer slam against the action but there was no bang. They did it to prove a point."

"Which was?"

"That they could kill me anytime they wanted. I remember the voice standing over me saying, 'Maybe you should leave town before something bad happens to you.' I didn't need to be told twice. I moved to Harrisburg a week later."

"Why didn't you tell the FBI or the cops?" asked Mike.

"What for? The only link I had died in the bogus holdup."

"It seemed a little too cut-and-dried."

"You got that right. Whoever it was had connections with the law. If I hung around, I might have hung myself too," said Bill.

"When you said 'whoever,' you made it sound like you had a name in mind."

"Oh yea, but, like I said, that's old news and all I have is conjecture—gotta deal with the facts in my business. Anyway, we got way off the Kepner thing. Got any idea who the lawyer was that represented the construction company that was paying Kepner under the table?"

"Dunn?"

"Don't say it as a question, my boy. Yes, Truman Dunn. Most of the time he gets away with it, too. Very slick and very deliberate. The owner of the construction company didn't want to pay Dunn's fee and went directly to Kepner. Then the cops find out once a thirty-foot geyser erupts on a city street. The best part is that Dunn Associates is leading a class action suit against Kepner and the construction company for damages to businesses they represent."

"You seem to know where all the skeletons are. Is that the reason you do all the stuff about Exeter for the *Harrisburg Post*?" asked Mike.

"Yes, and also why I'm writing a book about the Exeter race riots."

"You are? I wouldn't mind reading it."

"Sure, c'mon back to the car. I have a rough draft on a CDROM that you can take a look at as long as I get it back."

Darkness had fallen somewhere during the conversation. Bill and Mike made their way back to the parking lot. The hum of crickets was replaced by the hum of a streetlight. Bill fumbled through his leather attaché until he pulled a folder from the volumes of paper stuffed into it. Inside the folder were a jewel-cased CDROM and the small ream of paper that constituted Bill's manuscript. "Paper or plastic?" asked Bill with all the flair of a bag boy.

"Plastic is fine," smirked Mike.

Bill handed the CD to Mike after jotting Mike's name down on the manuscript's folder and said, "Enjoy it. Let me know what you think."

"I will. I'll give you a call and drop it off. Talk to you later," replied Mike as both men headed toward their cars.

Chapter 19

The desktop computer whirred to life. Mike popped the CD into the drive and the contents of Bill Renard's CD spilled onto the screen after a few clicks. Myriad little yellow folders filled the screen, causing Mike to hunt and peck until he found a folder named "Manuscript." Mike opened it, found the right file, and began to read *Exeter in Black and White* by Bill Renard. His labors got sidetracked when he looked down on the forlorn countenance of Abby looking back at him with the kind of begging eyes that no pet owner could refuse.

One serving of dog food and three hours later, Mike completed a very fast read of Bill's short manuscript. The book proved to be a history lesson on two summers of internecine warfare carried out on the streets of Exeter. Interspersed within the skirmishes and segregation were biographies of the principal players of the time. Names, dates and locations blurred together. Two exceptions stood out: Clayton Edwards and Vince Garmon. Edwards' name appeared several times as strategist, peacemaker and hero. Garmon's name appeared almost as a footnote and was simply listed as a victim of street crime. The content read just like Renard's newspaper articles—terse, factual and no nonsense. There wasn't a single page of rumor or conjecture.

The PC's clock ushered in a brand-new Friday somewhere along the way though Mike didn't notice until his eyelids grew leaden. Thinking of the probable penalty for a late night at work the next day, he decided to shut down the computer and get some shuteye. As he did, each layer of panels open on his computer winked out as he hit the X. The last panel showed the folder list he viewed to hunt down Renard's book. Mike's finger hovered over the mouse button to shut down the final panel until he realized just what he was looking at.

Dozens of folders lined the screen. Most of the folders went by name, some by date and others by town or street. Mike scrolled down the list scanning each name and occasionally opened up a folder to view some of the files contained within. A few random selections later, he figured out that he was not only looking at Bill's book, but also his research.

Leaden eyelids lifted with renewed curiosity as he opened file after file of old newspaper stories, scanned pictures and random thoughts Bill had seen fit to compile over the years. Mike copied the entire CD to his computer and began to sift.

Opening the first folder that piqued his interest, Mike delved into "Brenda Stabler." Not too many files, he thought. What few news articles there were mentioned her as part of the Houser staff or part of the Edwards staff, depending on the date the article hit the papers. Just as he was about ready to go to another folder, Mike spotted a file dated in mid-January and opened it up. The file was a scanned news-paper article from the social section of the Exeter newspaper dated December 12th, 2001, and it reported the story on the lobbyists' party. The pictures that accompanied the article showed a variety of named unknowns and a single shot of Brenda Stabler handing Clayton Edwards a drink. The caption read, "Freshmen Representative Clayton Edwards and his assistant enjoy a night out." *You got to love the irony of that*, Mike thought.

Not far from the Stabler folder was "Clayton Edwards," and what a folder it was. Mike gasped at the sheer amount of pictures and documents that Bill had managed to accumulate. Court cases, news articles and picture after picture came to life. All of the pictures fit the cookie-cutter posed shot of Edwards with so-and-so supporting such-and-such.

Rather than plod through each and every file, Mike skipped to the bottom of the list where the most recent dates resided. More court cases, news articles and pictures appeared, this time with Edwards as the defendant of his own trial and his fall from grace. Mike saw the same file name and mid-January date as in the Stabler folder and opened it up. It was the same picture as before, although he spent more time looking at the pair—their clothing kempt and crisp and their faces happy. *And a few hours later, you met Bennie Carlson and your world changed*, thought Mike. *All of our worlds changed.*

The slider bar pulled more folders into Mike's weary view. The urge to sleep grew with each passing minute, offset only by the gnawing curiosity to find some tidbit of interest. Most of the alphabet flickered by until the name "Truman Dunn" scrolled into view. The mouse danced over to the name as Mike thought about opening the folder. It was more than odd that there wasn't a single word about Truman Dunn in Bill's book, especially since he had regarded him as one of the behind-the-scenes big shots. Once Mike opened the folder, Bill's lack of references to Dunn became more curious. Like Edwards', scores of files came to life in front of him.

Mike started at the beginning and worked his way down each file. Renard's research skills were excellent, but his computer skills were lacking. Everything was dated the day Bill created the file, which made it difficult to keep things mentally in order. What he could keep in order wasn't pretty. The adolescent Truman Dunn appeared in an arrest report in 1955 for burning a cross on the front lawn of a Catholic church. A news article dated the next day listed him as being released on his own recognizance. Some days after that, charges were dropped. Another article, dated a few months later, showed the church breaking ground for a new rectory that had been gifted by an anonymous donor. After that, Dunn's next appearance was in his college yearbook followed a year later by a society page listing of one Miss Arlene Lillian Johnson to be wedded to one Truman Randolph Dunn. Mike looked on into folder after folder finding advertisements of legal and land titling services of the now partnered firm of Dunn and Arthur Johnson—evidently, the former Miss Johnson's father. Beyond those files were image after image of numerous land deals brokered, court cases successfully defended or dismissed against ACLU and NAACP suits, and criminal verdicts overturned in favor of Dunn & Johnson clients. That was, until the early 1970s where the files showed more than a few criminal cases and civil suits being lost.

By the late '70s "Dunn and Johnson" became "Dunn" after the death of Arthur Johnson and subsequent divorce of Miss Arlene. A few files after that and two deeds appeared, one for a Mrs. Arlene Dunn in the city of Exeter and another for a Mr. Truman Dunn along Valley Road in Muir Springs, Pennsylvania. "I guess that Arlene was done with Dunn, Abby," Mike said out loud to his snoozing pet. One groan and a reorientation of Abby's butt toward Mike told him what she thought of his remark.

Mike went back to his reading as the clock ticked past 2:00 a.m. The Dunn files meandered through every published and public aspect that could be gleaned out of the free press all the way to the recent class action suit on behalf of all the damaged souls that Dunn represented. At the end, nary a file connected Truman Dunn with the skullduggery that Bill Renard insinuated during their conversations. *That's why he's not in the book*, Mike thought. That was, until he saw the folder named "Vincent Garmon" right after Truman Dunn's highlighted icon. Sleep battled what little curiosity remained until Mike's heavy eyelids fought their way open to view one last series of files.

The list of files proved mercifully short. Mike clicked on the first, which showed a black and white photograph of a proud Vince Garmon, his very pregnant wife, and a few other local dignitaries cutting the ribbon on the brand-spanking-new Garmon's Market. A second picture showed the market some years later followed by a third shot showing the Exeter paper's coverage in the aftermath of the robbery, murder and subsequent arson at the store.

Beyond Garmon stood the bland manila Houser folder icon. Mike's eyes blinked more and more as the urge to sleep became a need. After taking a deep breath, Mike shook himself awake and double-clicked on the folder. Document after document yielded nothing more than public records of businesses started and closed by Houser in his early years as a businessman. The next time he showed was on the employment roster of the Muir County Commissioners. The lack of anything interesting made Mike's head bob lower and lower. The last few files came into view when a half-dozen uncoordinated double-clicks managed to open a scan of a newspaper article. One article looked like the nondescript little blurbs that Mike had seen a hundred times in the *Post* except that this article came from Exeter. The muddied scan read:

Commissioners Scuffle Over Rezoning Plan—County Commissioner Sam Houser was arrested by officers after they were called in to quell a fight that had broken out between Commissioner Sam Houser and Commissioner Arden Jackson over the prospect of rezoning a rural area of the county for low income housing. After a heated debate, it is alleged that Commissioner Houser assaulted Commissioner Jackson. County police refuse to comment on the case other than to say that they may charge Commissioner Houser pending further fact finding.

"I am so glad I've stayed up this late for this, Abby," Mike said to Abby, who refused to move a whisker. Mike somehow managed to open the last file, which turned out to be another scan of another newspaper article. He couldn't decide whether the monitor was bleary or if it was his eyes. Three blinks later and he figured it was both. The Exeter newspaper article couldn't have been plainer:

County Police Drop Charges—County Police announced today that Commissioner Houser has been exonerated of charges concerning the alleged assault that occurred during September's County Commissioners' Meeting.

Since both the files and he were exhausted, Mike shut down his computer and trundled off to bed with all the excitement of a zombie. He called to Abby, who was not where she had been most of the night. Mike found her forty winks ahead and probably happy to be out of the range of his puns.

* * *

To Mike, it seemed like fifteen minutes instead of four hours of sleep. All of his blood had been removed and replaced with lead that pinned his arms and legs to the covers. He had whacked the snooze button of his alarm clock repeatedly, but it came back to life each time, insisting on his revival with its reveille. In an hour he found himself parked at his desk in an almost catatonic state, lusting for sleep.

Three cups of Judy's forty-weight coffee later, Mike went to work. Of course, Lazarus himself would've awakened from the dead had he enough of Judy's coffee. It took until lunchtime to fully feel alive, although the caffeine headache he now had reminded him of his frail humanity. Over bites of his lunch and throbs of his head, flashes of Bill's research popped into his mind. Like his lunch mixing with Judy's coffee, something unsettling churned in his gut. He couldn't quite place it. Maybe it was how dry Bill's research was. After all, it was reporting. There were no rumors, conjecture or speculation—none of the things heard over whispered conversations along with knowing glances. It was like all the facts, forms and reports he either read on the web or at the ranger station. Of course, being berated by Ellie Edwards or body slammed twice weren't paper realities, he thought. Mike's thoughts wandered back over Bill's research and how it had been accumulated for people like Edwards and Dunn versus, say, Houser or Stabler. There hadn't even been a folder for Ellie Edwards. All Mike knew of her was a one-way shouting match outside a courtroom, and he still had no idea what that was all about. He guessed that it had to do with all the pent-up anger over the whole mess between her husband and Stabler. It must have been hard for her to accept the fact that Clayton had been chasing a staffer round the desk, so to speak. He wondered what motivated Stabler—*was it power or the excitement? Why did Edwards cover for her? Would Bill know?* He reached for the phone to make a call but found it ringing already.

Jen's voice made him forget the volatile mix of coffee and an over-mustarded ham sandwich. "You wouldn't mind walking Roxanne tonight, would you?" begged Jen.

"Roxanne usually walks me. Sure, how come?"

"I'm way behind on applicant processing and it will just get worse if I don't stay and catch up. You know how Roxanne is if I don't get home on time."

Mike grimaced at the memory of a past Roxanne tantrum and counted his Abby blessings, saying, "Not a problem." The word "applicant" hung in Mike's mind for a second before he made the connection. "Jen, what kind of applicants are you working on?"

"Summer interns mostly and some worker bees. Why?"

"Do you do anything like that when the new senators and representatives come in for their term?"

"You mean, like reference checking and stuff like that?"

"Exactly."

"Nope. If the voters are stupid enough to elect them..."

"Heh, heh. I get it—then we...they get what we deserve. How 'bout any of their staffers?"

"They have to fill out an application and pass a background check for security."

"So you would have run a background check on Clayton Edwards' staff, including his wife and Brenda Stabler?"

"Don't go there, Michael. I would lose my job if I told you anything about anybody. Besides, the State Police do that."

The use of the proper form of his name told Michael that he had gotten his hand slapped much the way his mom used to when he was caught doing things worthy of punishment. He apologized, "Sorry, I was just curious."

The conversation ended with a cold "goodbye" from Jen. Now, Mike had Judy's coffee, an over-mustarded ham sandwich and Jen's ire to contend with. Searching through his desk drawers, Mike hunted for antacids. His search ended with another ring of the phone.

"Do you have a pen and paper ready?" whispered Jen.

"For what?" questioned a clueless Mike Daniels.

"For the info you wanted."

"I thought you couldn't..."

"I had to put on that act for the folks around me. It's not like I can stand in my cubicle and spout off confidential information," said Jen.

"Have I told you you're wonderful? Go ahead."

"Not lately. First off, there was no background check on Elizabeth Edwards."

"None? What does that mean?"

"That means that she's his wife and wasn't on staff. That's typical."

"Oh, thanks. You'd better get going," said Mike.

"Don't you want Brenda Stabler's?"

"Whoops, sorry. I'm getting senile, Jen."

"No kidding. Memory's the second thing to go, Mikey. Stabler passed the check with flying colors. Her app shows her working for Edwards for a year, and for Samuel Houser for five years before that. No judgments, arrests, convictions, loan defaults or trips out of the country. It's all pretty clean."

"Anything else?" queried Mike as he took notes.

"Worked for the Muir County Commissioners for five years before the Houser job. Before that, Abbots Ridge College in Virginia, 3.5 GPA, Bachelor of Arts in Political Science. She got a poly/sci scholarship from Johnson Land Titling. Before that, she was a straight 'A' student in Stone Hills High School in Richmond, Virginia. Wanna hear about the boys she dated?"

"They tell you that on an application?" asked Mike as he continued jotting.

"No, but I figured that this girl is so boring that I had to spice things up."

"You're bad, Jen," kidded Mike.

"Isn't that what you like about me?"

"Yea. Was there anything else?"

"Not really. Listen, I've got to go. My boss is coming down the aisle. Remember, we didn't have this little talk in case anybody asks. Bye."

Jen's voice changed to the drone of a dial tone, leaving Mike wondering why everything he had been learning seemed to come out of Exeter.

"*Post*, Bill Renard speaking."

"Write any good books lately?" joked Mike.

"Just one worthy of a Pulitzer. Read any good books lately?"

"No, not really."

"Thanks. Did you even open up the cover or do you computer geeks have to scan everything in before you touch paper?" retorted Bill.

"Actually, I read it yesterday. Exeter sounded like a great place to take the kids back then."

"You don't know the half of it."

"True enough. That's what I'm calling about. Well, not exactly about Exeter, but Exeter politics. I read your research."

"I should have known that you'd poke around in that mess."

"Messy, but comprehensive. You've got a ton of stuff on that lawyer Dunn. How come there's nothing on him in the book?"

"Because, my boy, there's nothing to connect him to any of those ugly days despite any feelings I have to the contrary. You can't publish that sort of thing without getting sued, and I have much better things to do with my life besides appearing in civil court."

"Does that apply to the Edwards and Stabler story, too?"

"It sure does. Plenty of grist for the rumor mill but no hard evidence."

"I was surprised that your research didn't cover her a bit more," said Mike.

"That's 'cause there's precious little about her that's documented."

"You knew about where she worked and all that?"

"Oh yeah, word of mouth told me all that, but nobody's handed me a copy of her resumé."

"How about a job application?" asked Mike.

"I'm listening."

Mike looked at his notes and began, "She worked for Edwards for a year and Houser for five years before that."

"Nothing new there, my boy."

"Did five years for the County Commissioners..."

"Old news."

"...good student in a Virginia college, got an academic scholarship..."

"So did I, Penn State...," added an increasingly bored Renard.

"...from Johnson Land Management and..."

"Stop. Say that again," commanded Bill.

"Good student in..."

"No. Tell me again who she got the scholarship from."

"Johnson Land Management for political science..."

"Oh crap. How did I miss that? I need a copy of that."

"That won't be possible. I got it from a...an unknown source," said Mike, trying to obscure Jen's participation.

"Unknown source? Now you sound like me. What else did your unknown source tell you?"

"That's pretty much it," said Mike.

"You should be in the newspaper business."

"Too bad. Maybe you are getting old. Why did you make me repeat the scholarship stuff? I mean, why in world would Johnson Land be handing out scholarships to little girls from Richmond, Virginia?"

"I have no idea," said Bill, although he was lying through his teeth. "Well, my boy, thanks for these tidbits. Too bad you can't get 'em on paper. You don't suppose..."

"...that I could get you copies? No. No way, Bill."

"Then it is too bad. Well, it's Friday and my editor is reminding me of whom I work for. I'll see you later. Bye," said Bill.

Mike said his goodbye to a click. *Bill could hardly wait to say his farewells*, Mike thought. *Oh well, the weekend is here and thank goodness for that.* Maybe he'd ask Jen to the movies after walking Roxanne. Saturday, he could take another run in the woods at Sanford. He promised himself to stay way clear of the ranger station and everybody in it—just a quiet run at the break of dawn.

Chapter 20

The old wooden chair's spring protested with a screech loud enough to cause several of Bill Renard's coworkers to stop keying their weekend columns as they desperately tried to get out the door for two blessed days off. Bill, very much used to his chair's idiosyncrasies, tilted the chair all the way back, ignoring the animal cry beneath him. Looking at the drop ceiling above, Bill could remember when it had been plaster. It could have been termed a drop ceiling, Bill thought, by the way small chunks would fall into his typewriter when someone heavy walked on the floor above his rickety wooden desk. That was the way it was when he had started at the *Post* over thirty years ago. His typewriter had given way to his computer and his wooden desk was replaced with the stamped-steel sameness of cubicle walls. Plaster had given way to panels stuck in the metal grid work above him. Those changes evolved and were either enjoyed or endured, depending on his attitude at the time. Only his screeching old wooden chair survived.

Bill didn't fight change or wallow in reminiscences; it just was the way things were. Of course, that was what he told himself to avoid thinking about why he happened to be seated in the offices of the *Harrisburg Post* in the first place. That thought never sat well. Now, after Mike Daniels called, that reason was sitting even less so. The thought of Daniels' matter-of-fact three-word delivery made him laugh under his breath. Those three words connected him with his past the same way his old chair did. No, those three words went back before he ever occupied his old wooden chair, he thought.

The book had proven to be a kind of catharsis for Bill. It gave him a chance to revisit the old Exeter he used to know by lauding its heroes and chiding its villains. Exeter had changed for the better since the fever pitch summer of '69. It had only done so on the blood of martyrs, some white and some black, along with the Herculean effort of hundreds of living souls.

"Darcy, I want you to run something down for me," said Bill to Darcy Pell, a zealous journalism intern that was assigned to Bill's section for her final semester.

"What do you need?" replied Darcy.

"I need you to run down some scholarship winners for me by close of business today."

"Today? It's Friday," said Darcy with more than a little protest.

Bill could tell that Darcy's zeal evidently had ebbed by the end of the week. "Darcy, I need this today. It'll be old news by tomorrow."

"Yea, yea, yea. It's always old news by tomorrow."

"Darcy, I need it today." Bill's voice didn't carry a command. It carried a plea and Darcy responded.

"All right, what do want me to look up?"

* * *

Bill's thoughts were not about the looming deadline his colleagues were straining to meet. His column was done hours ago though he wouldn't forward it until late in the day. It was his time-honored ritual to wait to the last moment to submit his material then run like crazy lest his editor give him one more thing to do on a Friday, just like he had done to poor Darcy. It was that one more thing that he was waiting for when the phone rang its distinctive inside ring.

"City Desk—Bill Renard."

"Resident slave—Darcy Pell. Your list is in your email. Can I go home now?"

"No."

"No?"

"Not until I tell you thanks—thanks, Darcy."

Darcy's email opened with a double-click of Bill's mouse and eighteen names appeared along with the high school they attended. More than a few were familiar to Bill as he shook his head at the information displayed on the monitor. "I have you. I have you by the short and curlies," said Bill to no one in particular as he forwarded the email.

* * *

A British Racing green Mazda Miata purred along the narrow country road, hugging the curves and eating up the straight-aways. It was just the kind of driving Bill remembered when he put his old MG through its paces in the years after he left school and Exeter. It was funny, Bill thought, that he was in a similar car heading toward his past, rather than using his MG to escape from it.

A deer scampered off the side of the road and Bill reined in his foot, anxious to avoid a nasty encounter of a small car with a big animal. His car rolled to a stop at a break in the forest-shrouded road-way. Bill took another look at the directions he had gotten off the Internet, made the turn onto the asphalt-paved lane, and found himself almost immediately confronted by a large, ornate iron gate. "Here we go," said Bill as he tapped the steering wheel of the convertible.

* * *

Darcy Pell could barely hear her cell phone chiming over the throb of the music blaring onto the nightclub floor. The LCD number on the screen told her that it was the night desk from the paper and that she'd better answer it. After hitting the call button, she yelled in the phone. "Hold on a sec. I can't hear you." Navigating into the restroom, Darcy pressed the phone to her ear again and said, "Okay. Go ahead."

"This is Nick at the Night Desk. You're supposed to come in tomorrow in case they need some researching done."

"Aw c'mon. It's Saturday."

"Darcy. Listen, it's about Bill. He's in critical condition down in Exeter Central Hospital. He hit a deer and is pretty messed up. The boss wants us all in tomorrow."

"Okay," replied Darcy as if the wind had been knocked out of her.

Chapter *21*

Mike Daniels awakened early to prepare for his usual Saturday morning trail run. Abby, as usual, had not. The urge to return to bed hung heavy in Mike's eyes due to a late night out with Jen. Jen insisted on them having a date, especially since her hectic schedule left little time for social, and personal, activities. The word date brought a slight smile to his face. Dates belonged to teenagers and twenty-somethings, not thirty-year-olds. Still, this thirty-year-old went on a date and the reduction in sleep seemed a good price to pay. It was, until he looked into the mirror and realized that someone had replaced the teenager-on-a-date face with some old guy. "5:00 a.m. Saturday—reality sets in," Mike said to his reflection.

One of the realities happened to be that Mike was not used to dating. A lively Friday night included such exciting activities as opening his email, backing up his computer, and, if he felt wild and crazy, renting a movie. A date made the rental unnecessary, which left him with checking email and backing up his computer. A quick check of his watch told Mike that he had time to do one or the other. A flip of a mental coin told him to do the backup. He could stretch and have a quick bite while the computer burned his data onto a CD. Mike started the backup and went downstairs.

Eight stretches, two strains and a cup of coffee later, Mike returned to his computer that had opened the CD burner door and offered up his file backup. After putting the new CD into a jewel case, Mike checked the other CD drive for leftover CDs that should be put away. He spotted Bill Renard's CD and looked around for a jewel case to put it into. As he began to look for an empty case, he felt a gentle prod to his left thigh. Mike looked down at Abby who had finally awakened from her slumber and was in search of breakfast. Before he left the bedroom, he took a look at the desk clock and saw 6:32 a.m. Feeling an artificial pressure from his anal adherence to time, Mike began to rush in order to hit the trails precisely at 7:00 a.m. He slapped Bill's CD into the same case as his backup and tromped on down the steps.

Heading for the garage while still carrying the CD, Mike was cut off by a pair of accusing eyes attached to four legs standing in the way of his exit. That look told him that he could not pass. "I'm sorry, Abby," apologized Mike as he grabbed the dog's dish and filled it with food. He set the dish on the floor and gave her a pat on the head.

It wasn't too long after the garage door went down that Abby heard the front door open. Considering that her owner was often absent-minded or forgetful, she assumed that he had returned to pick up something minor or inconsequential like those stupid shoes he wore. *They didn't even taste very good*, she thought. Rather than going to the effort of checking on another set of his frenzied activities, she decided to continue the luxurious pace of eating her breakfast one luscious kibble at a time. There was no need to hurry like her owner. The bed upstairs would be there after she was done.

Strange noises emanated from the bedroom. Not the strange noises Abby normally heard when her owner and Jen were up there, but something else—something not quite right. What was also not right was that her owner's typical return usually lasted a few seconds before he was gone again. Rather than leave the better part of her kibbles, Abby elected to remain at her dish and try to focus on her dining experience. Leaving a good meal for curiosity would never do, especially if it meant devouring her meal like that heathen Roxanne.

Halfway through her meal the odd noises stopped, and Abby could hear descending footsteps on the stairs. She looked up to find that her owner had grown blonde hair and appendages like Jen. A cold rush of fear surged through Abby, and she pinned herself against the kitchen door in wild-eyed fright. Abby sat, frozen to the floor, as she watched a woman rummage around the kitchen, opening drawers and cabinets as though she were looking for something. To Abby's horror, the woman's gaze focused on her. What was worse, Abby realized that the intruder was reaching for her half-empty breakfast dish.

In a fierce frenzy borne less out of personal protection and much more out of the fact that somebody had the brazen nerve to take her food, Abby launched herself at the intruder with all the flair of the Hound of the Baskervilles. *Nobody, but nobody, messes with my food*, thought Abby, as her teeth shone between barks and snarls. The intruder turned tail and fled toward the front door with all possible speed with a seemingly rabid little sheepdog in hot pursuit. The door slammed in front of Abby and she knew that her efforts, although deeply tiring, had been worth the effort. She returned to her beloved kibbles and finished her meal uninterrupted. Satisfied in tummy and spirit, she retired to the corner of her owner's bed to bask in the blissful dreams of "Abby the Fierce." *Take that, Roxanne*, she thought.

* * *

A golden spring sunrise greeted Mike on his way to Sanford State Park. The trees were budding and the grass lining the trailside glowed bright green. Mike felt that it would be a fine day for a run. The radio that had been playing classical music now turned to a voice proclaiming the local news precisely as the Pontiac's fluorescent radio flickered 7:00 a.m. "A Harrisburg man remains in critical condition after colliding with a deer on Valley Road in..." was as far as the announcer got by the time Mike switched off the car.

Snapping his water belt on, Mike stretched again before heading off onto Sanford's Lakeside Trail, blissfully ignoring the signs that warned visitors that spring turkey season would begin on April 27th—today.

The sunrise poured through the forest around Mike as he ran along the trail. Each step added to the next until he found himself on the far side of the lake near the ranger station. Mike paused and listened for any sound or sight that might mean a ranger's appearance. Having heard none, he continued on. Mike's thoughts returned to the trail as he negotiated the rocks and roots. The woods were silent. Even the little hollow where he had met the mountain bikers proved to be quiet and uneventful. Mike dwelt on the quietness and lack of events. Squirrels hadn't run from the forest floor and scratched up the trees to chitter at him. Crows and jays didn't bay out alarms on his approach or departure. The only birdcalls he heard were the nervous chirps of wrens and finches. Rather than being comforted by the lack of noise, Mike found himself unsettled. He glanced around, looking and listening for anything out of the ordinary.

The trail soon emptied out onto the hard road near the parking lot where Mike had seen the red Chevy Blazer. A pair of old pickup trucks were the only occupants in the lot. Rather than continue on, Mike decided to stop at a nearby restroom. Any facility like that had a four star rating over having to deal with it in the woods.

Refreshed, Mike left the restroom and squinted into the bright morning light now set above the trees. His right arm lifted to shade his eyes as he prepared to run. In that instant, his mind stepped back to the night he watched the videotape of the news broadcast. He could see himself watching the broadcast and staring over the reporter's shoulder looking at the Blazer—looking at the Blazer. No, his eye wasn't looking at the Blazer, he thought; it was looking at the reflection of light on the Blazer's windshield. He blinked at the recollection and it brought him back to the spot he was standing near the restroom staring into the shade of his hand. After taking two short steps, Mike stopped, this time looking at a large painted map of Sanford State Park. Some diligent state employee had gone to the trouble of locating these four-by-eight foot maps around the park. Each one stood underneath a small, shingled roof, and each frame was painted in institutional green. The lake was portrayed in sky blue while each trail had been color-coded around the lake's periphery. Mike's eyes followed the dark blue legend of the Lakeside Trail until it met up with a "You Are Here" bubble. His view resumed along the path he had taken in December when the trail split off that fateful day. The map above the trail ended abruptly with a wide black line indicating the park's boundary. Above that, in a thin "X" was the compass rose, tipped over to denote North, South, East and West. Mike stood numbly, puzzling over the '"X." *By rights*, he thought, *the "X" should look more like a plus sign—the way the park map is laid out—N on the top for north and S on the bottom.* He looked again at the "X" thinking it was wrong. *It's not wrong. I am.* Each hair on the back of Mike's neck took a turn standing up and delivered an increasing chill down his spine. A numbing paralysis transfixed his jaw-dropped stance along with eyes staring at the compass points. The icy paralysis lasted only a moment and was replaced with the hot rush of fear pushing him to run.

Dancing in place, Mike feverishly tried to decide which way to take back to his car. If he returned the way he came, it might take longer and also take him past the ranger station again. That wouldn't do. The ranger station was the last place he wanted to be near. *No*, he thought, *the fastest way back happened to take him right past the place they buried Bennie Carlson*. That thought sat no better than the ranger station, but a dead man wasn't going to try to kill him.

Mike ran flat out until sanity and shortness of breath slowed him down. Before long, he had clipped off the park's boggy nether regions and bounded over the campground road with only three more miles to go. Each step closer to his car made him feel better.

Mike wouldn't have felt as good had he seen the two camou-flaged men on either side of the trail that were now following him. Distance played out between them until Mike slowed to a walk to take a drink from the bottle on his belt. Before the first swallow went down, the pain from a dozen bee stings stung his calf followed by the sound of a thunderclap. Mike tried to rub the hurt away until his mind caught up with pain. *That was a shot*, he thought. *Somebody shot me.* Mike pulled his shaking hand away expecting to see blood and found only measle-like welts.

Ka-pow.

Another peal of thunder went through Mike and another set of stings burned his right calf. Again, his hand rubbed the fire on his legs and there was still no blood. There was, however, a plume of smoke from a nearby somewhat lumpy tree. Mike stared blankly at the trunk and its strange contour until his mind began thinking again rather than dealing with the pain. The lump on the tree's side had eyes and was pumping the action of a shotgun.

Mike darted off the trail and ran into the woods, hoping to cut back to the lakeside trail he had abandoned in favor of getting to his car in a hurry. The shotgun-toting tree lump rose and began to run after him but was no match for Mike's fear-induced sprint—not that it mattered.

All of his body ached with the demands of his sprint, and it took his mind off the burning sensation in both of his calves. Mike hoped that he had gained a hundred yards on his assailant. He slowed again to take a pull from his water bottle when the third shot went off, this time peppering his back with more stings. Mike arched his back in agony as if he could twist away from the stings. Reason returned much sooner, and he looked around in vain for the person he had seen the first time.

Ka-pow.

A fourth shot mostly missed though stings were coming off his left hand now. That shot gave away its sender. Mike saw the man behind a receding puff of smoke. *His camouflage has a different pattern*, Mike thought. "My God, there are two of them," said Mike as he took off running, back toward the other man.

Shots rang out all around Mike as he tried to get to the lakeside trail or back to the campground. Every time he'd try, his pursuers would double-back and shoot at him. Sometimes the rounds would hit Mike, sending new stings throughout his body while others scratched off the trees and rocks. Mike knew his best bet was to bushwhack through the spring growth in order to keep most of the shots from hitting him.

Despite the growing fatigue, Mike forced himself to run as fast as he could. Any break in speed or in his serpentine course brought the stings back when his attackers drew near. From the look of his surroundings, Mike thought, it's only a mile and a half to the car.

* * *

A faded blue DCNR ranger car trundled to a stop next to Mike Daniels' car. The engine refused to die despite having had the ignition turned off. Tony Savastio stepped out of the aging Chrysler and into the parking lot. After noticing the Daniels Pontiac, Tony let his eyes scan the trails leading into and out of the lot. Tony's ears picked up the sounds of repeated shotgun blasts in the distance and looked around again for any sign of Daniels or any other passer-by—none were present. Tony opened the trunk and pulled out a scoped hunting rifle, flicked open the bolt and loaded the magazine. In minutes, he was running down the trail and into the woods.

* * *

After Mike gained some distance, the shots became less frequent, and he felt that he could slow down just enough to catch his breath. He could see that he was coming to the end of the denser forest and now had to contend with an open clearing on its way up a gentle hill. Steeling himself for more stings, Mike counted to three, and tore off up the hill.

* * *

A single eye floated on the lens of the riflescope. Following back along the scope's smooth black surface sat the projection's source, clad in tree bark camouflage and barely visible in the golden dawn of a spring forest.

The snap of a distant branch alarmed him and his masked head swiveled to track the approaching runner. Sweeping eyes surveyed the dense brush that bordered the dirt trail. His hands embraced the weapon's contours. Another branch cracked in the early morning chill, this time closer, louder, and imminently nearing. Embracing the weapon's contours, he brought it into readiness against his shoulder. He could see the sweat-drenched shirt clinging to the runner's chest as he positioned the crosshairs in the center of his target. He curled a single gloved finger on top of the gun's safety and clicked it off. With that sound, the rifle grew leaden as if deadliness gave it more weight. His eye returned to its projected perch within the scope as he drew in a breath.

The thump of sprinting feet announced the arrival of the target. He caught sight of it behind a tangle of vines and brush. A single nervous breath rose upward in a cool fog. He unsheathed a single pale finger from his glove and wrapped it around the trigger until he felt the cold metal push into his warm skin. The target overflowed in the riflescope as he took a breath in then let it out halfway.

* * *

Mike wasn't sure but he thought he heard someone yelling at him. He tried to listen but was running too hard to be able to understand. Mike figured it out when he spotted Tony Savastio standing on a hill and bellowing at the trees in front of him like a madman. Mike's heels dug into the dirt. Tony pointed a scoped hunting rifle at him.

Tony screamed, "You there. Put your weapon down. Now."

Put my weapon down? Mike watched in detached stupor as part of the forest floor rose up in front of him, toting a rifle and spinning around. Another pair of ka-pows shook the forest and a man dressed in a camouflaged suit resembling netting and dead leaves rolled down the hill toward him.

"Daniels, are you okay?" yelled Tony.

Mike stood and stared at the body sprawled out in front of him.

"Daniels? Daniels," yelled Tony again.

After running his hands over his body feeling for holes, Mike answered, "Yea. Yes. He was gonna kill me. Oh my God."

"Glad to hear it," said Tony as he walked down the hill and knelt down next to the shooter.

"Tony, there's two more guys out there taking shots at me. They must have been pushing me here the whole time."

Tony noted Mike's comment but was far more interested in the man under the hood of the suit. "Oh no. Damn it. Damn it all," said Tony as he turned the body over and pulled off the hood. Daryl Musser lay in front of them with lifeless eyes.

"Oh man. This just keeps getting worse. Listen Tony, there's two more of them..."

"Get a hold of yourself. They're probably long gone. Now settle down and tell me what the hell is going on out here."

"I was running like I always do and two guys started chasing me for the last mile and...," said Mike as he turned and pointed in the general direction of his pursuers.

Ka-pow.

Mike heard a wet thud hit Tony and a spray of blood slew into the air. Mike spun back around in time to see Tony hit the ground. Two more shots thudded into the ground nearby and Mike knew that the shooters weren't using the same kind of bullets they were using before.

"Get the hell out of here," gasped Tony.

Mike fought the easy urge to do as commanded and focused on the gaping hole in Tony's shoulder. He reached into the pocket on his water belt and pulled out a zip lock baggie holding a long length of just-for-woodsy-emergency toilet paper and stuffed the paper into the hole, sending up an agonized howl from Tony.

"Damn it, Daniels, that hurt. Now get the heck out of here before I shoot you for doing that to me."

Ka-pow.

Not needing any more encouragement, Mike sprinted off toward his car. Twenty yards farther and one loud report from the other shotgun owner told him that he wasn't going to make it. Mike's car stood at the end of a hundred yards of open field, and he knew he'd never get his keys into the ignition. Instead, he cut back around both attackers and began to bushwhack again.

* * *

Tony's feet kicked earth as he fought the urge to scream against the sheer pain racking his body. When he opened his eyes, a lone figure stood over him pointing a shotgun at his chest. The ranger reached for his pistol and knew that he'd never get his gun halfway out of the holster.

Ka-pow. Pow. Pow. Pow.

* * *

The sound of the four shots brought Mike to a halt and he knew what it meant. The crack of branches nearby warned him of the approach of the other shooter. Daniels gritted his teeth and ran hard, now more determined than ever to get to safety. His mind focused on any chance to get help. It came to him almost instantly—*the campground*. Mike figured that it was too early for any campers to be there but the phone at the registration office might give him that chance.

Only a half-mile had gone past when the shooting started again. Mike flinched and ducked as the shots slammed into trees, sending splinters flying. What made things worse, he thought, was that all of the cross country running slowed him down enough to be a target once again. It also forced him away from the lake and the easiest route back to the phone. Step after step carried him deeper into the forest, and Mike knew that he'd have to turn back to the campground. He caught sight of a small footbridge and knew he was getting close.

Ka-pow.

Another tree exploded in splinters near him, and he took off over a low hill. The far side of the rise was dotted in the remnants of an old stone wall. Mike hurdled the wall and came to rest peering into the eyes of a camouflaged man who had not yet brought his gun to bear on him. The latest camouflaged man's eyes bulged in fear at Mike's sudden appearance. One quick pull of the tree bark mask and the new assailant transformed himself into a half-boy, half-man. Mike looked at him for a long moment—like he had seen him before. It was the kid that had shot at him months ago—the same kid with the disagreeable father who reamed him out for being in the woods for deer season.

Mike grabbed the frightened boy by the shoulders and asked, "Is your father here?"

The boy feebly shook his head yes.

"Then find him and go call the cops. There's people shooting at me and one of the park rangers is dead. Go call the cops. Now. Tell them to go to the campground office. You got that?"

The boy's head shook up and down as he nodded yes and ran off in what Mike figured was the direction of his father. Mike then looked at the ground in disgust at his large amount of stupidity. *The kid took his gun with him.* "You idiot," Mike said as he chided himself.

The crunch of leaves and snap of twigs coming from the opposite direction told him that the chase was on again. "I'm really getting tired of being the rabbit in this," he muttered as he sped off. Mike came to a stand of hemlocks that bordered the confluence of three of the park's trails. Beyond that fork lay the single path to the campground office—and the phone. He stood, concealed by the trees, deciding to either continue his bob-and-weave in the brush or to run up the path to the phone. Mike decided to gamble and lost.

The wood-chipped path took Mike only a few yards when one of his pursuers stepped onto the trail and pointed his shotgun at him. Veering wildly, Mike plummeted through the trees. He could hear the cha-chit sound of the shotgun's action chambering another round, and he ran into the cover of some nearby brush.

The old toboggan run was arranged like two sets of huge white dominoes. Each pair of concrete supports stood erect and devoid of the wood track that used to bridge each pier to give winter visitors a thrill in days gone by. The piers were set into a modest hill to provide a decent ride, and the whole thing stopped next to a large boulder. Mike recognized the area and realized the value of what he saw. Each pier provided bulletproof cover. He tore off to get behind the first set to get out of harm's way. The move paid off immediately as the man chasing him ran and shot. Each round careened off the concrete and into the woods. Mike stopped at the last set, separated by a fair amount of open space between where he was and the big boulder at the end. Rather than jump, he almost stepped down into a gap in the rocks. Something moved down there in the leaf-padded recesses, and he yanked his foot back. Another cha-chit of the gun's action told him that he could jump while his pursuer was busy cocking his shotgun. Mike squatted down on his haunches and leapt for the boulder, scurrying over the top as another shot cracked off the stone. He looked down the other side that offered only a stony clearing and knew that he'd be a sitting duck the moment he tried to leave. Cha-chit sounded on the far side of the boulder and Mike knew he'd be seeing his assailant in just seconds. He looked around for a weapon; a rock, a pointy stick, a rabid possum, something. He found one. Hearing his pursuer take a breath in order to leap, Mike counted. *One-two-three* went by and Mike stood up right in front of the bounding man as he landed. Mike squirted him in the eyes with his water bottle. The man's left hand swatted at the stream and Mike rushed forward, shoulder lowered and football-blocked him off the boulder. The man tumbled down the rock and into the leaf-padded gully below. Mike walked to the edge of the rock and found the man winded and uninjured, flicking the safety off his shotgun—the weapon pointed at Mike. In that instant, the man began to twitch and struggle first to his right and then to his left. Soon all of his limbs were dancing in pain like some kind of witchcraft possessed him. Mike turned his head in revulsion when he saw the reason for the man's artificial epilepsy—snakes. He hadn't seen them during his jump. They had moved out of their sunning spot when Mike approached and hid in the crevices. The intrusion of Mike's pursuer proved too much for them to forgive.

Picking his way down the rock-strewn hill, Mike headed back onto the trail. The pause from running had tightened his already tired legs to the point of cramping, but he was determined to get to the phone. He figured it was his only chance considering the look on the kid's face. There were no guarantees that the teen's father would be any more helpful than he was before. The trail stopped where the asphalt began. The campground office and pay phone stood only fifty yards away. Mike dashed off the yards and grabbed the phone. Lifting the phone to his ear, he heard the blessed dial tone. He leaned his weight against the Plexiglas housing and gathered his breath as he tapped 9-1-1.

"Muir County Dispatch. Please state the nature of your call."

Mike breathed a sigh of relief and spoke, "My name is Mike Daniels. There are people trying to kill me. I'm at the Sanford Park Campground Office. Please send the police immediately."

The dispatcher seemed caught off guard and asked, "Would you repeat that, sir?"

Mike tried to repeat the same sentence but started to lose patience. "For the love of God, send the police to the Sanford Park Campground. I'm dressed in shorts and a T-shirt and I'm covered in dirt and blood. You can't miss me. Okay?"

The dispatcher replied, "We already have units en route, sir, but I'll pass this along."

Units en route? The kid must've called. He was about to ask the dispatcher when the police might get there, but he never got the chance. The surging of an engine drowned out the conversation as Mike caught sight of the old Ford truck bearing down on him. Tossing the phone aside, he tumbled out of the way. The phone disappeared in a lump of twisted metal, and the steel post it sat on folded like tin foil.

Attempting to get up and run, Mike put his weight on his left ankle and moaned. Somehow, he had wrenched it on the uneven ground while spinning out of the way of the truck. A heavy truck door slammed shut as Mike tried to crawl away. He didn't really see too much more of the man than his work boots. The sound of a pistol's action sliding shut told him all he really needed. Mike looked up at the barrel and started wondering who was going to take care of Abby. He closed his eyes and waited for the gunshot.

The blast seemed quieter than all the rest he had experienced during his harried tour of the park. *Maybe the afterlife isn't going to be so bad*, he thought. Something heavy slammed into him and pinned him to the ground. Mike could feel his breath being squeezed out by the smothering weight, and his nostrils could pull nothing into his lungs except the smell of dirt, grass and sweat. Lying on the ground for a bit, Mike wondered about the odd sensations that death was providing. Of course, that was until he opened his eyes and found a large man slumped over his body. He pushed the man off, and his hands came away wet with dark red blood. Sitting up, Mike resumed breathing, and found a Red Man hat lying beside him. *What in the world?* Beyond the Red Man hat sat a bloodied ranger sitting dazed by the road where the trail came out. Mike forced himself to his feet and hobbled over to the wheezing Tony Savastio as distant sirens wailed closer and closer.

"I thought they killed you," said Mike, quite relieved to see Tony again.

"They did...puff...Bastard pulled up on me with a twelve gauge... puff...and shot me smack in the chest before I could get my pistol out," breathed Tony.

"Bulletproof vest?" asked Mike.

"No, I didn't have mine on. It was the damnedest...puff...thing. He shot me and it stung like hell...ummmm...I saw the dust on my chest and realized what he shot me with about the same time he did," breathed Tony.

"And that was?"

"Rock salt...puff...Farmers used to drive off pranksters on Halloween with shells loaded with the stuff. You should have seen the look on that poor bastard's face when I shot him. He must have had the wrong shell chambered up. A damn shame."

"A damned shame, indeed, Tony."

"You know what, Daniels?"

"What?"

"Now I know how Stella must've felt."

"Oh, don't look so worried, Tony. I won't have you stuffed."

"Thanks, Daniels. I'm feeling better already."

Chapter 22

Mike's appreciation of the paramedic's zeal stopped short of annoyance. Their insistence that he be bound up like a side of beef boarding an amusement park ride didn't help. After all, Mike thought, all he did was turn his ankle over. While it was already sore, it wasn't the least bit black and blue although he couldn't judge his skin color through the air cast sticking out of the sheets. What worried him more was Tony's condition.

During the moment when Tony had been shot, Mike knew that he only had time to react. Now his thoughts of Tony's wounds squeezed around him like the air cast around his ankle. Four men had tried to kill him while he ran through a state park that had only ever given him poison ivy. All right, he allowed himself, a kid tried to shoot him, but that was an accident and he wished that was what this was all about. He knew it wasn't. Another man tried to protect him and got shot in the process. Mike managed to push the stiff sheets away from his chest to look at the blood spattered on his T-shirt. *How much blood is Tony's and how much came from the men that were hunting me?* he wondered as he focused on each tiny fleck of dark red. His head rocked back onto the gurney when fatigue and stress caught up with him. Feeling an urge to sleep, Mike drifted in and out of consciousness amid the din of the radio's chatter and the wail of the siren on his way to the hospital.

During a waking moment, Mike spoke to the male attendant who was otherwise occupied wisecracking with the driver and flirting with the female EMT. "Where are we going?" A flash of sunlight through the rear windows told Mike they were headed north. South would have meant Exeter Hospital, but north could mean about five possibilities.

"We're going to Harrisburg Hospital. Exeter put us on divert and—," replied the young attendant.

"Divert?" asked Mike.

"Yea, too many cases at Exeter. They pushed us up to Harrisburg. Don't worry, they're the place to go anyway."

"What about the ranger?"

"He's on his way to Exeter."

"How's he doing?" asked Mike.

Mike watched the EMT turn to the driver and ask. When the driver's lips stopped moving, the EMT's chin dropped and a serious face replaced the pleasant smiles of the earlier wisecracking. "Not good," was the EMT's reply.

Mike settled back onto the gurney and looked up at the rear windows of the ambulance. Daylight poured through the windows and reflected off the metal surfaces nearby. Each reflection he had seen around the park had warned him, in effect, that there was something wrong, particularly with Daryl Musser. Never in a million years had Mike expected Musser, or anybody else for that matter, to try and kill him. He had an idea why Musser did it. *That idea opened up the proverbial can-o-worms*, he thought. Now, with Musser riding home in the coroner's van, like Bennie Carlson back in December, those reasons supporting his idea would be hard to find.

The ambulance rolled to a jerky stop, and the crew went to work delivering Mike into the arms of the Emergency Room staff. An ER physician took one look at his injuries and consigned Mike to a curtained alcove while the ER crew tended to the real emergencies. Mike watched the curtain swirl with the passing of sexless feet clad in green or blue booties as they walked their muted, hurried steps. Voices murmured from anonymous groups of people speaking the language of desperate lifesaving. Occasionally, moans would drift through the room along with the sound of a scuffle as some poor patient thrashed in their bed. It all made Mike wonder how Tony was doing. He wished that they'd both be in the same hospital so he could know what was happening.

The fluorescent light above flickered. Each sputter flashed Mike back to the sunlight flooding through the trees as he ran in utter fear. The horrifying image of Tony pointing a rifle at him, and Daryl's body twisting from the impact passed by in his mind. There was the wretched dance some unknown man performed to the accompaniment of angry snakes, remembered Mike. Then there was the sound of the dispatcher asking him "Would you repeat that, sir? Would you repeat that, sir? Would you repeat that, sir? Sir? Sir?"

"Sir? Sir? Excuse me, sir?" prodded a doctor who had neared Mike's bed and caught him in his daze.

Mike snapped out of his recollection and gave a confused look to the woman prodding the cast around his injured foot.

"Hi," said the doc as she tugged on Mike's wrist to make sure his ID bracelet and chart matched whom she should be seeing to. "I'm Doctor Gable and I'm going to check your injury if that's okay. That's the one with the cast, right?"

It seemed quite obvious to Mike that it was and it took him a moment to realize that her statement was less about the doctor's power of observation as it was a test to see if he was lucid. "Yes, that's correct," he said to pass the test.

The physician removed the air cast and began her examination. Various movements of his ankle produced various contortions on Mike's face. She noted the flexibility and the amount of pain he demonstrated then pronounced he had a "mild sprain. Somebody from x-ray will be over to shoot some pictures just to make sure."

Time dragged on until an x-ray technician came in pushing a cart that looked futuristic and medieval at the same time. The tech weighed Mike down with a lead vest. "Too bad I didn't have this on at the park."

The tech smiled absently, having no clue of the kind of morning Mike was having. He took his pictures and wheeled his medical siege weapon away.

Another hour went by until Doctor Gable returned toting a large green folder that contained Mike's ankle, or, at least, the pictures of it. "I'm back, Mr. Daniels. Sorry for the wait, but it's been a bad afternoon. We had a nasty car accident to take care of. Stupid kids—drunk and high all at the same time," the doctor said as she pulled the film out of the folder and held it up to the light. "Yep, just what I thought. Mild sprain. Stay off it and ice it. Take two aspirins and call me in the morning," she said with a smirk.

Mike was not looking at the doctor or the x-rays. His attention had been compromised by the sight of a straggly-haired male teen dressed in a not-entirely-closed hospital gown shuffling aimlessly through the confines of the alcove. The doctor didn't see him until she noticed Mike's complete lack of interest to what she was doing.

"Oh holy cow. Nurse. Nurse. Somebody get over here. Six has gotten out of his restraints. Get over here now!" yelled the doctor.

Mike watched a muscular male nurse throw open the curtain and speak to the teen in a calm, quiet tone. The young man's vacant eyes showed no sign of recognition of the nurse's presence. He did, however, follow the nurse's quiet instructions to go back to his bed. Something about the scene tugged at Mike's analytical sense—something familiar although he couldn't quite place it.

"Sorry, Mr. Daniels. That kid came out of the wreck without a scratch. He's higher than a kite. Too bad everybody else in the car wasn't as lucky. Now, about your film here—mild sprain. Not even enough for crutches, really, but I can get you some if you prefer."

"No. That's fine. How about something for the pain?"

"Take whatever painkiller, aspirin, Tylenol or ibuprofen that suits you if it gives you any trouble. If you think it's real bad, I can prescribe some Tylenol with codeine. Put some ice on it to keep any swelling down. Questions?"

"Then I can go?" asked Mike as his attention focused on the doctor's comments.

"No. Security needs to talk to you."

"Security?"

"Don't ask me. I have a check box here on your discharge that says you need to go through Security before you leave. Anything else?"

"Thanks Doctor, no." Mike stood and winced a bit as his weight settled on his injured ankle. It felt better with each step he took as he followed the doctor out of the ER.

With forms signed and possessions returned, Mike hobbled over to the security desk near the exit and said, "Hi, my name is Mike Daniels. Doctor Gable told me to see you."

The dark-suited security man looked over Mike in his T-shirt and shorts. *He's probably wondering what cat dragged me in off the street.*

The man flipped through some papers on his desk and found Mike's name listed along with another name and a phone number. "A State Policeman wants you to call him as soon as you get home." The security man handed Mike a handwritten sheet of paper with the name, "Trooper Alvin Hoover—555-8532."

Walking out of the ER, Mike came to the unhappy realization that giving Al a call when he got home was going to be tougher than he thought. His car sat back at the lake along with his wallet and credit cards. Not having cab fare, bus fare or enough change to make a call, Mike decided that he needed some help.

The security guard looked up to find that the cat had dragged Mike back into the ER.

"Sorry to bug you, but I need to make a phone call," said Mike to the guard. "A phone call" turned into two phone calls. Mike's first call to Jen netted an apologetic answering machine which Mike asked, "Jen, pick up. Are you there?" She wasn't. The second call proved more fruitful. "John, this is Mike. I'm over in Harrisburg Hospital. Can you give me a ride?"

Twenty minutes later, a Jaguar XKR pulled up under the large awning of the ER's entrance and Mike did a double take when he saw John at the wheel. John did the same when he saw Mike, the walking train wreck, head toward his posh car's leather seats. "Now I know where the blood, sweat and tears of my hard labors go."

"Image. It's all about image. Speaking of image, what the heck happened to you?" asked John.

Mike gave John the short version of what had happened during the morning on the drive back down to Sanford State Park to get Mike's Pontiac.

A short while later, the Jag rolled to a stop short of the stone and dirt parking lot where Mike's car sat.

"That's a heck of a thing, Mike. A heck of a thing. So you have no idea why this guy Musser and his buddies tried to kill you?" asked John.

"I have an idea, but I'm going to keep that to myself until I talk to the police," said Mike.

"All right. You going to be okay?"

"Yea, John. I'll be fine once I get a shower and some rest. Thanks for the ride. Hope the smell comes off the leather."

"See you. Call me if you need anything. If you're not in on Monday, I'll know why," said John as he took out a hanky.

"Thanks, boss. See you later." Mike literally hopped into his Grand Prix and started it up. He watched John as he wiped the passenger seat of the Jag and then held the hanky out the window like it contained toxic waste.

A wave of relief spread through him when he got home and shut the car off. *There is no place like home, no place like home,* he thought as he clicked his running shoes together three times. A return to Kansas was not in store. Upon opening the kitchen door, Mike's mouth flopped open at the sight of open cupboards and abused belongings. The ransacking continued into the living room and all the way upstairs. Mike stepped through the mess, devastated at the state of things. Being shot at was bad enough, but to have his place ransacked just added to his misery. He had no idea where to begin or even if he should begin until the police would arrive. He took a moment and debated calling Al Hoover or just dialing 9-1-1. Getting the local police involved might muddy waters that were muddy enough as it was. *Besides*, he thought, *nobody had been injured here and Al will want to see...Where in the heck is Abby?* "Abby. Abby," screamed Mike as a lump formed in his throat and a leaden feeling descended on his shoulders.

Abby heard the ardent screams from on top of Mike's bed. She immediately jumped down but knew she had been caught red-pawed. Rather than run and hide, she moved to the bedroom door, lowered her ears and prepared to get punished.

Mike tossed debris aside in the den, opened the closet doors and kept yelling for Abby. He feared the worst until he caught sight of her, ears and nose pointed at the floor in a despondent pose. Mike ran at her, overjoyed and pitying all at the same time.

Abby watched Mike run at her and thought that her owner must be extremely upset with her being on the bed. She pointed her nose lower in penance and awaited sentencing.

Mike rushed up the steps and took Abby in his arms. "Thank God you're okay. Thank God."

After their reunion, Mike and Abby surveyed the house together, first in his bedroom and then on to his den. The bedroom was a complete mess with all of his drawers opened and clothes strewn about in much the same manner as the kitchen had been when he walked in. The den was another matter—his computer was missing. The other rooms seemed to have all of his possessions, albeit arranged by an insane interior decorator, but the beige metal case of his computer was nowhere to be found. All of the cables that had met at the back of his machine lay around like the disconnected life support equipment he had seen in the ER. Glancing around to see if anything else was missing, Mike pushed through the clumps of papers, finding knick-knacks and odds and ends. He almost overlooked it—the black plastic shelf where he kept all of his CDs wasn't there. It wasn't that the shelf had been knocked over and contents tossed all over the house. It just plain wasn't there. There weren't any CDs at all—no software, no reference materials, no operating system CDs. Even his collection of free software CDs that he used as drink coasters was gone. Mike surveyed and mentally inventoried the rest of the house, trying not to disturb anything else.

Fumbling through his pocket, Mike found the slip of paper with Al Hoover's name and number on it and reached for the phone. The phone rang before Mike lifted the handset off the cradle.

"Mr. Daniels?"

"Yes. If this is a sales call, you can stick it up your...," said Mike.

"No, Mr. Daniels, it's not a sales call."

"What's that supposed to mean?" asked Mike, who caught an inflection in the voice he didn't necessarily like.

"It means that you have a disk, a CDROM that I want."

A rush of anger washed over Mike as he figured out that whoever destroyed his house and took his PC was now on the phone with him. "You have all of my CDs," yelled Mike.

"Temper, temper, Mr. Daniels," said the voice.

"You have all of my CDs. You have my computer. You can kiss my..."

"I don't want your CD, Mr. Daniels. I want Mr. Renard's CD."

"Oh—so this is what it's all about. Why don't you ask Bill for it?"

"Mr. Renard can't answer that question."

"What does that mean?"

"I take it that you haven't listened to the local news. Mr. Renard had an accident last night. Something to do with a deer, I believe. He told us, before the accident, that you had his CD."

Mike felt a squeeze like the air cast surround him all over again. *What happened to Bill*, he thought. *CD—what CD? His book? That CD?*

The voice continued, "Mr. Daniels. We know you have Mr. Renard's CD. Please bring it to..."

"How about I bring it to the police and they can figure out just who this is and why that disk is so important to you," countered Mike.

"How about you bring me the disk, and you will avoid Mr. Renard's fate?"

"No, I like the police idea much better. Especially with all of the dead guys showing up all over Sanford Park."

"Then I would encourage you to think not only of yourself but of the lovely Ms. Stevens," said the voice like a poker player laying down four aces.

Mike went silent. A knot in his stomach added to the squeeze.

"I take it by your silence that you are considering my offer. Bring the disk to the State Game Lands at the north end of Sanford State Park—the shooting range—noon tomorrow. Say nothing to the police or the press. Come dressed in those awful running clothes of yours so that we can tell you're not concealing anything. Do you understand?"

Mike let his silence carry on a moment longer and finally said, "Yes."

"No surprises, Mr. Daniels, or Ms. Stevens and you won't have to worry about work on Monday. Tomorrow at noon."

The voice on the phone hung up without waiting for a goodbye, not that Mike would have offered one. He was too busy trying to unravel the knot in his gut, and far worse, remember where he put Bill's CD. *Surely*, he thought, *it has to be with all of the CDs they stole. There wasn't a single one of them upstairs.* "No, the CD wasn't up there or they wouldn't have bothered to call and threaten me," he said to Abby, who nosed around her dish the way she always did when she wanted dinner.

The phone rang again and Mike steeled himself for more instructions from the mystery man on the end of the line.

"Daniels?"

"Yes," answered Mike.

"Trooper Al Hoover here. Glad to hear that you're safe and sound at home. I need to get your statement right away. Things are all screwed up with the ambulances splitting up and all that. I'm down here at Exeter Central and I'll be up there as soon as I'm done here."

Caught off guard by Al's statement, Mike knew that the previous caller wouldn't like the idea of him meeting with Al. Mike resorted to adlibbing. "Al? Al Hoover? Um, er, Hal did you say?" Mike said with a spacey tone.

"Trooper Al Hoover—State Police. Remember me?"

"Yea, uh-huh. Yea, Al Hopper. Sorry, I'm really beat and they put me on this codeine stuff. Sorry, I'm kinda in and out right now if you know what I mean." Mike hoped that the statement of somebody under the influence of a mild narcotic would put off Hoover.

"Painkiller eh? Dang. I need to get your statement. Can I come by later today and speak with you after you've had a chance to rest?"

"Sure, sure, Hal. C'mon by anytime after noon. Hey, how's Tony?"

"The rifled slug that hit him almost put him away, but he's as strong as a moose. If you hadn't stuffed that wad of toilet paper in the hole, we'd be burying him for sure. Sorry I missed you at the hospital, but we figured you both would be down Exeter way. Stupid diverts. Look, I gotta go. I'll see you later. Stop taking the codeine, okay? I'd hate to bust you. Heh heh."

"Sure, Al. No more drugs. Gotcha. See you later." A warm rush of pride pushed back against the knots and tension pushing in on Mike. A "wad of toilet paper"—a stupid wad of toilet paper had saved a man's life. The weight returned an instant later with the thought about Bill Renard.

Mike watched Abby's head resting on her paws in front of her dish. He misjudged her body language and thought that she was sympathizing with him. "It'll be okay, girl. Now, where is that CD?" He said. Closing his eyes, Mike thought back to the early morning when he had last used his computer. He could see himself carrying the jewel case down the stairs, then preparing to leave for his run. The problem was that he couldn't see where the jewel case went after that. Then it came to him—*my running bag*. It sat on the kitchen table where he had placed it after seeing the chaotic state of his house. Mike pulled each item out and set it on the table, then went through it all again. *The CD isn't in here*. He closed his eyes again and, for the life of him, couldn't remember where it went after he brought it downstairs. It had to be somewhere in the mess that was his house.

Abby stood up, circled to the side of her dish and thumped her tail down. Mike heard Abby's thump and realized that it was way past her usual suppertime. "Sorry Ab, let's get you some supper," said Mike as he raised the dish. His fingers pushed against something plastic and foreign under the bowl. There, underneath the dish, lay a CD jewel case. He snapped it up and opened it, looking at the two CDs inside. After looking at the CDs, Mike realized that he had a dilemma. He wanted to see what was so important on Bill's disk but his PC had departed to places unknown.

Mike thoughts raced about whom to call, where to go and what to do. *Maybe I should just grab Jen and run. Maybe I should just sit and wait for Al to show up. None of this sounds right. Things have been totally screwed up ever since I found Bennie Carlson. I should call Al and have the police meet the person on the phone. If they showed up, then I'll be living in fear every day until the police bother to catch the person—and that was a big if. No—no living in fear. Bill Renard lived in fear for thirty years. See where it's gotten him? No. No running—at least not running in fear. It's time to run at this one, not away.* Mike picked up the phone and made a call.

Fishing through the piles of stuff on the floor in the kitchen, Mike managed to find three of his electronic timers. He went through the house plugging lamps into the timers and setting them at intervals to pretend he was switching lights off in different rooms of the house. Next, he keyed the TV remote and set the Sleep Mode for an odd number of minutes that fell just short of when the living room light planned on shutting off. With that mission accomplished, he grabbed a clean set of clothes and a set of running clothes for tomorrow's appointment. After gathering some toiletries, Mike shoved the whole mess into his running bag. Finally, he found Abby sleeping near his bed and snapped a leash onto her collar.

Mike hefted Abby over the chain link fence that bordered his backyard. Five minutes later, the pair stood at the corner of 19th and Wharton Street waiting for John's arrival. Abby was exhausted from the two-block walk.

John's Jaguar cruised down the street, seeking its riders until Mike waved at the oncoming car. John hit the power window button and said to the waiting man and dog, "You know, I feel like I'm picking up a gay lover and his pooch for a little rendezvous."

Mike covered Abby's ears and replied, "Would it pay more than you're paying me now?"

Ten minutes passed as Mike explained how his house looked and the phone call he had received.

"So, we're going to the police?" asked John.

"No. Not yet, anyway. I shouldn't have told you a thing either. I need to find out some stuff first. What I need is your key to the office and your car."

"My car?" protested John.

Chapter 23

The hot shower at Bleeding Edge had been mostly a blessing except for the painful stings renewed each time the soap seeped into Mike's broken skin. The salt imbedded in the wounds added insult to his injuries. *At least the pain was temporary*, Mike thought as his mind wandered to those in greater pain—Tony and Bill. Mike leaned his head against the tile while the shower poured down upon him and thought, *I can remember talking to Bill yesterday. What happened?*

The faucets shut with a defiant screech. Mike left the shower behind to get dressed and order a pizza. Once the pizza arrived, he returned to his second floor office to find Abby seated nearby, hoping for a handout. Both man and dog ate their fill as Mike fired up his office computer and loaded Bill's manuscript.

While the CD loaded, Mike surfed the *Harrisburg Post*'s web page for news on Bill's accident. "They must've missed the deadline, Abby," Mike said to the now dozing pup. On he keyed until he pulled up the WBWY web page and read the short article.

> A Harrisburg man remains in critical condition at Exeter Central Hospital following a collision with a deer last evening along Valley Road in Muir Springs. The driver, William Renard of the 600 block of Third Street in Harrisburg, was rushed to the hospital after firefighters freed him from his automobile.

Of course, reading about Bill's accident might have been a whole lot easier if WBWY hadn't allowed the half-dozen or so pop-up advertisements to crowd up the screen. Each advertisement disappeared with a click of the mouse. The screen now clean, Mike read the small blurb about his day in the park.

> Police in Cummington Township reported a quadruple homicide at Sanford State Park in Muir County today. The bodies of four men were taken away by the Muir County Coroner for examination. The coroner later identified three of the deceased as Roy Graves of Durham Township, James Straub of Exeter, and Craig Arnold of Hereford. State Police declined to comment on the identity of the other deceased individual, saying that the case was "pending further investigation."

"So, those are the killers, Abby," said Mike to the very asleep pooch. Abby's slumber looked like just the ticket to Mike as food and stress seduced him toward just a little nap. Instead of sleeping, he strolled out to the office kitchen and made a strong pot of coffee. He wasn't sure if he'd need it the way his heart surged every time he thought about the events of the morning and of Bill's accident. Shaking his head, he forced himself to take a breath while chanting a mantra of "Think. C'mon, think."

With a cup of coffee in tow, Mike returned to his desk. The CD had finished loading all of its files onto his hard drive and he was ready to begin. *Being ready to begin and knowing where to begin are two different things*, Mike thought. He opted to take a look at the spreadsheet he had saved as a cross reference just a few days before. His review proved mind numbing—it was nothing new. The fact of the matter was that every fact might matter—or not. *It's like being in the forest and not seeing the trees,* he thought. Instead he resorted to searching Bill's CD for clues.

His first search centered on the name "Brenda Stabler," since that was what he had told Bill the day before. A list of files materialized that he had skimmed over before. One of the files contained the picture of Clayton Edwards standing alongside Brenda at the party. The next happened to be the previous year's outing showing Stabler standing with Houser alongside a lawyer named Truman Dunn. *So many names*, thought Mike. The thought of so many people being involved along the way troubled Mike. He needed a way to thin things down and organize his thoughts. An idea came to him a moment later—the whiteboard.

After Mike raided the conference room, the whiteboard stood in his office—a stark, bleached rectangle against a sea of beige drywall like an office dweller's Rothko. The board soon listed as many people as Mike could remember since the day he saw Stabler, Edwards, and Bennie Carlson's feet at Sanford. He drew a circle around each name and then started connecting each name to any other name where a relationship occurred. When it was all said and done, the whiteboard resembled a confused chemistry diagram of protons, neutrons and electrons. The diagrams also showed him about what he expected. A little more study and Mike picked up on the amount of lines connecting Brenda Stabler to names like Carlson, Houser, Edwards and Daniels. The marker paused over the name Musser and how he should connect the dead ranger to Bennie Carlson. Mike settled on a dashed red line to Bennie's name.

When Mike returned to his computer, he noticed the throbbing icon of an envelope expanding and contracting on the bottom of his screen. He decided to allow himself a slight diversion to check the office mail and return to connecting the dots. Most of the mail proved to be the usual batch of office memos, jokes and junk. One by one, he deleted the spam offering such things as lower mortgage rates, stock tips, and travel offers. "Hey Abby, did you know that you can increase penis size and enlarge your breasts at the same time? I should send this to Monica," said Mike as he forwarded the message to his ex. "She wouldn't need her new husband."

Twelve messages went into the electronic trash can until he came across an email that looked like real correspondence. The problem was that he didn't know the name "Brenard" from a hole in the ground. "Brenard...Brenard. Abby, do we know a 'Brenard'?" Mike said to Abby. Mike watched Abby remain motionless on the floor. "Thought so," said Mike, mousing his way up to the "Delete" key. His finger hovered over the "Delete" as the name finally sunk in. "Brenard" was "B. Renard—Bill Renard," and Mike pushed the mouse away. Brenard@HbgPost.com showed in the address window with the subject "Research." Mike's hair stood on end as he checked the date and time—April 26th 16:15:33. *4:15 p.m. yesterday,* thought Mike as he opened Bill's email and read what short sentences appeared. The icon of a paperclip hung in the upper right of the email telling Mike that Bill sent an attached file.

"Hey. Got a list of Johnson Land Management scholarship recipients. Have some fun and match them up with my research. Give me a call on Monday and tell me what you found. CYA."

"No, you won't, Bill. No, you won't," replied Mike. The attachment spilled onto the screen in a haphazard manner. It looked to Mike as though the text had been cut and pasted from a wide variety of sources. Most were high school newsletters. Some were from college publications and others were just lines of typed text. The one thing that coupled all of them together was that each news item listed a name as the winner of a particular year's Johnson Land Management Political Science Scholarship. The first two names had no meaning to Mike as he passed each one by, although he recognized one of the schools listed. The third name, on the other hand, did—Daryl Musser—Salem High School Class of 1999. "Oh my God," said Mike. Bill's list now had his full attention. He followed more unknown names down the page until he hit a section cut from a Richmond area high school paper.

It doesn't look like her really, Mike thought. *Then again*, he conceded, *nobody's senior picture looked the way they did fifteen years later, especially when they are burying a body in a state park.* There, on the monitor, stood a happy Brenda Stabler receiving the 1987 Johnson Land Management Scholarship for Political Science from her high school principal.

Mike hustled over, in spite of his tender ankle, and wrote "Johnson Land Management" on the whiteboard, connecting lines to Musser's and Stabler's names. Mike stood back and looked at the new connections as he tried to remember what Bill had told him about the company. It came to him a second later when he remembered talking to Bill about Houser's lawyer, *Truman Dunn, running Johnson Land Management*. Mike drew a line from Johnson Land to Dunn. More names followed Stabler's, and Mike had to pull the scroll bar to see them all come into view. As before, none were familiar except that a large portion of the names were from high schools and colleges in Muir County. One last pull of the scroll bar and a final name appeared in the same kind of plain text that Daryl Musser's name had appeared—Samuel Houser 1972 Recipient of the Johnson Land Management Scholarship for Political Science. "Twenty-seven names, eh? What do you think the odds are, Abby, that I'd know even one out of twenty-seven names on a list of scholarship winners that spans thirty years from places I haven't ever heard of?" Abby made no response, and Mike figured that she was too far under the influence of pepperoni to answer his question.

A line was connected from Houser's name to both Brenda Stabler and Johnson Land. "I'm beginning to see a pattern, Abby," said Mike. The problem was that he didn't know what the pattern meant. Rather than dwelling on it, Mike took the remaining names on the list and started searching Bill's CDs for any reference. Three-quarters of the names Mike searched on Bill's CD turned up nothing more than a scanned image of a deed recorded in Muir County and authored by various people employed at Johnson Land. The remaining seven names turned up varying amounts of files—some with real estate transactions brokered by Johnson Land while others were named in court cases defended by Truman Dunn's law firm. What piqued Mike's curiosity was that most of the names listed on the court cases were involved with affirmative action and civil rights lawsuits. Clients represented by Clayton Edwards brought all of the lawsuits. "The plot thickens, Abby," said Mike as Abby shifted her sleeping position to orient her tail toward her owner.

Mike glanced through the legalese of the court documents, understanding very little. Fortunately, the articles scanned from the Exeter newspaper told him that Dunn's clients usually lost. The last name Mike came across, Dean Ebersole, turned up the only criminal case that Truman Dunn represented. Both Dean Ebersole and Roy Graves were being prosecuted for criminal mischief for arson—the arson of an African Methodist Episcopal Church during the summer of 1973. "Both men were acquitted in a jury of their peers," said the accompanying scan of a newspaper article from later that year. The criminal case was different from Dunn's civil actions and it seemed out of place to Mike. Something about the case tugged at him though he couldn't quite place what it was that bugged him. He read the names "Ebersole" and "Graves" over and over until it finally set in—Graves. Mike went back down the list of names that Bill had sent but didn't see Roy Graves. "No, it wasn't on the list. Where did I see his name? Yes, yes, on the WBWY site," Mike thought out loud. Several mouse clicks later, he was back on the WBWY site reading the news brief. "...identified the deceased as Roy Graves and..."

Adding all of the names from Bill's list to the now-crowded whiteboard, Mike connected each one to either Johnson Land or Truman Dunn. He had thought that all of the connections were going to lead to Brenda Stabler, but he now knew just how wrong that was. All of the lines were leading to Johnson Land and Truman Dunn.

Returning to Bill's CD, Mike searched for the name "Graves" and turned up seven files. The first file turned out to be the same file he had found when he searched out Ebersole's name. It was also the most recent. Next in line came a deed for a property Graves purchased in Exeter dated March 4, 1965. "Gee, imagine that, Abby. Johnson Land handled the transfer." A scan of a newspaper advertisement for Graves' Auto Parts followed and was dated a month later. Mike selected the next file and tried to read the federal form gobbledygook—something to do with disaster funding and dated during the fall of 1969. Mike left that one behind and scoped the next file. It was another court document having to do with a class action suit brought by six people, including Graves and represented by Dunn's firm. Mike read the form and found that those six people were holding the county and city responsible for negligence in the loss of their property. The sixth file was another Exeter paper's short article on the victory of the six litigants and their large settlement from the case. One last document turned out to be another deed, brokered by Johnson Land, for some acreage in Durham Township.

Mike mulled over all of the data that had passed before him, and he wasn't sure whether the concentration or the caffeine was making his head spin. The whiteboard quit looking like a diagram of molecules and now looked more like the musings of a disturbed physicist. He closed his eyes hoping that he would wake up and realize that the whole thing had been a nightmare. The words "tomorrow at noon," roused him from his near-nap and his heart started thumping against his chest.

Mike settled down and looked again at the whiteboard. "It's not what I'm seeing—it's what I'm not seeing." Realizing that the crux of the matter wasn't all the connections leading to Johnson Land. It was the lack of connections leading to Edwards. There were four connections leading to Edwards—Carlson, Stabler, Johnson Land and Daniels. Both Carlson and himself had no other connection to Edwards other than Carlson's murder. Stabler, on the other hand, was connected to a variety of people on the board. Johnson Land, and its owner, Truman Dunn, seemed to be connected to everybody.

It was almost funny to Mike how much he had been absorbed by all of the other details and how he had forgotten about the man crying at the side of Carlson's grave. He thought about his eloquence at the courthouse and the way he was led away to prison. Then Mike thought about the aftermath and his confrontation with Ellie Edwards.

"Just leave us alone now. You got that?" screamed Ellie, inches away from Mike's very surprised face.

Mike remembered her anger and his complete cluelessness. *What in the world did she mean when she said that?* Mike wondered. A reason crept into his mind as he shook his head in the affirmative.

"Tomorrow at noon," said the voice welling up in the back of Mike's mind. Mike rested his head on his hand and thought about what Ellie said. It clarified some things and muddied up others. His concentration waned against the need for sleep, and he soon found himself dazed and confused.

* * *

The morning sun shone down on him, and he attempted to block its brightness with his hand. His hand wouldn't respond as it was pinned under something heavy. Thunk. Mike felt the weight of the stone being placed on top of him. Moving his head, he could see Clayton Edwards reaching for another rock to add to the pile that he was under. Brenda Stabler stood nearby showing him which rock to pick up and where to put it. Standing at the wall stood Sam Houser and Truman Dunn, both in three-piece suits, filling out forms and throwing them at him. The sound of stacking rocks stopped and he found himself alone in the woods, seeing sunlight through the cracks in the stones above him. He could feel wetness on his exposed foot.

It wasn't rain or water, it had a slimy feel—a feeling like some animal was licking it. Mike twitched violently to chase the animal away but it returned again and again. He allowed his eyes to close from the sun and let the darkness surround him.

Mike woke in a cold sweat as his nightmare subsided into waking. He found Abby licking his foot. Harsh sunlight flooded into the office and spotlighted him through the slats of Venetian blinds. He shook off the awful dream and bent to pet Abby. That proved to be difficult because his arm had fallen asleep when it got pinned between his body and his chair. He glanced at the clock when all the reasons he had slept there in the first place came surging back—6:47.

Mike slipped on some shoes and took Abby for a quick walk. Getting her a meal was another problem. He hadn't brought any dog food with him, so he took a sprint across the street to a convenience store for a small box of her favorite kibbles along with a bagel and a copy of the *Sunday Post*.

The front page of the local section told the story of Bill's accident, complete with pictures and commentary by his peers. A small map on the page put an arrow on the spot near Muir Springs where the crash had occurred. Mike closed his eyes and wished he was able to make sense out of everything he had seen. Looking again at the paper, Mike stared at the town name of Muir Springs. The town name stuck with him until he sifted Bill's research once again and found a deed made out to Truman Dunn for property listed as 737 Valley Road, Muir Springs.

Mike brought up a mapping program, gave it the street address of Bill's accident, and typed in the location of the Dunn property. Five-tenths of a mile separated the two locations. "Bill was out there Friday, Abby," said Mike.

A flurry of thoughts raced through Mike's mind. *Why would Bill be out there? Bill's book—but Bill's book was nothing but a dry narrative of the Exeter race riots. Dunn wasn't in Bill's book. No, he wasn't, but Bill researched the heck out of him. So Bill has a near-death experience with a deer and I just about got my behind shot off. Coincidence—I don't think so. Somebody doesn't want the book published. So why was Bill out there? He got excited when I told him about Johnson Land—Johnson Land is owned by Truman Dunn— the same guy whose property is less than a mile from where Bill supposedly wrecked. So why does the guy on the phone want Bill's CD? Oh crap. Bill always carted his research around with him—and he put my name on the manuscript folder at the park.*

Mike's thoughts distilled into keystrokes as his fingers tapped and clicked their way into Bill's manuscript. To his disappointment, nothing jumped out at him. There were no connections to Dunn or Stabler or Edwards in Bill's book. One by one, he closed the open files until he was left with a faded photo of an aproned grocer and his wife—Vince Garmon. It was the same man that Bill told him was going to go to the FBI. Both figures posed in front of a big banner proclaiming a Grand Opening. He almost missed the sign on the store next door to the grocer because its name was partially obstructed— "...raves' Auto Parts." "Graves' Auto Parts," said Mike.

Considering that both stores were next-door neighbors and would soon be next-door embers, Mike went back through the files that Roy Graves was involved with. One by one, he looked for anything to tie them together and found nothing. Mike found his way through the court documents that Graves had been a part of when it hit him. The further he delved into the class action suit, the more he realized that Garmon wasn't mentioned, and the grocer's absence seemed odd. Mike ran back through the files looking for documents from the same time frame and found land deals by Dunn, Graves and Ebersole, all within a year of the suit. All three had purchased sizeable properties, with Dunn's acreage easily being the largest. Mike rocked back in his chair as the past came into focus. He knew what led Bill down there, and to his accident. *The same thing is going to get me killed around noon today,* he thought. Looking at the convoluted lines on the whiteboard, Mike traced an imaginary line from Johnson Land through Brenda Stabler to Clayton Edwards and onto his own name. "Yes. Stabler. How do I...," murmured Mike until an idea came to mind.

"Wake up. Come on, sleepyhead, wake up," Mike said to the ringing phone.

"Um, hel...lo," answered a groggy Jen Stevens.

"Jen, this is Mike. I need a huge favor."

"Do you know what time it is?"

"10:02. I need you to do something for me."

"Okay, call me later and I'll..."

"No, Jen. I need you to do it now."

"What? Oh, lemme go back to sleep and then we..."

"Jen. This is life or death and I am not kidding."

"What?" said Jen, now quite awake.

"I need a copy of Brenda Stabler's application. I need it now."

"I told you, I can't do that. I could get fired," protested Jen.

"Jen, there are worse things than being fired. If you don't think so, ask Bill Renard."

"Bill hit a deer."

"Bill's in intensive care. I'm going to end up like Bill, or worse, unless I find out enough to stay alive."

"What are you talking about?"

"Just listen to me. Get dressed, go to work, fax me at the office with her app and stay there until I call you. If I don't call by 3:00 p.m., call the police and stay with them. You got that?"

"But I don't..."

"Jen, just listen to me. Fax me the app and stay there. I don't want you hurt," pleaded Mike. He hung up the phone and headed into the bathroom to get cleaned up. He paced the floor for a half-hour until Jen called.

"I'm here and I've got it. What's the fax number there?"

"555-3948 and thanks," said Mike.

"Are you going to tell me what's..."

"No. Right now, I wish I didn't know what I know, and I don't have enough time to explain it all. Remember, if I don't call you by 3:00 p.m., call the police."

The fax machine at Judy's desk rang and the fax rolled out to the accompaniment of electronic gargling. Mike's eyes danced from box to box of information. None of the demographic information seemed useful and he tossed the page aside, waiting for the next page to arrive. Stabler's work history appeared next. Each job of her life appeared on the page all the way back to her days in a shoe store in

Richmond. Each box listed the company name, address and immediate supervisor. Mike started reading the page again and focusing more on each tidbit in front of him. A name came into view three-quarters of the page down in the box marked "Immediate Supervisor" for her stint at the Muir County Commissioners. The name was "Houser, Sam."

It took a few seconds for "Houser, Sam" to sink in but sink in it did. There were too many connections to ignore, but still not enough to figure out how Edwards was involved. It just didn't fit, and Mike knew time was running out. He started to close down all of the open windows on his PC. Each screen disappeared with a click of the little "x" in the upper right corner. An annoying Internet pop-up ad declaring a cheap source for penis enlarging drugs came into view for the deletion. The ad also said that it was a great source for all sorts of other bargain pharmaceuticals that would attract women or render them senseless enough to want to date a person that would buy cheap penis enlarging drugs over the Internet. Mike ran the mouse up and got ready to get rid of it when he thought of the kid that wandered around the emergency room, tanked up on coke or Ecstasy. The image hung in his mind, and he clicked on the ad rather than deleting it.

The ad took Mike to a site that looked far more dubious than he thought possible. All manner of drugs, herbs and weird concoctions were available. What caught his eye were the drugs available to get a date in the mood. All of the items available proclaimed their legality in every state except Rhode Island and touted that they contained no Rohypnol or GHB. Mike had seen Rohypnol somewhere before, and it caught his eye. He searched the web and found its better-known nickname: Roofies—the date rape drug. "Now, I get it," Mike said to Abby, who wasn't getting anything except forty winks. He wanted to pursue the drug information more until the clock added another minute to 10:50 a.m.

Mike paced around the office trying to think of what he should do next. *Going to the police seems like the best idea, but I don't want death threats for the rest of my life. Besides, who would take care of Abby?* Time eroded away in useless thoughts until it was time to go. He reached down into his desk drawer and fumbled around for his keys. In doing so, he pushed his cell phone and interview case into view. He stood motionless, looking at the case as an idea took shape.

"John, Mike here."

"How is my car?" replied John Weaverton.

"It's fine. I need a favor."

"You have my car. What more do you want, my wife?"

"Does your cell phone have three-way calling?"

"Yep, so?"

"I need you to connect me up with a three-way call around noon today. John, I really need this favor."

John didn't like the tone of Mike's voice and asked, "Does this have anything to do with yesterday?"

"It has everything to do with yesterday. John, please, no questions. Just connect me with the number I give you, okay?" Mike slipped the office gear into his sports bag and then searched for the first page of Jen's fax. On his way out the door, Mike spied a row of phone books behind Judy's desk and hunted down the Exeter directory. He fanned the pages until he located the number he wanted, copied it on the back of the fax and hustled out the door. Ten seconds later, the office door burst open again and Mike yelled, "C'mon, Abby." Within a few minutes, Abby sat in the passenger seat of John's Jag looking like a dog of leisure.

Mike parked the Jag out of sight and ushered Abby into his still-wrecked house the way they left the previous evening. Cupping Abby's muzzle in his hand, Mike gave his dog a pat on the head. "I'll see you later, girl—I hope."

* * *

Abby wasn't entirely sure what she sensed from her owner, although she was sure that she didn't like it. The odor was part fear, part adrenaline and part nervousness. It reminded her of the way some of the dogs smelled when she was at the veterinarian—especially the ones she never saw or smelled again. With that thought, her ears drooped and her tail lowered as she made her way out of the kitchen. She looked at the steps leading up to her owner's bed and sighed.

Instead of going upstairs, she made her way over to the couch and curled up at the spot where her owner usually put his feet. The aroma of him was strongest there. It gave her a bit of comfort as she spun around and faced the door, awaiting his return.

Chapter 24

The dashboard's neon clock shaved another minute away from Mike's life, or so he thought. Only five minutes remained until his rendezvous with whoever made the call yesterday. Mike didn't need a lot of imagination as to who made the call. He knew who it was.

"John? This is Mike," said Mike on his cell phone.

"Edna's Pizza," replied John.

"Not funny, boss," said Mike.

"How's my car?"

"The Jag is around the corner from my house."

"Are you going to tell me where you are?"

"No. You'll know where I am if I don't show up for work tomorrow—just read the papers. Please, just call that number I gave you about ten minutes from now and hook my phone into the three-way."

"All right. Are you sure you don't want me to call the cops?"

"Just call the number, boss, please?"

The Game Lands parking lot stood empty except for a hulking black Ford Excursion. One man sat at an oddly shaped picnic table peering at a distant target on the range through the scope of a heavy-barreled rifle. The man's head turned toward Mike's car as it pulled into the gravel-covered lot and rolled to a stop.

"Mr. Dunn, I presume?" asked Mike as he left the Pontiac and thumbed the remote to lock his car.

"Mr. Daniels," answered Truman Dunn, who gently squeezed the trigger on the rifle, sending a tha-wump through the air.

"Pretty clever of you to invite me to a shooting range. I mean, who's going to question hearing gunfire out here? Do you want me to hand you the disk or just fling it into the air when you yell, 'pull'?"

"Come closer and turn around."

Mike obliged and felt a hand rummaging around his body. He caught a glimpse of elderly fingers appearing from time to time between his legs and wondered how he'd explain something like that to Jen.

"I'm glad to see that you're not wired," said Truman, waving at a grove of trees across the parking lot.

Mike saw movement at the base of one of the trees as a woman rose from the turf, toting another scoped rifle. She came near and Mike greeted her. "Good afternoon, Ms. Stabler. It's nice to meet you—formally," said Mike to an ignoring Brenda.

"He's clean, Brenda. Wait over in the truck. This won't take long," said Dunn.

"I think she looked better in the party dress," said Mike.

"Don't make small talk, Mr. Daniels. I'd like the disk now."

Mike walked over to the shooting table. His hands fumbled for a pocket to put his keys into, and, having none in his running shorts, he decided to toss his keys on the table next to Dunn. Mike waved the CD in the air.

"Just set it down and start walking toward the end of the target range. Once you get to the end, wait five minutes and then you may leave," ordered Dunn.

"And if I don't? Do I get a deer in my windshield?"

Truman opened the bolt, and laid another cartridge in the action, saying, "Nobody autopsies a deer, Mr. Daniels—even ones that reporters run into."

"That's about as clever as the turkey shoot you organized. Did you think a coroner would overlook a bullet in my chest?"

"Yes, Mr. Daniels, they would—especially if a park ranger reported the accidental shooting of a jogger that didn't know enough to stay out of the forest during gobbler season."

"Trail runner," corrected Mike.

"Trail runner?"

"Yes, trail runner. Jogging went out of style in the '70's—probably ten years after you went out of style, Mr. Dunn."

"Get going, smart ass."

"Or what? Don't you get tired of leaving bodies all over the woods?"

"No one will look for a body in the berm behind a target range. It always looks dug up," replied Dunn as he slapped the bolt down.

"Point taken, Mr. Dunn," said Mike, who started walking away from the table. Five steps later, he heard the rifle's safety click off. Rather than moving another inch, Mike turned and faced Truman.

"So that's it, no explanation?" asked Mike.

Dunn peered into his scope and shouldered the weapon, yelling, "Walk."

Mike didn't budge. He knew what Truman wanted—*a distant kill. Nothing personal—no face to remember or guilt to associate.* "You'll have to shoot me right here. Right here, where you have to look me in the eye and pull the trigger."

"I said walk," yelled Truman again.

"Tell me, Mr. Dunn, what's it like to actually see the face of the person you're about to kill?"

"There won't be a third time."

"How can you be sure that things won't come back to haunt you?" said Mike, who caught the subtle change in Dunn's mood. "Things like Exeter in the sixties. Things like Clayton Edwards. Things like me?"

Truman's eye moved away from the reticule as he sized up Mike's comment. "What's that supposed to mean, Mr. Daniels?"

"Things like me? In my case, a dead man can tell a tale."

"Just get walking, Mr. Daniels," ordered Dunn.

Mike focused on his bluff. He hadn't had the time to print off or create a copy of Bill's CD. Still, what did a sixty-something lawyer know about computers and email? "I've emailed the contents of Bill's disk to an address that only I know. In three days, the contents of that email get automatically forwarded to the police—unless I change the date," said Mike.

"That's bullshit and you know it."

Mike inwardly blanched at Truman's comment. *How could he know that?* he thought, and decided to stick with his story. "Pull the trigger and see how much bull I can shovel, Mr. Dunn."

"How about I shoot your girlfriend instead?" threatened Dunn.

"How about I don't change the date?" countered Mike.

Truman thumbed the safety back on and pushed the stock aside. "Then we're at an impasse, Mr. Daniels."

"Yes, we are. You know what's funny, Mr. Dunn?" asked Mike.

"What's funny, Mr. Daniels?"

"That you're about to put a bullet in my back for Bill Renard's book."

"So?"

"The funny part is that it isn't just about the book, is it, Mr. Dunn?" Mike could see Dunn's thin colorless lips straighten into the closest thing to a smile the man could probably make. "It's about Bennie Carlson and Clayton Edwards, isn't it?"

Truman said nothing and smiled the coldest smile Mike had ever seen.

"Clayton Edwards didn't hit Carlson, did he?" asked Mike.

"You're too smart for you own good, Mr. Daniels," said Dunn.

Mike knew he was on the right track. Over Truman's shoulder, he could see Brenda Stabler looking down and fumbling with something in the truck cab. His watch read 12:10—*show time*. "Was it Rohypnol or GHB?" asked Mike.

"How did you...Get walking, now," ordered Dunn anew.

"Edwards supposedly got roaring drunk at the party. He's a large man. That would have meant that he arrived drunk or pounded down drinks at the party. When Bill saw him, he was gone already. By the time I saw him at the park, he was all sleepy-eyed and doing everything that Brenda, over there, told him to do. Heck, I'm willing to bet that she shuffled him off to the hotel room to keep him awake. Both drugs bowl you over on the first drink and then you want to sleep like a baby. Those drugs also leave you open to suggestion. You'll do things you'd never ever want to do if you're on that stuff. So which one was it, Rohypnol or GHB?"

"Does it matter?" said Dunn.

"I bet it matters to Stabler over there in the truck. She had to dose him and shepherd him. I bet she drove to the corner so you could load up Carlson's body. Then she wakes up Edwards and tells him he hit the poor drifter. The police get their evidence from the back of Edwards' Blazer. Funny how there wasn't any sign of impact on the outside. You had to really relish the whole thing when he confessed and kept her out of jail."

"That was the best part, Mr. Daniels. Why didn't you tell the police?"

"Because I didn't know it till yesterday. It's funny how the sun reflects light at dawn, Mr. Dunn. I kept seeing something wrong from the get-go, but I just didn't get it. When I did see it, I knew Musser had to be involved. How else would a brand-new ranger know where the body was when I gave him the wrong place to check? There's a bunch of old farm walls in the park and he goes right to Carlson's body—like he knew where it was. I told him 'southwest.' I was wrong. Carlson was buried on the southeast side. I remember Tony calling him a rookie. No rookie could be that lucky."

"Which means that you have nothing but supposition, Mr. Daniels. Walk—I won't ask again."

"I don't need supposition, Mr. Dunn, I have Johnson Land Management."

Mike's words changed the smiling indifference on Truman's face to a darkening frown.

"What's the matter, Truman, did I say something wrong? Actually, I wrote it in that email I told you about, so I'm not taking a walk," said Mike.

"Then I'll shoot you right now," hissed Dunn.

"Is that what you're going to do to Stabler? She's the last one that knows about your scheme. Too bad the blackmail part didn't work."

Truman's face passed from red to ruddy.

"You had already called Edwards, hadn't you? Musser didn't get to tell you what happened because he had to stay with Tony and do paperwork. He probably didn't warn you until it was too late, right? You know, I spoke with Ellie Edwards a while back. She said that somebody told her husband to 'play ball.' I bet you couldn't wait to turn the screws on him. Then Musser calls you and tells you that I hosed everything up."

"You know too much..."

"That's really what this has been about all along, hasn't it? Not just now, but thirty years ago. Man, when I read who's gotten started and helped along the way by Johnson Land Management—your Johnson Land Management—I got the picture. You wanted Edwards in your hip pocket so you could control him. What better man to have under your thumb than the guy you've been losing to—and a black man to boot. That must really chafe your behind."

"You chafe my ass, Mr. Daniels," said Truman.

"Temper, temper Mr. Dunn. All of your secrets are safe with me."

"All of my...?" questioned Dunn.

"Does Stabler know you—I mean, the real you?" asked Mike, looking over Dunn toward the Ford.

"What's that supposed to mean?"

"Does she know how deep she's in? Does she know that you've killed before just to keep people quiet? Does she know that Musser and Graves are dead? Does she know that she'll be next if she doesn't mind her P's and Q's? Does she know about Vince Garmon and Bill Renard?" said Mike as he waited to see how his guess affected Dunn.

"Garmon was killed by a black robber during..."

"...Now we both know that's not true, Mr. Dunn. That's the part of Bill's book that has you running scared, isn't it?" taunted Mike, who knew that Renard's book only reported the facts. Watching Dunn's growing anger, Mike knew that his hunch was dead-on. He wished that Bill could be here to see Dunn sweating bullets instead of shooting them. "We both know that you had him killed because he was going to tell the FBI about the little house fire you were planning."

"Damn Renard. I should have killed him when I stuffed that gun in his mouth."

Mike watched Dunn's simmering anger explode into a white rage and felt it was the color of rage that suited him. "What's the matter, Truman, afraid that Bill figured out just how much money you made on that deal? Is that why he had his accident? Heck, you got federal money, insurance money, and then turned around and sued the city just like you're doing now. All you had to do was kill one guy who didn't think it was right—and you've been killing ever since. I gotta hand it to you, Truman, you've got the biggest set of balls I've ever seen."

"You wish your balls were this big. Now walk and I'll make it quick. Screw around any more and I'll start at your ankles and work my way up," threatened Dunn.

"Just make sure you save one bullet for Stabler over there. God knows you won't shield her the way Edwards did. She's the last one that can tie you to it—after me," said Mike as he focused on Stabler's silhouette. "You'll have to kill her just so she won't turn state's evidence on you."

"Walk!" screamed Truman.

Mike stood still for a moment, staring at the windshield of the Ford. He started walking, waiting for the crack of a rifle and a voice guiding him to go to the light. The voice arrived before the bullet.

"Put it down, Truman. Put it down, now," ordered Brenda Stabler as she pointed her rifle at Truman's head from inches away.

"What in the hell...Get back in the truck, Brenda."

"Put down the gun now or your head is going to come off."

"My dear, why are...," muttered Truman, who heard his words being repeated through the tinny speaker of the cell phone clipped to Stabler's belt. Truman's head spun round as he looked for Mike in the distance. He glanced around at the table where Mike had thrown his keys. A single red LED glowed out of one of the remotes on his key ring.

"You son of a bitch," cursed Dunn as he re-shouldered the gun to aim it at Mike. The safety never made it off when Brenda butt-stroked him with the stock of her hunting rifle.

Mike rushed back to the table. Brenda had finished hitting Dunn and brought the barrel against the unconscious man's head. "Brenda, don't do it. Don't do it. Put it down. It's not worth it. Not now. Not after everything you've been through. Trust me, it'll be better to put him away and take away everything he's ever done than to just kill him," pleaded Mike.

Brenda responded by slamming the safety off and grasping the trigger.

"There's a way out of this, and killing him isn't it." Mike watched Brenda's finger quiver between pulling and letting go until a single tear rolled down her cheek. Mike slowly walked over and took the gun from her. After unloading the gun, Mike laid the rifle on the ground next to his Pontiac. He hit the remote to open his car door and reached under the seat, smiling at his jerry-rigging. Taped together were his dictation machine and his cell phone. Pulling the wireless microphone on his key chain to his lips, Mike said, "Hi, John. This is Mike. It's over." The dictation machine broadcast his voice into the cell phone and he nodded his head in satisfaction. Peeling the tape back, Mike spoke to John. "Thank God you got Stabler's cell phone number right, boss."

"Well, thank God you're all right. I was afraid I was going to have to replace you," said John. "I suppose you're not coming in tomorrow."

"I think I need a day off."

"Okay, if you insist. Maybe I'll take off too and we can go golfing."

"Are there any windmills on the course?"

"No."

"Then I think I'll pass, boss. See you on Tuesday," replied Mike as he said his goodbyes and hung up.

Dialing another number from the back of the fax, Mike spoke to a man who was all too willing to help out. Mike made his way to the sobbing figure of Brenda Stabler. "I made a call to some people. They'll take care of Dunn and protect you until the police come."

A half-hour later, Jorge Rembez pulled up in a classic Chevy muscle car. Mike introduced him to Brenda and showed him where Dunn's unconscious body was. Ten minutes later, Mike stood alone on the target range, basking in the spring sun. He keyed the directory on his phone until he found Trooper Al Hoover's number and made a call.

* * *

Abby had watched the sunlight dim in the windows until the streetlamp came on. She hadn't stirred an inch since her owner headed out the door earlier in the day. Dinnertime had come and gone. Occasionally, her belly would growl, reminding her of the missed meal. It didn't matter—she didn't have an appetite. She almost mistook the whirring of the garage door motor for yet another stomach growl, and a bolt of joyous lightning surged through her body. She ran to the garage door and ran circles around the kitchen table as her haggard owner came through the door.

"God, did you get into the chocolate again, Abby?" asked an incredulous Mike.

"Yip, yip, yip," replied the Shetland sheepdog doing a full-out happy puppy dance. She stopped long enough to get a good ear rub and nuzzled up to her owner.

"It's all right, girl. I'm home. I'm home."

Abby heard the soft words coming from her owner. She tossed herself onto her back with reckless abandon—it was belly-rub time.

Chapter 25

The neat type on the title page of the hardback *Exeter in Black and White* stood in ordered contrast to the erratic scrawl of a signature and a single sentence, "See you at Gavin's, Bill." Mike pursed his lips and drew them into a smile, thinking of how fast Bill's book made it into print. *Time flies*, mused Mike as his eyes glanced at the June calendar page on the desk beside him. Of course, it didn't hurt that the whole Edwards affair made it to the national news and more than a few publishers wanted to cash in on the event. It also hadn't hurt that Clayton Edwards had hosted a party the night before to kick off the book where former invalids Bill Renard and Tony Savastio took the limelight.

Flipping through the pages, Mike happened upon a picture depicting a formal portrait of a man in a fine suit. A wry smile formed on Mike's lips as he remembered talking to Trooper Hoover the day after he met Truman Dunn.

* * *

"Thanks for your statement," said Trooper Al Hoover as he wrapped up his report.

"That's it? Now you go pick up Dunn?" asked Mike.

"I don't have too. Exeter police have him under lock and key. Seems as though somebody handcuffed him to the marble pillars of the courthouse early in the morning."

"Oh, yea?" said Mike.

"Yea. Handcuffed him buck naked to the marble pillars of the courthouse early in the cold, cold morning," continued Al.

"No," smiled Mike.

"And here's the best part—the same somebody tattooed the word 'Racist' across his butt. He's going to be very popular in prison."

* * *

The memory of the conversation ebbed as Mike thought about handing Dunn over to Jorge Rembez and company. *I never did tell Al that Rembez ran a tattoo shop*, thought Mike.

Clapping the book shut, Mike stroked a sun-basking Abby behind the ears and headed down the steps to meet Jen, who was reading the newspaper and having some coffee. Jen had accompanied Mike to the book's gala and stayed the night.

"You ready to go, Jen?" asked Mike as he grabbed his car keys.

"No."

"No?" said Mike as he raised an eyebrow.

"No. Last night reminded me about the murder."

"And?"

"Do you remember the morning you woke me up and made me fax Brenda Stabler's application to you?"

"Yea."

"And, how did you know she'd turn on Dunn?"

"I took a risk."

"You? You took a risk? That's not like you, Mikey."

Mike smirked at the "Mikey" reference and said, "It was actually the least risky thing I could have done. Dunn sent four guys after me, so I knew that he wasn't going to stop until I was either out of the picture or dead. Look at Renard's life—he left Exeter because of that. Dunn tried to kill him thirty years later. That's what I call holding a grudge."

"But that doesn't tell me why she turned on him."

"I did what the people of Exeter did."

"Which was?"

"I put my faith in Clayton Edwards. Think of it, Jen. Stabler starts out on a Dunn scholarship and gets jobs based on Dunn's little network of insiders. Little by little, she gets in over her head—all the time owing favors to Dunn just like everybody else on that scholarship list. One day, Dunn hatches an idea to frame the one man he can never seem to beat. Then, the very guy they're framing turns around and protects Stabler by taking the fall."

"That's all well and good but you took a heck of a risk."

"I guess so, but I didn't think of it at the time. I just figured that she needed a bit more data—something to think about once I was dead."

"Only a geek would think that way."

"Geek? There you go using four-letter words again. No, as Spock on *Star Trek* would say, 'Logical'."

"Only a geek would quote *Star Trek*."

"Hmmm, you got me there. I just thought things through to a conclusion. All of Dunn's henchmen..."

"Henchmen?" leered Jen.

"Henchman—a gang member..."

"Only a geek would know that."

"All of Dunn's henchmen were dead. I prodded Stabler into thinking that she would be next," explained Mike.

"So you gambled."

"Yes, I suppose I did."

"And you got lucky."

"Very. I'm hoping to get lucky again."

"Yeesh. Last night wasn't enough for you? God, you give a geekboy a cookie..."

"And he wants a glass of milk," replied Mike, eyes lowered in a begging pout.

"Funny. Hey, you promised me a walk in the woods."

"Can we pick up some hot fudge on the way home?"

"Dream on. I'll take Roxanne home and we..."

"Ah, don't worry about it. She'll be fine here," said Mike as the pair headed for the car, bound for a long peaceful walk at Sanford Park.

* * *

Abby, upon hearing the garage door close, rose from her spot in the den and headed upstairs to catch the last of the morning sunbeam on her owner's bed. Sixteen steps later, she arranged the blanket the way she wanted and snuggled into its soft wrinkles.

The sound of nearing footsteps woke Abby from the placid embrace of the cushy mattress and warming sun. She could hear feet moving from room to room as if their owner was looking for something—or someone. The steps drew nearer as Abby heard the familiar creak of each step leading up to the bedroom. She peered out over the bed, looking for the intruder. A golden bolt of four-legged madness leapt from beneath the bed's horizon, causing Abby to recoil in surprise—Roxanne.

Jen and Mike never heard the long plaintive howl emanating from his bedroom...

THE   END